# Cartridge in a Pear Tree

# Cartridge
## in a Pear Tree

# Merry Holt

WordCrafts Press

**Cartridge in a Pear Tree**
Copyright © 2021
Merry Holt

ISBN: 978-1-952474-81-1

Cover concept and design by Jonathan Grisham for Grisham Designs

Published by WordCrafts Press
Cody, Wyoming 82414
www.wordcrafts.net

*He who pursues righteousness and loyalty finds*
*life, righteousness, and honor.*

*Proverbs 21:21*

# CHAPTER 1

Angel's agoraphobia begged her to stay, but the claustrophobia demanded she leave.

As she dashed toward Cookie's Café to meet Etta, light snow fell. In the globe, it never hit the ground because the climate control wizards maintained the higher air colder than street level. The town lowered their budget by not needing snow removal crews, and no ice built up on sidewalks for slip-and-fall claims.

It was early November, but local children had not displayed Halloween decorations last week, thank God. Witches and goblins roamed her nightmares; she did not want to encounter them in the grocery store. Winter ruled the calendar no matter the month. Angel remembered the mayor's hissy fit the first time a shop owner stuck large sunflower heads onto an evergreen. For years, the townspeople referred to it as "the incident."

She searched her pockets for her phone and realized she had left it on the charger. "Fiddlesticks," she said out loud. Her mind was sharp, but her memory was weak. Thoughts piled up in disorganized heaps she later sorted through like bargain bins.

A gust of bakery-scented warm air brought Angel to a standstill as she entered Cookie's place.

"Close the door!" a tourist who had not taken the constant forty-degree weather into consideration shouted.

Angel complied and headed for the table her best friend had staked out for them. The music broadcast through hidden speakers would have soothed patrons if played at a lower volume, but

1

Cookie was hard of hearing. Crossing the room, Angel noticed two customers had kept their fluffy earmuffs in place.

She offered an apologetic smile for being tardy, and Etta nodded her indulgence. Before Angel had shrugged free of damp outerwear, a loud confrontation caught her attention.

"You won't get away with it, mayor."

Benny, the man she planned to have dinner with tonight, stood red-faced with his fists clenched. She felt trapped and embarrassed to witness the unfolding scene. The globe was a tranquil place, built on peace and goodwill toward men, a visual reminder to keep the holiday spirit all year long.

Angel's heart froze. All eyes watched the angry man, and everyone wondered if violence would erupt. Distress seared her chest, and she stood, mortified. The coat came off in a move, but it did little to help the heat pouring off her skin. She measured the distance to the door and contemplated making a run for it.

The man's tangled hair and unshaven chin made him appear unstable. Etta looked at her in panic, and Angel knew she would get an earful about her choices in men.

"You think I'm going to put up with your crap just because I'm new to town? You're dead wrong." Benny pushed past without recognition. If he saw her, he didn't care.

Angel watched her date's retreating back and heard the murmur of shocked voices around the almost-full café. She considered following him, but was too much of a coward. The villagers did not yet know about their may-be relationship, and it seemed wiser not to announce it at this moment. Etta tugged at her sweater sleeve, and Angel dropped into the wooden chair with a thump. The other patrons would have heard it if they had not been so intent on talking about what had just transpired.

Her mind felt full of wool, and her cheeks burned. Angel liked Benny, or she had thought she did. Confrontation twisted her insides. She had not been involved in the fight and had almost fled. What if they had been a couple—would she have deserted him?

2

"What's Ebenezer's problem?" Etta asked. Her friend's face was dainty and doll-like. Blonde hair tumbled out from underneath the chunky cable-knit cap she had probably whipped up last night to match today's outfit.

"Don't call him that," Angel said, and her voice came out sharper than she intended. Dark to her friend's light, she noticed the moisture had made her hair frizz instead of forming perfect ringlets like Etta's. Next to her bestie's sparkle, she always felt a little drab and, on occasion, invisible. Men intent on meeting the beauty nudged their way close, pushing Angel out of the circle until Etta pulled her close.

"It's his name, isn't it?" Her wide, blue eyes looked innocent, but Angel knew better. They had grown up together, and early on, Etta had earned a black belt in feminine ju-jitsu. Angel's ordinary looks had forced her to rely on intellect.

"Sure thing—Jeannetta."

Etta studied the hot chocolate in her hands, and Angel felt a pang of guilt. She wondered why she would launch a missile on Benny's behalf. It was not like they were an official couple. Yet. Etta had proven her commitment to their relationship, and the man who moments ago made a scene had not.

"I'm sorry, but I worry about you. We don't know this guy." Her friend looked up at her. "I think he's dangerous," she whispered in full voice.

The word triggered Angel and caused her mouth to go dry. She reached for the red mason jar of water and took a drink, careful not to swallow any ice cubes. People choked to death on the slippery assassins.

"We can't all marry an all-around good guy." She wasn't jealous of Etta—Angel was her biggest fan—but come on, already. Eric and Etta had been together since they were the high school "it" couple, while she remained stubbornly single. Angel had been what her mother called a "late bloomer." At twenty-nine, she still yearned to wake up and discover she had blossomed overnight.

3

Her hopes dwindled with each new dawn as she attempted to keep the faith.

At the mention of her husband, Etta's face lit with the smile which had won over him and everyone else. It touched Angel, too, and she apologized. No shadow returned to Etta's heart-shaped face. She did not hold grudges, a trait Angel admired but had not yet mastered.

"Forgotten, but seriously," she looked around to see if anyone was listening, "what's going on with him?"

Angel hesitated. She did not know if Benny had given her the information in confidence. If so, why had he unloaded on the mayor in public?

The line between gossip and soliciting advice eluded her. Was it always disloyal to talk about someone else's affairs? What if she could help Benny? Etta ran a successful business. She knew things Angel—and possibly Benny—did not.

Before she had decided whether to answer the question, Cookie arrived with her order pad in hand. "What'll it be, ladies?"

They each ordered a French Hen—herbs de Provence chicken salad on a buttery croissant. Cookie swaddled each poultry-shaped sandwich in striped paper and placed a tiny beret on top. A cigarette and mustache would have completed the caricature.

"These are amazing!" Etta said. "I've never seen anything so cute."

Cookie beamed with pride at her artistry. She took full control of the café not long ago and struggled to put her stamp on things. "Come back next week, for the Pah-rum-pum-pum-pum."

"What's that?" Angel asked as she unwrapped her lunch.

"Pumpkin pancakes decorated like snare drums with honey-dipped drumsticks." Leave it to Cookie to make chicken and waffles more festive. The woman had a touch.

Etta ripped off her bird's head while Angel waited to make sure no disgruntled employee had poisoned her food. After five minutes, she dug into the substantial tail feather section. Around mouthfuls, the women discussed the town's number one priority: plans for the holiday light show.

For the last two years, national judges had the gall to rank the globe as the second-best Christmas town in the country. It shamed the residents and made them angry. No other village existed in a permanent dome dedicated to the holidays; they should be the decisive winner. Angel had heard the rumors about the mayor's cost-cutting measures being the cause of their downgrade but felt they all needed to shoulder some responsibility.

The townspeople had banded together and made a New Year's resolution to reclaim the tree-topper award. Besides a short summer lull or two, the locals had worked with diligence. To do her part, Angel had joined the committee. The meetings set off her fear of groups but assuaged her terror at being alone.

Etta's family ran the lighting store, and the bulk of the task had fallen to them and a few volunteers. Ordinary civic displays used thousands of twinkle lights to brighten the night, but thanks to Etta, the globe would boast of hand-turned neon sculptures.

The number of bake sales and car washes hosted to cover the cost staggered the hardiest among them, but every mom and pop shop would profit. The top designation would bring in new families who would pass the tradition along to future generations.

"It took all year, but we're getting there. I'm a little tired of those lords leaping all over my shop, but they beat the cows the milkmaids needed."

"I'm meeting the arborists in the morning. They want to make sure the pear tree's roots have taken well." As the first stop in the Twelve Days of Christmas, it had to be impressive.

It had taken three months of cajoling to convince the tree guys to move it to the park. At twenty-five feet tall, it had been a massive undertaking involving an entire crew of men. Cookie had rewarded them all with lunch after they had completed the job. The tree surgeons had warned Angel transplanting such a mature tree could kill it, but she believed in their skill, and they had proven her right. It did not bear fruit this year, but it survived.

Angel was pleased with their progress. As an ornithologist, she assumed the burden for the twenty-three birds listed in the song. As Etta's friend, she contorted into awkward positions to support the sculptures in progress.

The city council scheduled the exhibit to go live on the fifteenth and remain open until January 2nd. It would draw more tourists during the already busy high season. Next year, they needed to brainstorm how to even-out their annual income streams.

Angel looked at her watch and said, "I've got to get back." Before Monday, she had to finish her syllabus, work on the geese-a-laying, go to the grocery, and help her father before he did something else foolish.

"Me, too," Etta agreed. If they were to get the installation finished in the next week, no time could be lost.

The dessert case with its rows of sugar cookies sprinkled with red and green crystals beckoned. "Have one on the house," Cookie offered.

They sighed in unison and walked past the temptation with a quick, "No, thanks."

Angel obsessed over the scale while fasting to overcome her latest feast. She could not allow fat rolls to develop, because someday while trapped in a cave, they would block her narrow passage to freedom.

The friends hugged in the doorway. Angel smelled the bright citrus in Etta's perfume and considered buying a new fragrance before tonight's date. She had not worn any since a notable over-application fiasco in high school. The thought of a reoccurrence made her nauseous.

Benny made Angel's heart flutter, and she was not sure if fear or anticipation caused the palpitations. It could be a cardiac issue. As the first single man to relocate here in five years, Benny was an anomaly. He opened a store he called the Lump of Coal in the spot the Vegan Fudge Kitchen had tried but failed to make a go of it. His shop sold free-standing fireplaces and stockings filled with anthracite. Angel thought he was smart to cater to both locals and visitors.

Families looked forward to time spent in the winter wonderland of the globe. Children loved the idea of endless tinsel and gingerbread men, but their parents drew the line at a steady diet of Christmas carols. Benny was brave enough to embrace them.

Though not as pretty as Etta, Angel had dated quite a bit in her twenties. Now near thirty, the boys she had gone to school with had either left or became part of the town's cast. The dating pool had dwindled to a puddle. She waved to guys she once knew as she walked. Angel was not attracted to the men dressed as elves or polar bears. She worried whether bugs lived in the costumes and what would happen if the zipper got stuck. The blacksmith had caught her attention, but a ballerina from the nutcracker had danced off with him.

Maybe God never intended for her to find a husband. She did not have time for one, anyway. Her parents needed her help, she served on the committee to win the Best Christmas Town competition, and her dual roles at work kept her busy.

The College of Christmas Knowledge, like all structures in the globe, had been modeled after a Swiss chalet. Angel's office in the building's interior did not have the beautiful beveled glass windows visitors admired from the street. Many more vital people than she occupied those spaces. She held her breath before entering the building because shared hallways meant any number of free-floating bacteria. The college's history department employed the most staff and was renowned for its archives of sacred and traditional documents. Scholars made pilgrimages here to view them.

The music department provided her a home. An accomplished organist, Angel played in the gorgeous cathedral downtown each Sunday and in concerts throughout the year designed to entice visitors in the off-season.

She had feared boredom and being locked into one career, so she obtained a second degree in ornithology. Joining the two disciplines brought her joy.

As she unlocked the door, Prancer said, "Good bird. Good bird."

Angel let out her breath and drew in another in shock. Her resolve to accomplish every item on her over-expanding to-do list died when she took in the crime scene. Ribbon-sized pieces of paper littered the floor several inches deep. She wondered if the shredder had come to life in her absence and vomited out its stomach contents. The textbooks for the upcoming session, the Birds of Christmas, no longer sat on her desk. Someone had knocked the stack to the floor and reduced them to confetti.

She looked from the mess to Prancer, who ducked his head in an unusual display of subservience. "What did you do?" A lump blocked her throat and breathing became impossible. Her coat slid down dejected arms. She let it fall to the floor and followed, every bit as limp as the cloth. The scarlet macaw scurried branch-to-branch on his stand until he reached its base and hopped to the floor.

Angel heard his nails click-clack as he made his way across the tile but did not reach out to him. The one being who loved only her had dismantled her class materials and cost her a thousand dollars she did not have.

"Good bird," Prancer said as he climbed onto her leg, seeking forgiveness. Angel refused to acknowledge him. He was the furthest thing from good, and he knew it.

She had chosen the most elaborate version of the textbook due to her sheer excitement about the course. It included fabulous glossy photos, anatomical charts, migratory maps, and other extras the basic volumes did not provide. Full-color reproductions lay in tatters all around her, and Angel's heart felt every bit as slivered.

"How could you?" Angel knew what it felt like to be trapped, a flighted creature constrained by circumstance. Her parents helped found the globe and played Mr. and Mrs. Claus. They were, therefore, small-town royalty. The village's "magical powers" lay heavily on the entire family.

Her father had expected Angel to take on his role, and so did everyone else. Her idea of a fulfilled life did not include the spotlight, and years of pain and disappointment followed for them all. They accused her of abdicating the throne on a whim and failing to fulfill her responsibilities.

Prancer wanted to make decisions for himself, too. He did not relish being Angel's companion only when it was convenient for her, and he strove to assert himself just as she had done. Both now sat in a mess of their own making.

"Lord, please help me. What am I going to do?" She would not ask her dad to bail her out with the college bookstore, but had no savings. The budget deficit kept her up at night as she ran various scenarios of homelessness. Living single cost Angel as much as any of her coupled friends paid out of their joint accounts. She believed half would be fair.

"Please, Lord," Prancer repeated. The two-pound weapon of destruction scampered up her limp body and sat on her shoulder. "Are you alright?" Prancer imitated Angel's voice because he heard hers the most. The bird brushed his warm beak along her hairline.

Some might assume the bird was concerned with Angel's well-being, but he wasn't. Parrots mimicked. They sometimes joined phrases together to make sentences. Prancer did not ask if Angel was okay; he thought she should ask him. "Are you alright?" he asked again.

She ran her hand down the soft brilliance of his red feathers and held back a sob. The macaw knew nothing of money or her professional obligations. He would not have to tell his boss about the loss of study materials or his inability to replace them.

Co-workers voiced amazement when they learned Angel allowed Prancer to roam free. These same people kenneled their dogs for ten hours a day while they worked. The bird's actions overwhelmed her, but she never considered locking him up for the offense. Her fear of small places would never allow it. When she had first met him, Prancer had been cage-bound for years. Selfish owners who thrilled at having a talking animal had grown weary of the care he required. They gave him water and cheap seed, but no stimulation.

In protest of never being able to expand his four-foot wings, Prancer had screamed. Macaw vocalizations clocked a hundred decibels, equal to an outboard motor or a jackhammer. Non-deaf people could not handle it for long.

The constant screeching caused his owners to abuse Prancer, an all-too-common scenario. By the time they surrendered him, he had bitten anyone who tried to coax him out of his cage. He had spent so much time inside it, he became both territorial and fearful.

Angel had taken on the challenge and spent over a year rehabilitating the bird. Now he lived unrestricted, but on occasion, Angel paid the price. She lifted him to face her.

"I love you, but you are a bad bird." Sadness had replaced the shock and anger she had felt. The parrot was as intelligent as a toddler, but small children flushed cellphones.

Prancer disagreed. "Bad Angel," he said. "Good bird." Angel sighed. It was useless to argue. Each believed the other to be wrong.

She spent the next hour cleaning her office and searching for a way to make things right for Monday's class. In the end, Angel did what she must and returned the Christmas gifts she had bought. The first to go was the new tree stand she had gotten for Prancer. She canceled her layaway orders and received a refund. Only one payment had remained on her parents' new high-definition television and the brand-new coat she had looked forward to wearing.

The woman in the bookstore did not ask what had become of the first shipment of textbooks. Something in Angel's tone had warned her off being too inquisitive. She used her credit card to pay the bill, and profound anxiety took root.

Angel went home and prepared for her date with Benny. Before witnessing his temper at lunch and Prancer's antics this afternoon, she had been buoyant. Now, she felt deflated. They had agreed to go bowling. Angel had not mentioned it to Benny, but the sound the pins made frightened her in their ferocity. Smashing things for entertainment did not seem reasonable.

The snow had stopped, but the air was chilly. Multi-colored bulbs lit Angel's path. On special occasions, simulated northern lights flickered across the globe's sky, but not tonight. The globe drew visitors from across the world. A technological wonder, the encased village ran on thermal power, but was far from a greenhouse. Everyone celebrated Christmas year-round, and windowpanes frosted over in the middle of July. The town held snow and ice sculpture building contests each summer weekend. Snowmen creeped Angel out; their dead eyes bored into her soul, probing for soft spots. She always covered her face and hurried past.

The lanes were popular on Friday evening. League players wore coordinated shirts emblazoned with team names: *The Rollers*, *Living on a Spare*, *Dolls with Balls*, and her favorite: *We Don't Give a Split*. Neither did she.

Benny had not arrived yet, and Angel felt a flash of irritation. People who considered their time more important than others' irked her, even though she often ran late. She prided herself on her scheduling abilities and worked ridiculously hard at fitting everything into the day planner's slots. Angel's system broke down when she failed to hold things to their time limit. Undisciplined events sloshed out of one block and into the next. It was not her fault if others were undisciplined.

She went to the counter and arranged for a lane. The guy sprayed a pair of size tens and handed them to her. Angel looked for a place where it was not so obvious she was alone and always would be. An open table sat behind where the Dolls with Balls practiced. She took off her coat and sat. Too late, she noticed the mayor's wife was a member of the girl group.

Vivian Harrison spearheaded the committee to assure the village won the Best Christmas Town in America award. They had worked together throughout the year, but their relationship remained shaky. Angel's dad—aka Santa—wielded real power in town. Still, the mayor pretended the globe was a metropolis, and he, its king. The two had been partners for decades, but their friendship had dwindled with the years.

Glacier Harrison's wife wore her bowling shirt Betty Boop style, with the ends of the pink button-down tied in a center knot above her naval despite the cold. Blonde waves of hair reached mid-back in volumes never seen outside shampoo commercials. Angel wondered if it was a natural gift of God, or if Vivian wore extensions. The woman owned the most decadent salon in town, so the latter was a good bet.

"Well, hello, Angel. We don't usually see you around here. Come to roll a few?" The woman's sweetness was a prop. She checked people with it like a hockey stick.

"I thought I might give it a try." After Benny's run-in with Vivian's husband this afternoon, Angel wished she had chosen to sit at another table.

Glacier Harrison came from money. When drunk, he bragged about how he had lifted Vivian out of poverty and set her on a throne. Angel's stomach turned every time he alluded to it. A man should never treat his wife—no matter how grasping—like a rescue animal. Vivian, though born poor, outclassed the Italian-loafer-wearing jerk at every turn.

Angel slipped off her snow boots and put on her rented tricolor shoes. Even inside the globe, red and green shoes lacked excuse. They did nothing to minimize a big girl's feet or make her feel pretty.

She heard a cell phone and glanced to make sure it was not Benny calling. Vivian swiped hers open and said, "It's my night. What do you want?" Angel pretended not to eavesdrop and busied herself with her laces.

Vivian listened for a few seconds with an impatient expression on her face. "We have a deal. You're not to bother me on Fridays, and I don't care about your so-called emergency."

People only spoke to their spouses with such disdain, so Angel assumed Glacier was on the other end. The happiest marriages were battlegrounds, as far as she could see. People often warned her off the experience, but it was selfish on their part. Each of them presumed upon their husband or wife. Angel wanted to be comfortable enough to take someone else for granted.

Benny entered the far door, and she gathered her belongings to meet him. The dark curls hanging over one side of his face gave him a somewhat brooding look. Her hair, longer and less controlled, made her look like a Muppet. He walked with purpose, each stride confident and direct. Angel's shuffling step sometimes confused her pedometer into thinking she had not left the couch in hours.

Her heart picked up its rhythm when he grinned at her. The move transformed his face, making him appear boyish and eager. Benny's smile made her insides squishy and warm. He hugged her in greeting, and she melted a little, then stiffened.

"You nearly knocked me over earlier today," she said and allowed the reproach to color her tone. People may not yet know they were dating, but he knew; he should have acknowledged her.

Picking up her lunch tab would have gone a long way, too. The eight dollars plus tip would not have put a dent in the thousand dollars Prancer had eaten, but as a gesture, it would have worked wonders.

Benny looked at her and cocked his head to one side. "I don't know what you mean." He smiled again, but this one flickered at the edges, and she wondered if he was sincere. Angel did not know him well enough yet to tell.

She looked at him hard, searching his face. "At Cookie's." His face remained blank. "At lunchtime?"

"We didn't have lunch together."

The man was dense as fruitcake, and the scary Christmas confection with an identity crisis frightened her. "No, we didn't, but I was there. So were you."

A scowl settled on Benny's features. "I only stopped in for a minute. Glacier's secretary said I could find him there."

As they talked, the pair moved to their assigned alley, lucky number seven. Angel did not feel fortunate. She was in public with a man who had failed to recognize her existence.

"It sounded like you found him."

Benny set down his bowling bag and looked at her. "The man is scum. How can you live in a town that chose him as mayor?"

Angel busied herself finding a ball without touching any of them. She had voted for Glacier in the last election. He wasn't in it for the money, and he championed environmental causes. Logging, which supported most economies in the north, did not influence his decisions.

"He's not so bad." She calculated whether her fingers would fit in a green ball with swirls.

"Not bad? He's trying to put me out of business."

It was not the first time they had discussed the mayor, and Angel resented Benny always putting her on the defensive. "That's an exaggeration," she said. "It's just a tax."

"I went to a lawyer today. He thinks I should sue."

Angel swallowed hard and looked at another rack. The globe was not a litigious place, and maybe Benny did not fit in here. She could not be with a man who started trouble. The idea warmed her cheeks, and she squirmed in discomfort.

"On what grounds?" She kept her voice level while cleaning a ball with disinfectant wipes. Angel didn't wish to appear as judgmental as she knew herself to be.

Benny took a practice roll while she put their names into the automatic scoring machine. He got a strike, and the excess power behind his ball sent the pins flying.

"Singling me out. Taxes should apply to everyone equally."

Angel picked up the blue and white polka-dotted ball, took three steps, and launched it. Ten feet down the slick wooden surface, it veered off into the gutter.

"They do." She paid taxes; everyone did.

"Not this one. Glacier is punishing me for not being green enough, and it's not right. I'm not selling drugs; I'm keeping people warm."

Angel was of two minds. Of course, coal was legal, but so were cigarettes and alcohol. The mineral made her think of miners trapped underground, gasping for air. If they surfaced, they had black lung disease.

"What about pollution?" The globe had proprietary filtration systems whose schematics were worth billions. The villagers breathed the cleanest air on the planet. The exhaust must vent to the outside world; she was not sure. Angel had no plans to venture there.

Benny snorted and shook his head. "You work for the natural gas lobby? My coal burns clean. It's the most efficient and time-honored way to heat small spaces. I'm not saying large cities should burn it exclusively, but a shop stove is no big deal."

Angel did not buy it. It was the worst of the fossil fuels from what she read. "Why not sell more pellet and wood stoves, and discontinue the coal ones?" Her solution would work. Win-win.

Benny made a derisive noise and said, "The store offers the others; you know it does. I allow people to choose, and the wood burners aren't as harmless as you think."

Angel turned her back to him and tossed the ball. Five pins fell in a slow arc to the left side. "You walked right past me," she said as she waited at the ball return. Angel feared being a doormat and congratulated herself for having brought up his actual crime.

Benny's face hardened. "If I did, it was because I didn't see you. I was focused on not losing my life savings because of some idiot's power trip."

She threw her second ball and picked up another three pins for a total of eight. As Benny passed, he reached out to touch her arm. "I'm sorry." He had not meant to slight her. Angel forgave him in an instant.

"You're right; Glacier wasn't fair. He didn't put a tariff on fudge or hot chocolate, and sugar is a killer." It did a number on her thighs, anyway. She sighed.

The grin Benny gave her repaid her loyalty ten-fold. "There's no ugly sweater tax, and those things should be outlawed." Benny rolled another strike, and it was Angel's turn again before she had a chance to sit. The game and banter continued, and she found herself having a good time. Prancer's destruction of her office did not cross her mind.

Before they parted ways in the parking lot, Benny kissed her and said, "Let's see where this goes. I think we're good together." Was he asking her to be his girlfriend and to make things official?

"There's something you need to know," she said.

Benny looked at her with interest but no fear. "Do you have a child?" he asked without blame or trepidation, and her heart skipped a beat.

"I have a macaw," she said, and Benny laughed. He wildly underestimated what the statement meant, but they had time. He had just said so. Angel watched her breath come in short puffs, and knew it was cold, but felt only warmth. She experienced hope for a shared life with someone, and it was foreign and euphoric to her. Up until now, when she saw her future, the only male in it had been Prancer.

# CHAPTER 2

Saturday morning arrived too soon. Angel had stayed up late to knock out her course syllabus for work. After the textbook catastrophe, she did not need her boss to think any worse of her. When she finished, Angel stored the document twice in rapid succession and laughed. If the save function failed the first time, why would she expect any better the second? Just in case, she emailed a copy to herself and said a quick prayer.

On her single morning off, she liked to sleep in and pretend a life free of responsibility. Getting out of bed spoiled the fantasy.

Prancer singing, "Rise and shine and give God the glory, glory..." drove her from hiding after a single round with the snooze button. Her record was five times, unless someone counted the times she shut it off and fell back asleep.

Angel had chosen a two-bedroom duplex for the extra space. She could always find a flat mate to improve her cash flow if necessary. Her current roomie paid no rent and ate half the fresh food from her fridge. He never came home drunk, though. She had turned the second bedroom into an aviary, and Prancer occupied a mansion instead of a cramped sleeping cage.

Her father had donated left-over reindeer fencing, and she used it to line the walls. The wire mesh gave the bird's long toes something to grasp onto and kept him from eating the wooden trim. The idea of losing her damage deposit gave Angel palpitations.

Climbing ropes, hanging toys, and various shiny objects kept the macaw engaged. Without stimulation, Prancer became vocal and destructive, and Angel could not always be with him.

The bird hung on the wire, waiting. "I love you," he said, happy to see her. Prancer relied on Angel for everything, and without her care, he would die. On some level, she thought he understood this. It made him clingy.

"I love you," Angel replied. He was not the husband she yearned for, but the bird filled a hole in her core. Her loneliness vanished the moment she brought him home.

They went through their morning routine of cleaning, feeding, and playing. She had trained Prancer to relieve himself in a single area and kept his food in the opposite corner to avoid contamination. While Angel worked, they sang "Take Me Out to the Ballgame," one of Prancer's favorites. He loved to "root, root, root for the home team." The bird bobbed and weaved, and his enthusiasm energized her.

The pair put on their fan gear and watched games together in the summer. Angel once slipped up during the playoffs and called the opposing team "lousy buggers." Prancer had never forgotten it, and she learned to moderate her language.

"I've got to go, buddy, and you can't come." She had a date with a horticulturist. Maybe he would be cute. After finishing in the park, her father expected her help with some painting. So much for a life free of responsibility.

When he realized Angel planned to leave without him, Prancer changed his tune and sang about Bobbie McGee being busted flat in Baton Rouge. He sounded as mournful as Janice Joplin on a down day. Angel involved her friend in her life as much as circumstances allowed. Five days a week, she brought him with her to work. The church had yet to admit him to the choir, so he stayed home Sunday mornings.

She instructed Alexa to turn on Prancer's playlist, and the opening bars of Lynyrd Skynyrd's "Free Bird" filled the house. "I'll be back as soon as I can," Angel said and grabbed the backpack filled with water, snacks, and the tools she would need.

The globe prohibited the use of gas-powered vehicles. No one used a full-sized car; everyone owned or rented golf carts. Bicycles came in a close second, and walking shoes got most people where they wanted to go. Angel jumped into hers. The backpack went next to her on the empty bench seat where her husband should have been. One day, she hoped to see an infant car seat behind her, ready for a family outing. She checked her hair in the rearview and sighed.

She arrived first and stood at the pear tree's base. The group had picked this specimen to anchor the Twelve Days of Christmas display, and it was magnificent. Angel tilted her head to admire the view and screamed.

❄❄❄

The tree sheltering her did the same for someone else, but the dead guy took no notice. The body lay face down over a large branch, his legs dangling on one side and arms on the other. She recognized the face. It belonged to Glacier Harrison, the town's mayor.

Horror froze Angel where she stood. "Dear Lord, help me, please." Her hopeful mind tried to transform the sight into something benign, but the blood dripping from his head wound made it impossible. She fumbled for her cell phone and dialed 911. "There's been a murder." Vomit followed the words from her mouth.

The woman asked her to repeat herself. Angel wiped her lips on her shirt and did so. The village based its existence on goodwill toward men, and even non-violent crime was rare. No one would ever visit here again. Nor should they. Of all her phobias, being murdered ranked near the top. She imagined herself in a landfill, a burned-out car, or an abandoned building. The globe did not have these things—and Angel never left—but still, she worried.

Her legs shook uncontrollably, and she sat in the cart to wait. It would not take long; the globe stretched a single mile in each direction from its center point. She spent the time in prayer.

The chief of police arrived with four deputies. At this hour,

19

most visitors luxuriated in their overstuffed beds, buried under a mountain of faux fur blankets softer than the real thing. Later, the disciplined would linger over spiced tea and scones while everyone else feasted on a multi-course brunch.

Angel may never eat again. She kept her back to the deceased but could not un-see the tragedy. Frank sent his men to establish a perimeter and approached her.

"Are you okay? Do I need to call a doctor?" The man was her parents' age, but his frame reflected a disciplined lifestyle. In contrast, her dad embodied his character: soft, round, and stuffed full of cookies.

She had never been so afraid in her life. The policeman asked her several questions, but she had no answers. Angel had driven here to meet the tree guy and found death. Frank told her appointment she would need to reschedule.

Angel did not remember the drive from the park to the North Pole Complex. The golf cart knew the way. Being Saturday morning, the roads were not busy yet. The complex occupied the central plaza of the globe. Every road and person ended up here by design. City codes limited buildings to two stories except for this one. The castle's spire provided the highest vantage point in town. It was a good rule. Cranes and scaffolding tended to fall on the unsuspecting people below them, and she felt unlucky. The dome protected her from errant space labs dropping from the sky. The thought had brought her comfort until this morning when she discovered terrible things could happen within the walls.

She parked in the employee's lot, full at this early hour. Townspeople took vehicle personalization to a whole other level. The cart next to hers wore gigantic reindeer antlers, false eyelashes, and a swishy tail. She bet the horn tooted jingle bells—most did.

Unobtrusive but always present security restricted the curious to the public spaces. On occasion, the nutcrackers did what they were designed to do. Sometimes, they appeared in Angel's dreams with their mechanical jaws ready to chomp. Angel walked past the bucket lift truck used for hanging Christmas lights on tall trees and wondered who had left it there instead of returning it to the garage. Her father did not appreciate sloppiness.

"Good morning," she said as she peeled free from her mother's hug. Her mom's face appeared splotchy from crying. In her role as Santa's wife and grandma to everyone, she knew all the gossip. "How did you find out about the mayor?"

"Vivian called me. Glacier never came home last night, and the police came to her place first thing this morning. It's terrible. Things like this don't happen here."

Her parents' magnetic presence drew people to the globe. The self-contained village with everlasting winter contained a lot of charm, but Mr. and Mrs. Claus provided the vital element: love. The gargantuan task of creating holiday magic had become impossible once someone spilled blood. The murder threw off Angel's sense of equilibrium. The safest zip code on earth transformed into a suffocating plastic bag over her head. She prayed for Glacier, his wife, the killer, and the town.

Her dad embraced her in a bear hug. His beard tickled Angel's ear, but she did not resist. The man smelled of pine and pipe smoke, a manly scent. Benny's cologne had reminded her of open blue water, also lovely, but more modern. "Why in the world were you there?" he asked, and she heard the agitation in his voice. She was his little girl, and he worried about his only child.

The globe did not contain sketchy neighborhoods. Working-class people made up most of the population; the wealthiest residents arrived on a seasonal basis. Her father helped found the community to assure her of a safe place to grow-up.

"The Twelve Days of Christmas is due to open, and I needed the final okay to use the pear tree."

Angel's emotions had not settled, and she rotated through the worst ones in rapid succession, looking for a fit. Tears had threatened, but she pushed them away, unsure of their honesty. Falsehoods of every kind disturbed her. She experienced outrage at the mayor's end, but didn't trust genuine grief would follow. They were not close friends; a rivalry existed between the families due to their respective positions. Seeing him had shocked her system. Americans hid death in sterile places; they did not confront it.

"Excuse me," her father said and left, an orthopedic brace on one foot. Angel looked at his retreating back in confusion. She had expected him to hold her hand as she related every gruesome detail and cried.

Instead, she and her mother had tea. The phone rang so many times, Angel shut off the ringer. Everyone wanted to speak to her parents and express their sorrow. Some wanted to gossip. They could all wait. Her father had not returned after an hour, and she asked her mom to check on him. Angel considered going home, but did not wish to be alone.

Her mom returned and said, "He's not well. The news has him out of sorts." Of course it did. Angel's father had dedicated his life to making the globe a wholesome place filled with joy, and someone had shattered it.

"Is he okay?" Angel did not remember the man ever presenting a less than boisterous face to the world, and it rattled her. He could not even bring himself to hear what she had been through; it hurt him too much. She felt as if the air system had malfunctioned and failed to deliver oxygen.

While lost in deep teenage angst, the man's chipper idealism had driven Angel to distraction. She ordered him to drop the façade and admit life sucked. In her despair, she found his cheerfulness to be the worst form of betrayal. Now, Angel wanted to snatch the hurtful words from her memory. Her father's steadfastness had led her through the growing years, and she yearned for a return to optimism.

"He'll be fine, dear," her mother said, but she didn't believe her. Caring men did not overcome senseless death. This morning had traumatized them all.

"Maybe you should have someone fill in for him this afternoon," Angel said when she could not think of anything else. "Take the day."

Her mother agreed, nodding her head, and all her chins followed suit. "It's a good idea. Maybe we'll go outside for a while."

Angel's heart seized, panic filled her chest, and the ground turned into quicksand. She could not remember the last time her parents ventured further than the outer wall. Maybe they never had.

Guests entered through control portals, which allowed for screenings and population control. The environment sustained a specified number of people, and if the village reached maximum capacity, security halted the influx. The village held every amenity from theaters to a zoo. A walk to the library solved every bit of wanderlust Angel had ever had, and now her mom wanted to leave. She did not know what she would do if they never returned. They must fix this and restore tranquility. No one must go.

"Go to the park. He could even fish." Angel did not want her parents outside the protection of the globe. It felt like abandoning God. She did not wish to consider it had never been safe inside and would never be so again.

"We'll see," her mom said.

Back in August, her father had asked Angel to retouch the wooden doves on the gingerbread eaves. They carried holly branches complete with red berries, and she had always loved them. Last week, her dad had tired of her procrastination and determined to repaint them himself. An hour after his decision, Angel received a phone call that shocked the selfishness out of her. The three-hundred-pound man had fallen from halfway up a ladder. Guilt pummeled her, and she berated herself for being an ungrateful daughter.

"I'll do the painting; you two take the day." It made her ill, but Angel did not wish her parents to know about her fears. The globe's ambassadors could step outside without getting mugged. She hoped.

In truth, she believed her parents' kindness left them defenseless. They had invested their lives fashioning a fantasy. No one could have found people better suited to their roles, but they remained naïve. Angel had not traveled, but she read. Online news reports told of arson, burglaries, and violent kidnappings. Living in such an insular community protected villagers from all but petty strife, but going out in the wild was dangerous.

Her parents did not wear padding in their portrayal of Mr. and Mrs. Claus. Neither needed to augment what God gave them. Angel watched her mother walk down the hall, and an invisible band constricted her breathing.

A vicious murder had bloodied the safe space they had created, and it was beyond repair without Divine intervention. With a sudden vehemence, Angel hated the killer and his execution of their dream.

She went to a decorative cabinet and picked up a set of keys for the boom truck. Her mother's neat handwriting labeled each spot on the pegboard, and she had no trouble locating the right set. During summers and school breaks, Angel had performed most menial tasks around town. Her father had encouraged it, and she learned many skills. Climatologists and electricians held the best jobs in the globe; everyone else worked in the service or maintenance fields.

The truck's electric engine fired on the first attempt. Angel maneuvered it along the open walkway, careful not to bump any of the outsized Christmas ornaments hung from the rafters. She stopped and set the stabilizers and wheel chocks. Her father had drilled safety first into her head.

Armed with her backpack of supplies, Angel climbed into the bucket, heart pounding. Levers on the inside allowed solo operation, and the arm extended upward in a smooth motion. Angel held her breath. She thought of falling and fought back nausea. Situated near the top of the spire, she could see across town. Besides an owl or two, the vista belonged only to her. Angel turned to scan the opposite direction, and an invisible fist slammed into her gut. Out of instinct, she closed her eyes to block the grisly sight. The pear tree two blocks away shone in the blue glow of emergency vehicles.

Horrified and fascinated, she opened her lids and swayed as if wind buffeted her. Breezes blew in the globe, but the controllers never allowed anything close to a gust. The bucket lurched downward a foot, and she caught onto the railing. A short scream escaped her lips in the form of a prayer.

"What the heck?" She used this piece of equipment to replace strings of Christmas lights, hang garlands and new signage, and sprinkle tinsel on the tallest trees in town. It had never malfunctioned before this moment. Angel looked down and saw Merry. "Stop it!" she yelled, both relieved and incensed. Her father would have a conniption fit if he caught anyone monkeying around, and it ticked her off, too. Thirty feet of elevation gave her a new perspective on the mandatory safety trainings he held each quarter.

Her cousin's plump face grinned up at Angel as she pressed the red lever once more. The unenclosed box flew upward this time, and Angel muttered under her breath. "I mean it," she said and hurled a paintbrush. It bounced off the truck's metal frame.

Angel had left herself open to this, and it irritated her. Even idiots locked out the lower controls when working alone. She had allowed the murder and her father's reaction to distract her. Calamity needed a spark, and Merry fit the bill.

"Don't be such a spoilsport," the prankster said with a pout. "You get to have all the fun."

Hours ago, she had found a dead body, and her cousin thought it was an adventure. "You're welcome to take my place," she offered. If Merry wanted to kiss up to her uncle so badly, Angel would let her.

"You know I can't. I get vertigo on a step stool. Basil puts away the dishes in cabinets above my waist."

Merry's foolishness knew no bounds. As children, the older girl insisted on playing the role of mother. She ordered the other kids around, and for every gumdrop handed out, her pocket got two.

"Basil's a saint." The queen bee expected all lesser drones to serve her, and the good man did. Ninnies like Merry had tainted Angel's view of providence. The lazy, greedy woman did not deserve a catch like Basil. Angel's cousin was cute in a frivolous, childlike way, but a terrible life partner.

"He is, isn't he? It's a shame you never managed to find a man; your father can't live forever, and hope is not a strategy."

On occasion, Merry said something intelligent as well as mean. For twenty-nine years, Angel had not done much more than wait for the right relationship. She chased professional goals and a life separate from her parents. Why not men, the way Etta and Merry had? Her passivity and fear had failed her.

"You're wrong," Angel said. "I have a man." As soon as the words left her mouth, she regretted them. Merry would tell her parents and the rest of the village. She did not keep confidences, as Angel knew from experience. For years, they had been best friends, almost sisters. They spent their childhoods together opening the stacks of prop gifts and unscrewing lightbulbs to bedevil the staff. The fun stopped when her cousin realized Angel's birthright made her special.

"A man?" Merry jumped at the words, and Angel cringed. She had gotten out ahead of her skis again, a maneuver sure to end in a humiliating, arm-twirling fall.

She had made two major mistakes this morning, and Merry exploited both. Angel's temper flared to boiling. Her cousin offered a target for her not-yet-categorized emotions, and she took aim. "The mayor's dead. Why don't you go harass the city council? Maybe they'll vote you in to run things."

"I had thought about it, you know," Merry said in a thoughtful voice. "Toyland needs a leader with a firmer grip."

If Angel had stood on the ground, she would have applied one to Merry's thick head. Non-violence was the globe's golden rule, but breaking it would help them both. Memories of Merry tricking her into doing all the chores came back in a flood. Each time her cousin cozied up to her, Angel let her guard down, and bad things happened. Merry wore white gloves to stir up trouble and never left a trace of evidence. The grown-ups had loved her.

"Are you accusing Dad of something?" Advertisements and billboards featured her father's face, and, while not a religious leader, he served as the globe's moral compass. Couples often came to him for counseling.

"He's too soft," Merry said without hesitation. "Expecting the best from people is simple-minded. Look what happened to the mayor. I'm sure he trusted the townspeople not to kill him."

Angel stuttered and searched for words to hurl. How could someone be so disrespectful when the man's dead body lay a few streets away from where they spoke?

"There you are, babe," Basil said as he made his way across the plaza. Tall, with broad shoulders and a quick smile, Angel liked him. He walked like Paul Bunyan, rough and ready to protect. "Hey, Angel. Working Saturdays, huh?"

"Angel asked for my help, and I clambered up here like a champ," Merry said.

"But now I can't get down." She raised her arms like a child wanting to be carried. The strong man scooped Merry up, kissed her forehead, and set his wife on the ground. Angel's heart clenched tighter.

"I've got a surprise for you," Basil said. "Something to take your mind off the terrible shock you've had."

Had a collectible figurine gotten broken? Her cousin did not seem distraught over the murder, so it must have been something far more consequential.

"You spoil me rotten," the true princess protested, and Angel agreed.

Basil tipped his head in humility and said, "It's more than a month until Christmas, and a woman like you should never go that long without a present."

Merry giggled and looked at her in triumph over Basil's shoulder. Angel wondered if she could direct her vomit at one and miss the other. The lovebirds said their goodbyes, and Angel got ready to work. A craftsman had carved the doves out of soft basswood and included feathers and feet. His efforts turned generic shapes into art. The task demanded concentration, and she kept her mind and eyes far from the grisly scene playing out in the distance.

As a rule, Angel did not involve herself in politics. The college's historians loved to discuss past intrigues and current events in the cafeteria. Due to her deep-seated fear of boredom, she didn't join them. Her father played a pivotal role in the village, and people looked to him for guidance. In watching out for the residents, he placed himself at odds with the mayor and city council.

The globe's continued viability depended on its idyllic reputation. Visitors wouldn't return if they found roads in disrepair, uncollected trash, or substandard goods. Worse still, they would leave scathing reviews warning others to skip the experience as well. No perpetual grouch sought out the globe's unrelenting joy and merriment, and Angel had never met someone with enough hatred to kill. It must have been an outsider. The idea gave her the shivers.

In a final tribute to the deceased mayor, Angel gave the last dove a soul-patch and goatee. She smiled and moved the red lever to lower the bucket. Nothing happened, and her impatient finger tried again. No response. Angel's gut understood the problem before her mind did. Merry had overridden the controls. She swore. The bad habit flared up around her cousin, and Angel did not believe in coincidences. Not minding the elevation when she chose it differed from being stranded three stories off the ground. Her pulse rate increased, and she whimpered. At least the bucket did not sway like those on a Ferris wheel.

One of the snowflakes came into view, and Angel waved to get her attention. Before she understood genetics, Angel longed to be part of the elite group. The dancers wore elaborate hairdos with white fur and pearls. They were the most glamorous ladies in the globe, and everyone loved them. Angel explained what she needed and soon lowered her prison to street level. She thanked her savior and grabbed the backpack.

After returning the truck to its rightful spot, she went home to get Prancer. The bird yelled, "Hi, hi!" when he heard her key. He did not care if she taught class, played the organ, painted doves, or worked on the lighting display. Industry did not interest him; he yearned for connection.

Angel loaded him into the insulated carrier that stood two feet high and was long enough to accommodate his tail. Macaws lived in warmer climates, and she did not want him to take ill. The pair got back into the already-warm golf cart and drove to Etta's shop because she had promised to help finish the six geese a-laying today. Angel entered without announcing herself and regretted it.

Etta and Eric faced each other, hands on their hips. Etta's pale color had deepened in anger.

"Sorry, guys. Should I come back later?" Angel wished she had knocked first.

"No, Eric was on his way out," Etta said. Her husband narrowed his eyes, and without saying a word, he returned to the retail side of the store.

Angel sat Prancer's carrier down and looked at her friend. "Are you alright?"

"Peachy."

The woman ran deeper than those who looked at her cherubic face supposed. This workspace belonged to her, not Eric. The high windows brought in natural light to the austere room filled with shelves and open areas.

Etta wore overalls and a welding hood, which made her appear both fierce and feminine. In an identical outfit, Angel would have looked like a man. She still wore her painting clothes and felt drab.

"You've heard about the mayor?" Angel asked as she placed Prancer on his portable stand. She thought about Benny for the first time this morning and felt uncomfortable. Did part of him think Glacier deserved what he got?

"Lousy bugger," Prancer said, and Angel looked at him in shock. Parrots repeated random phrases at inopportune times. She gave him a toy filled with almonds to occupy him while they worked. Etta moved to a pile of long white tubes and handed one to Angel, who had pulled on heatproof gloves. The pair had completed four of the six geese so far, and Angel knew the rhythm. Shattering glass scared the wits out of her, but her friend was a pro.

"I heard," Etta said. "It's unimaginable."

Angel felt a rush of nausea. "I found him. He was in the tree." The idea unsettled her. Why go to the trouble of making a public spectacle out of the death? She understood someone felt they must kill him, but humiliating the corpse and his family afterward seemed cruel.

Etta ran to her. "I'm so sorry. I only heard he died. No one told me you found him." The women hugged, and Etta said, "Go home. I can do this."

"No, I'm trying to keep busy." Ticking off items from the to-do list seemed a useful occupation. Angel feared what horrors her mind might conjure once alone and still.

They said a prayer and got to work. "Who do you think did such a thing?" Angel asked.

"I have no idea. Eric is in a hot lather about it, though I'm not sure why." Etta placed an outline of the goose on the table for them to follow. "They weren't friends. He didn't like the guy."

Angel had never thought about it, but the two men must have done business. Eric ran the bank and Glacier Harrison, the city. Their careers were bound to have crossed paths.

"I'm sure it's you he's worried about," Angel said. "He feels like he can't protect you, and it scares him."

Etta looked up, and her face relaxed. "Do you think so? He has a funny way of showing it. It's like he doesn't trust me out of his sight."

"It broke the taboo. Once we've had one murder, who's to say it won't happen again?" She had not acknowledged the thought before now, but it was true. People felt bad for Glacier and his wife but worried about their families and businesses. Her concern lie with her parents. No one took notice of her—especially men.

Angel steadied the tubing as Etta fired up a blow torch and softened it with the flame. Too much heat and it would burn through; too little, and the glass would not be malleable—like love.

"It might be wrong to say, but Glacier was a fool. There've always been rumors of affairs." Etta's safety visor was down, and Angel could not see her face.

Prancer said, "Fool. The man's a fool."

"Sorry," Etta said. In everyday conversation, it took more than one repetition for Prancer to parrot. But like a toddler, he picked up off-color phrases the first time. There was no point in being irked with Etta. It was too late; Prancer heard the word and would use it. Good thing Angel did not take him to church. Humiliation was a constant fear.

"Sex isn't worth killing for," she said and fed the soon-to-be-goose through her hands.

"Then you're doing it wrong." Etta bent the now flexible tube into what would be the arch of the bird's back.

Angel laughed because she was not doing it at all. "People kill to have sex. Or have sex and kill. Sometimes with the body." Etta tipped up the bulky shield and grinned at her. "No one ever wanted Glacier that much." The women set the glass onto the pattern. With a set of six, they had to keep things symmetrical.

Angel said, "He was rich, and wealth is a turn-on."

"You couldn't pay me enough." Etta spun the sculpture around to work on the bird's feet. Keeping the conversation light helped Angel come to grips with the morning's darkness. Both existed simultaneously. Remembering the destroyed textbooks and the resultant debt, Angel wondered how far she would go for financial security. She would not commit murder, but a lack of money made people do terrible things.

When finished, Angel found six missed texts from Benny. Her heart melted a little, and she agreed to join him later for a drink though exhaustion threatened. After several hours of glasswork, she needed a pick-me-up. She dropped Prancer off and met Benny at the Celtic Inn. The fiddler played and danced as if gravity did not affect her. Angel admired lightness in all forms: those with a sense of humor, the pond's ability to reflect the sky, and flight. She plodded like a draft horse with a heavy load on the brightest of days, and today did not qualify as one of those.

Benny hugged her and ordered beers. "I had a great day, how about you?" he said with a smile.

Angel's jaw dropped. Someone had murdered the mayor and put him in the pear tree for her to find. The news made her father so ill he called off work, and her mother considered leaving the globe. Merry stranded her in the bucket of the boom truck, and one of the snowflakes had to help. Etta and Eric got into a fight—which they never did—the day was a complete loss, and her date was an idiot.

"It was horrible." She took a sip of the Guinness. Angel had not eaten, and her stomach rumbled. "You know I found the body, right?"

"No. I didn't. I'm so sorry." Benny looked contrite. "I heard he was dead was all. We don't have to talk about it; I'm not from here. In Chicago, fifty people get shot in a weekend."

Angel started. "Was he shot?" The idea unnerved her. She had seen the injury but not considered the source. Knowing someone had killed him overpowered her without searching for more detail.

Benny stuttered. "I guess I don't know. I just assumed." His face turned red. He shuffled his feet and not in time with the music. The town's original charter forbade guns. As far as Angel knew, no one ever brought one into the globe. Even police officers did not carry them.

"Wouldn't someone have heard the shot?" Now he had planted the idea she could not shake it.

Benny shook his head. "Don't you watch TV? They could have used a silencer."

Loud noises made Angel jumpy, but the idea of soundless projectiles terrified her. She looked around as if one might be headed her way. "Do you think the killer's still here?" Angel's voice was not much more than a whisper.

Before Benny could answer, streams of people stopped by their table to discuss the murder. She should not have gone out in public. Everyone but Benny knew she had been the one to stumble across the corpse. People had blown up her phone all day looking for information.

"Bet your dad's glad Glacier is finally gone," one said.

Angel's head spun; she should leave. "No." She took a breath. "Of course he's not. Why would you think that?" They had been partners for almost twenty years. The globe wouldn't exist without them.

"Well, now he wins the head-charge argument. And a few others, I'll wager."

Glacier Harrison had wanted to change the fundamental way they marketed the village. Poinsettia Point had always operated like any other community. It made its money from tourist dollars spent in the shops, restaurants, and attractions. Most activities were free for everyone. Villagers wanted visitors to celebrate special occasions with them. Those who lived close should be able to pop in for dinner or a show without paying an admittance price.

"It's a stupid idea. We want to be a town, not an amusement park. People live here," Angel said.

"The mayor was onto something. That money could have funded improvements."

Another guy sided with him. "My shop doesn't make as much as the bigger ones, and charging a fee could spread the wealth a little."

The man ran a boutique selling high-end nutritional supplements. Not every storefront in the globe catered to Christmas or to the tourists, but the draw for vitamins ran low in a place known for its sugar consumption.

"I agree," Benny said. "It makes more sense than taxing the daylights out of us to pay the freight for free-loading outsiders."

There was a lot Angel did not know about the man she was dating. Turns out, he only hated some of Glacier's politics. For a guy who just got here, Benny considered himself a local in record time. Angel bit back the uncharitable thought. She could not complain no new singles moved to town and then fault them for doing so. The law set no probationary time limit before one could express an opinion.

She cut the evening short and retreated to her bed with Prancer and a bowl of popcorn. Staying there for the next week or so crossed her mind.

# CHAPTER 3

Sunday morning, Angel attended both morning services at the cathedral. The sunlight prismed off the stained glass and elevated her mood. Her faith remained a constant but soared and became a living entity when she played the old hymns. Glacier laid heavy on her heart and had troubled her dreams. She had kept her hands busy since discovering the body, but her mind kept returning to the horrific scene. For the few hours she spent in church, Angel looked forward to eternity even though it meant passing through death. The condensed course she taught started the following day, and Angel wanted to be ready. The idea of being caught unprepared had given her nightmares since she was a child. She picked up Prancer after church, and the two returned to her office. The building was quiet. Anyone else catching up on work did so from home. Angel liked the idea of getting things accomplished while in her pajamas but never managed to do so. Working from home felt as wrong as tobogganing in a thong, and a refrigerator filled with comfort food lurked too close.

"Nut! Nut!" Prancer demanded as soon as Angel settled him on the tree stand. He received a toy instead. Treats needed to maintain their effectiveness, or she would be at his mercy.

She spent a few hours on her lectures for the upcoming course and felt pleased with her progress. Angel had designed the class to interest both biology and music history majors and hoped the fusion would work.

Her cell phone rang, and her mother's picture appeared.

"Nut! Nut! Nut!" Prancer grabbed a braided rope and shook it until the bells sounded like Santa had parked all eight reindeer in her skull. To buy a minute's peace for the call, Angel tossed the parrot a chestnut. He caught it in a three-inch beak capable of breaking small bones. He would never bite her but had nipped on occasion.

She faced the wall and tipped her chair up in juvenile rebellion of the rules. Her mother said, "Dad needs your help."

Angel put her feet back on the floor, worried. "Is he okay?" Her father had taken the murder as hard as she had. His soft heart hated evil and what it had done to the globe's future.

"He ate breakfast," The news sounded trivial but was not. Her father only lost his appetite in times of extreme stress, and he had refused all food yesterday. "But he's not himself. He says he's up to the day, but I know better. This is one of those times a son-in-law would come in handy. Maybe you could ask Benny…"

Merry had wasted no time passing along the fib she had told about being involved with a man. Angel's insides froze. What if her cousin quizzed Benny about their relationship? Mortification settled over her in a slimy green cloud.

"I'm sure I can manage whatever it is." Angel had only gone out with the man a few times; she would not ask him for a family favor. Darn Merry to heck. Didn't the woman have anything better to do than make her miserable? There had to be a small country in need of a coup.

"It's your father's turn to read at the library. I would do it myself, but I have to interview the seasonal help plus get the baking done, and I agreed to…"

Angel sighed and stared at her hands while her mother listed a schedule Fed Ex could not deliver. Although the rest of Angel's body was far from delicate, she had once modeled rings in a jewelry ad. Maybe she could again; it would bring in a little extra Christmas cash.

She glanced at her watch and started with the realization her mother had given her no time to get there. "Mom, I can do it, but I would have to go now."

Angel received instructions and gave assurances to her mom. Prancer would have to wait alone in the office for an hour while she was gone. She grabbed her coat off the hook and looked for the office keys. They always sat on the edge of the desk, next to where she used to keep the textbooks. Losing things caused a domino effect of cascading fear within her. First, she lost the keys, then her job, then who knew what? Angel always took care on the very first stair. She believed it kept from plunging down the entire set.

A hand on her soft stomach kept the flaps of her unbuttoned coat from blocking Angel's view as she bent over to look on the floor. No glint of metal caught her eye, so she swung around and scanned the rest of the room.

"Prancer, you rat!" The sought-after objects hung from the thief's talons in place of the discarded chestnut. The agile bird must have left his perch while she spoke with her mother. He was fast on his feet and as sneaky as they come. The bird cocked his gorgeous red head to one side and issued her a challenge. If she made a move, he would take flight and roost somewhere high enough she could not reach him. Macaws lived a hundred years and had more time to play games than she did.

"Good bird," Prancer said, daring Angel to disagree. He mimicked her kindest voice, but she heard a tinge of sarcasm in his tone. To anyone outside the door, it would sound as if she talked to herself.

"Of course you're a good bird," she said. "Can I have my keys back?" The bird brought the set to his beak. He tried to separate them from the ring while watching to make sure she came no closer.

Prancer hated not being included in her endeavors. She never should have put on the jacket before she reached the door. Angel needed a ploy. Like all bullies, the parrot would lose interest if she did not react.

She took off her coat and hung it back on the peg. "I'll call

Mom and tell her I can't help. It's too bad; I was going to stop at Cookie's for pineapple upside-down cake."

Prancer's intelligent eyes flicked to hers. "Pineapple," he said.

"Maybe next week." She leaned back in her chair and kicked off her boots, not bothering to untie the laces. The computer absorbed her full attention now.

"Pineapple," Prancer repeated. He loved all fruits, but the tropical varieties made him happiest. His sounds of appreciation always gave her a laugh. Whoever coined the phrase "ate like a bird" had never known one. Like his owner, food motivated most of the flyboy's decisions.

Angel ignored him and responded to an email. She tamped down her growing desperation because Prancer picked up on non-verbal cues better than any crime novel detective.

"Pineapple! Pineapple!" She gave no indication she had heard him. At last, in frustration to have his needs acknowledged, Prancer dropped the keys. Having no arms, the bird could not hold them and walk.

He used his beak to latch onto the tree stand, swung to a lower branch, and dropped onto her desk. His feet, better suited to tree climbing, slid a little on the slick surface. Prancer waddled across the desktop and stepped up onto her hand. Angel closed her fingers around his toes to prevent escape and to assure his stability. Macaw talons were an inch and a half long and sharp enough to cut. Every two weeks, she filed them with a drill.

Angel lifted the large bird to her face and kissed his smooth beak in love. She stood up carrying her friend, retrieved the keys with her free hand, and deposited him back on his tree stand.

"I'll bring you a treat, I promise!" Angel said as she snatched her coat and boots and hurried out of the room.

Prancer yelled, "Me, me," through the closed door, and it hurt her heart a little. He only wanted to be where she was. No other male tried so hard to do so.

She leaned against the wall and slid her feet back into the boots, tugging up their fake-fur lined tops up as she did. The effort made her breathe harder, and Angel thought about starting an exercise program. Too bad Prancer did not need to be walked.

The library lay on the opposite end of town from the college, and she had not driven in today. The air was a bit nippy, but not cold, and it was dry. Unlike outsiders, people within the globe could rely on the weather forecasts. The engineers posted the schedule on the website, and no one had to carry an umbrella just in case.

Her budget did not allow for a taxi or horse-drawn sleigh, so she waited for a tourist trolley. Being a Sunday six weeks before Christmas, the shuttle arrived full of tourists. Small children looked in wonder out the windows.

"Look, Mom!" a boy of about five pointed in excitement to a live seal performing on a platform. A group of people had stopped to watch him do a handstand on his flippers. Angel smiled as the pair got off for a closer look. The penguins waddling down the street a block away would elicit the same reaction from another family group. The trolley was not the quickest form of transportation, but it allowed locals to re-experience their home with new eyes.

The children's section took up an entire floor of the library. Soft pillows and low chairs catered to small bodies. Parents looking to curb the non-stop stimulation of the globe came here for respite.

The librarian greeted Angel with as much enthusiasm as if she were her father. Being the daughter of the town's most important man colored her life. People treated her better than the average citizen based on nothing other than who her parents were. Angel wished it were true of all Christians. It would be. She did not deserve the honor and feared people would figure it out any day. Angel contributed to the community, but no more so than any other resident. The attention and occasional jealousy made her uncomfortable.

The staff rounded up the fifteen or so children present, and they sat in a semi-circle around her overstuffed chair. Angel loved kids, but their directness intimated her.

"You're not Santa," said a disappointed four-year-old wearing elf ears and pointy shoes purchased from a souvenir shop.

That much had been clear her entire life. She could never fill the big man's boots. "No," she said. "I'm his daughter." It might have been different had she been born male.

The best a girl could hope for was the role of Mrs. Claus. The town expected her to find the perfect replacement for her father and marry him. It felt incestuous, and Angel had no wish to play a secondary character.

"Why didn't he come?" The kid was relentless.

Angel could not talk to the child about murder. This was the first time in memory anything sidelined the man. A week ago, when her dad had fallen from the ladder, he had not missed a step.

"He's very sorry, but there are so many more good children this year he's behind on making all the toys." Lame, but the standard go-to line in the globe.

"Santa doesn't make the gifts," a little girl with long red pigtails said. "The little people do. I saw them!"

She cringed. The globe employed more people of short stature than any other single city. Her father instituted a union and made sure their benefits and wages matched or exceeded those of like positions, but it still made her uncomfortable.

Angel had lost control before she began, and the librarian came in to assist. "Children, this is Angel. She gets to live with Santa." It was no longer true, but Angel let it slide.

"Who would like to have a reindeer for a pet?" The children's hands shot up in the air. "She's going to tell you a story about one who got to sleep in the house."

After she read, Angel fielded questions about whether she ate fudge for breakfast and got presents every day. The kids missed some of the particulars but nailed the joy of her childhood. Stepping free from the Currier and Ives painting had her caused pain. Remaining within it would have been so easy. She shook off the thought and gathered her belongings.

The librarian thanked Angel again and begged her to return.

Benny had texted, thanking her for last night. She returned one to him. The excitement of someone new made her a little buzzy. The trolley delivered her to Cookie's. She heard "Deck the Halls" from the sidewalk, and the place stood almost empty on a busy weekend afternoon. Angel bet she knew why.

"Hey," she said as she spotted the woman. "Can you turn it down a bit?" Angel waved a hand in the air to indicate the assaultive sound.

"No," Cookie said, and Angel gasped. Globe citizens hated rudeness; many listed it as the main reason they lived insulated from the wider world. Kindness was currency. "You don't get to call all the shots."

No one thought Angel ran anything; she didn't. It took her a minute to recover from the blow. Two days ago, Cookie had no issue with her. What had changed?

She wanted to leave without Prancer's cake or the answer to her question. When possible, Angel avoided anger and difficult conversations. Cookie was not a close friend, and Angel could frequent a different bakery. By the same token, she did not stand much to lose. She fought the unproductive fear and gathered her courage. "Are you okay? What's wrong?"

"The town chose Glacier to run things, not the Clauses. Put your face on as many billboards as you want. The mayor is in charge, not you."

Angel's parents had pressured her into taking part in this year's advertising campaign. Their three smiling faces shone down on the town and in television ads. Non-photogenic from birth, it had not been her idea.

"We—we don't think we're in charge, and our name isn't Claus. Dad just—" People liked her family; they were good people. No one hated them. Glacier Harrison had been the only person who did not worship her father.

Cookie ran up to her with clenched fists, and Angel stepped toward the door. "Glacier was a good man, and you offed him."

The woman had gone crazy. Cookie's eyes were wild and streaked with broken blood vessels.

"You misunderstood. I *found* him, not killed him." The rumor mill had run off its track if people thought she murdered a man. Angel wished she had never gone to the park.

"Get out!"

Her resolve melted. She ran.

It took Angel over an hour to stop shaking. She sat in her office, stroked Prancer, cried, and prayed. Until today, she believed only Merry resented her parentage. How had she been so blind? Growing up, she had not been aware of town politics, much less involved in them. The prodigal daughter had opted out, gone to college, and started a different career. Her destiny did not lie in the family business.

Angel realized how naïve it sounded. Last night in the bar, she learned some townspeople agreed with the mayor. Today, Cookie accused her of killing him. It made no sense. She had voted for Glacier and defended him to Benny. Angel sided with her father about the gate fee because it would change the nature of the village. The town's Christmas spirit was more than a gimmick to draw tourists; it was a shared philosophy. Monetizing Christ's birth invalidated it and would turn them into nothing more than a bunch of greedy merchants.

Prancer said, "Pineapple." She had forgotten the promised treat, and Cookie would never welcome her again. The office mini-fridge held some goodies, and Angel gave the bird a piece of fresh mango.

"Mmmm," he said. The soft orange flesh smeared his white beak, and she laughed.

"You're a mess." Prancer ignored her and kept eating. He did not allow people's opinions to interfere with his enjoyment.

The mayor's death had unhinged Cookie, and Angel could only guess the effect it had on his wife. Sudden violence had swooped out of nowhere and stolen her husband. The couple did not seem close, but Vivian would not have wanted him dead. Angel wondered who did.

She called Benny and told him what had happened at the bakery. "Where does Cookie get off treating you like that?" Angel liked the protectiveness in his voice, but his vehemence seemed overwrought. The woman had not struck her.

"It's a bad time for everyone. No one ever imagined—" Angel stroked Prancer's head, admiring the bone structure covered with soft feathers.

"Why are you making excuses for her? She attacked you—there's no reason to be nice about it." He sounded angry with her, not Cookie.

"I—I'm sorry."

"Stop apologizing!" Benny shouted, and Angel cringed. She set Prancer on his stand and gathered her things.

Angel did not want to escalate things with Cookie. "Maybe I'll send her some flowers." Her credit card limit might accommodate a small bouquet.

"Over my dead body! If someone comes for you, you hit back harder. If you're too chicken to do anything about it, I will."

"No! Don't!" It was too late. The line had gone dead, and Angel stared at the phone. She felt sick. Benny accosting Cookie would worsen the rift between them, not narrow it. She fired off a text begging him to do nothing.

Prancer said, "Go. Go." He was right; they needed to get out of here. The office walls had closed in, and she could not breathe.

Angel loaded the bird into the carrier and headed outside, where twilight caused the automatic lights to flicker. She looked around, wondering which direction to turn. All roads led to the North Pole Complex, so she went there. She waved at the couple playing Mr. and Mrs. Claus. The crowd had thinned, but several children wished to sit on Santa's lap. Puppet shows, dancers, and elves on stilts kept their attention while they waited.

The nutcracker sentry nodded as she passed into the inner sanctum. Her parents had not changed the door code within memory, and it opened with quiet ease.

In the plaza area, the decorations dazzled with brilliance. Her parents' home shimmered with soft candlelight and mid-century ambiance. Angel had always loved their old-fashioned bubble lights. Her parents looked up in surprise when she entered unannounced. For the second time in two days, Angel wished she had knocked. Her mom had aged twenty years overnight and made a quick movement to hide the bottle she held.

Drinking did not factor into daily life for any of them. Angel looked to her father, and her heart dropped. "Dad, Mom, are you guys alright?" She had come to seek help with problems and found someone had ground the rocks she relied on into sand.

Her father wore a wrinkled and stained Santa suit, though Angel knew he had not worked since the murder. He must have slept in the thing—if he had slept at all. Her parents' home often smelled of cinnamon and cloves. Today, the locker room odor of old sweat nauseated her.

Neither answered for a minute, and Angel's heart beat like a toy soldier's drum. She set Prancer's carrying case down and hurried to her dad. He had shrunken and did not fill out his clothes. His wrinkled hands sat in his lap as if he had forgotten how to use them.

"Tell me." The words were the plea of a broken woman or a scared child. She needed to know but was certain she could not handle the information. Angel felt like Eve, her teeth poised above the apple.

Her mother no longer attempted to disguise the whiskey in her glass. She threw it back in a neat shot, and Angel was the one who choked. "They're going to arrest him."

Angel's hearing had fled her when she needed it most. A buzzing rang in her ears, blocking all sound. The clock on the mantle struck six, but the Westminster chimes did not cut through the static in her head.

"Who is? What are you talking about?" This alternate universe of murder, hatred, and drunken parents did not suit Angel. She wanted to go back to where things made sense and maintained order. Hallucinations had never been part of Angel's psychosis. She suffered from panphobia—fear of everything. Abandonment flared hottest now, followed by paralyzing chronophobia. The future appeared as a flaming pit, and she backpedaled from it in haste.

Her mother, the professional grandma whom everyone loved, sneered at her. Angel backed off another step. The woman had gone feral—like Cookie.

"The police, you moron. A fat lot of good the fancy college education did you." She chuckled at her mirthless joke.

"Lousy buggers," Prancer added in agreement. Angel stared at the bird and did not recognize him. No one in the room looked familiar, and she felt threatened. Her childhood home, full of nurturing memories, rotted before her eyes.

Her father had not spoken and slumped, semi-comatose. "That's crazy. Arrest him for what?" Angel's mind could not keep up with the transformations occurring in front of her.

"Murder." Her mother refilled her glass.

❄❄❄❄

Angel commandeered one of the carts from the plaza and dared the nearest nutcracker to stop her. She drove Prancer home, not swerving to avoid tourists. They scattered in front of her with looks of panic on their faces.

She spent a few minutes performing the parrot's evening chores to soothe him into compliance. "God, my friend," Angel led with the first line of her childhood prayer. She remembered kneeling next to her bed, heavy with quilts, small hands clasped in front of her and reciting the same words.

Prancer supplied the second, "It's time for bed." Routines brought order to the chaos in her mind and made her feel a continuity much needed in stressful times.

"Time to rest my sleepy head."

The bird bounced as if dancing. Knowing what people expected and being able to provide it made even a bird happy. Angel wished she experienced the feeling now. "I pray to You before I do."

Their voices joined for the final request, "Please guide me down the path that's true." She emphasized the last sentence and doubled down on it in her heart.

Birds were prey animals, and their instincts sensed danger. The ritual had calmed her as well, and by the time she left, Anger felt more in control. Her parents must have misunderstood; she would straighten things out, and life would return to normal. God would fix it all; He had always blessed them. Today would be no different.

Due to the hour, she drove to the police chief's home. The station served milk to children who had wandered from their parents and handed out maps to tourists. They did not solve crimes.

Frank opened the door and stepped back when he saw her. She passed into his living room. The man needed a maid. "My folks are as messy as your house. What's going on around here?"

The globe's force helped people, not arrested them. Policemen escorted shoplifters to the wall, not a jail cell. High-end jewelry designers or banks had never been hit, and fights were all but unheard of except on weekend nights.

The top cop's posture led Angel to believe he had a military background. He moved a stack of newspapers and indicated she should sit. Angel stood. He sighed and dropped into a reclining chair facing the television. A basketball game was on, and he muted the sound.

"A murder investigation." The man had not grown up in the globe but had lived inside for fifteen years.

"Why are you scaring my parents? They had nothing to do with it, and you know them. There's no way my dad would hurt, much less kill, Glacier."

"There's video."

Angel sat because she feared her legs would not hold. Her mouth went dry. If the police had tapes of her father committing a crime, they would have charged him. The buzzing returned to her ears, and she concentrated on lip reading. Something smelled moldy, and she pushed a pizza box off the couch. Bacteria crawled and spread, but she had no idea how fast it traveled. As soon as she could, she would research the answer.

"Of what?"

"Him driving the bucket truck near the park." Frank met her gaze without blinking, and Angel broke their eye contact. She believed the academy must teach courses on mind-reading, and the man did not hold a warrant for her thoughts.

"So? We use that truck all the time. I drove it yesterday." The vehicle got used several times a week. Seeing it run errands around the globe had never raised an eyebrow before today.

Frank sat straighter in his chair. "I need details. Start from the beginning."

Angel had watched enough television to know she did not have to tell him anything; the idea her father had been involved in the mayor's murder was ludicrous. She could not have ever imagined having such a conversation. Maybe this was a dream.

"You saw my dad in the truck? What time?" They could both ask questions. Frank wanted to use a flimsy coincidence to bring down her father. Did he hold a long-standing grudge for some reason? She made a mental note to check around and see why he would target Santa.

"Around 2 a.m."

"Are you sure it was him?" Her father had always been a morning person who nodded off in his chair before 10 p.m. The man did not cruise the streets late at night.

"Why were you driving the truck? You work at the college."

She would not allow him to drag her into this. "I did some painting for my dad. He fell off a ladder and is wearing a boot."

Frank picked up a cat Angel had not noticed. The tabby looked as worn as the furniture, his skin hung on him as if he wore an oversized fur suit. "It's him in the video. Hard to miss the suit."

He stroked the animal, and Angel's perception changed when she realized he loved it.

"There are a dozen stand-ins for Dad on a slow day." She breathed easier. It had all been a mistake.

"This one is wearing a special boot."

Angel felt sick. "Then, he had a good reason." She had no idea why her father went to the park at 2 a.m., but it did not involve murder. The man emulated a saint, for goodness sake. No one ever spoke against her dad—ever.

"If he does, he's unwilling to share. I don't want to arrest him, but I may have no choice. You need to convince him to cooperate."

The do-not-disturb setting on her phone silenced spam calls. Angel's cell only chimed if someone from the contacts list called, which allowed her to sleep through telemarketing attempts. The morning after meeting with Frank, she found two texts from an unidentified number. The first read, "Call off the dogs." The second, from the same sender, read, "Your mom knows everything." Angel's blood ran cold, and she deleted the messages. Had Benny threatened Cookie? Was he the rabid dog? Why drag her mother into it? Angel had not introduced the man to her parents. She always dreamed of a man to fight her battles, but yesterday made her reconsider. Angel suffered from phobias, but she was not weak. Benny had hung up rather than listen to her pleas not to intervene in her life. If this is what relationships were like, she didn't need them.

Benny did not answer his phone, so she sent a text asking what he had done. Cookie would think she sent him, and it was not the case. There would be no pah-rum-pum-pum-pums in Angel's future.

She pushed the problem from her mind and planned a condolence call on Vivian Harrison. Neighbors would visit and bring casseroles, but the widow did not eat. Food interfered with her

perfect figure. The woman had found a man worth marrying—
something Angel only dreamed of—and he died. Someone had
robbed Vivian of her husband, and she would be steamed.

Angel puzzled over what to take with her and decided on wine.
Day drinking seemed the most reasonable thing to do when the
world unspooled. Remembering Cookie, Angel put a second bottle
in her cart. The woman at the checkout counter insisted they were
on two-for-one special, but she had not seen a sign.

The Harrisons had never invited her to their home. Before now,
Angel had never questioned the lapse. They worked together on
committee business but always met at City Hall. Why didn't the
two most powerful families in the globe socialize, and why had
it never occurred to her they should? Angel had awoken from a
long nap. As a pampered child, she had bought into the globe's
pristine image, but adults examined things. Town business affected
all residents, and no matter what the decision, someone lost. Her
family had never yet drawn the short stick.

Who stood to lose enough they would kill? Angel knew it was
not her father. The man portrayed an icon in public and stayed
true to it in private. He cared about the globe's residents and their
families; politics could not turn an idol into an assassin.

Angel parked at the curb and took a deep breath. She pushed
the second bottle under the golf cart seat for safekeeping and
approached the house. The Harrisons had built a mansion meant
to rival the North Pole Complex. It fell short and would have
looked ridiculous if they had managed it.

The symmetrical evergreens lining the long sidewalk got replaced
if they failed to keep pace with the others. Glacier had insisted on
uniformity and reliability. Those who did not measure up found
themselves uprooted. Professional decorators had used only blue
bulbs when trimming the eaves and windows. The newspaper called
it classy, but it left Angel cold. No warmth radiated outward from
the home, only an icy chill. She shook it off and forced herself to
keep going. The doorbell echoed as if the house were empty. After

a minute, Vivian answered. Shock showed on her face when she saw who it was.

"Hello," she said. "What a surprise."

She shuffled her feet and wished she had not come. Angel thought of herself as friendly, but not sociable. Conversation was not her forte, and unfilled silences intimidated her. She lifted the bottle of courage. "Mind if I come in?"

Vivian, whom Angel expected to be in her pajamas, looked pulled together but tired. Wrinkles lined her face. She held the door open, and Angel passed into the foyer. The entryway opened to the second floor with the grand staircase set back to allow room for parties. Angel had seen pictures, but the photographer had not done the space justice.

She followed Vivian to a glass sitting room more like an indoor garden. It was as if someone dropped her into a terrarium, and Angel would have loved to be a plant. If a giant snail approached, she would not blink. A birdhouse and feeder sat next to a small fountain, and the walls were covered with stunning nature photos.

Angel handed the bottle to the widow and said, "Shall we?" Dropping in on someone while they mourned required skills she did not possess.

Vivian looked uncomfortable and glanced around for help. None came. "It's 9 a.m."

"Sorry about the time," Angel said and slipped off her shoes. Her hostess noticed the move and sighed. "But I have to teach class later."

Vivian brought stemware and a corkscrew. When they each had a glass, she sat. "As you can imagine, I have many things still to do." Angel picked up on the hint but ignored it.

"I'm sure Glacier's staff will be a big help to you with details." She did not have a secretary, file clerk, or receptionist to field her calls, though she had filled those positions in the past.

Angel received a wane smile. "I have a wonderful support system, and I appreciate you coming by, but…" Vivian let the words end. Even in grief, she was unwilling to be outright rude.

"I know we're not close. It's why I'm here." Vivian looked at her in confusion, not understanding Angel's point. "There are things you can't tell family. You don't care about my opinion, and I'm not a gossip. Be as nasty as you want. Say anything."

The widow considered the offer and sipped her wine. Angel felt she had overstepped. Some buddies shared every embarrassing detail of their lives, but most did not. Loving someone meant protecting them, and Angel loved Etta too much to let her see all her ugly. Maybe Glacier's widow felt the same. If Vivian trusted those closest to her with random dark thoughts, they might come to hate the man—or her. Things would change, maybe forever. It was a big risk.

"What makes you think I have anything bad to say?" No chink appeared in the armor, but Angel did not buy the act. Everyone harbored thoughts they hid from the respectable world. Airing them diminished their power and cleansed the soul.

"Glacier was your husband, but he was a living, breathing man. He could be a jerk. Now, because he's dead, people act like he was wonderful."

"He was wonderful," Vivian said. She waited a moment and added, "And a jerk."

Angel did not smile but understood. "Aren't we all?"

"My friends are so concerned I want to puke. They sit here like vultures, expecting a suicide." Vivian lost her drawl and sounded more authentic than she ever had. Angel nodded her head in encouragement.

"I bet they tried to spend the night." Audiences expected a performance, but Vivian did not wish to display her private hell. Grief was an internal war, fought on a cellular level.

"They think of me as fragile. If they knew me at all…" Vivian drank more wine, and Angel waited in silence. She had opened the door and need only listen without judgment.

"Who do they think handled the real stuff around here? Glacier? Don't make me laugh." She did so, but the result was a lifeless mockery.

"More ornamental than useful, huh?" Angel tucked her feet up underneath her and relaxed, wanting Vivian to do the same. The woman needed to unburden herself of conflicting emotions and did not want to taint the relationships closest to her.

"I did it all. Handled our stocks, the business, his political campaigns."

"Of course you did." In Angel's experience, women carried the brunt of the work. Men played the frontman with little understanding of what it took to keep them there.

Vivian made a noise between a chuckle and a strangled sob. "And he told everyone I was a trophy wife." Her body jumped, rocked by a hiccup or a giggle. "He was the diva, not me. He demanded constant attention and adoration. From everyone." She took a gulp of the wine, her lady-like sips forgotten.

"Did you fall short?" The question cut to the quick, but Angel needed to know the private man. It was the only way to prove her dad did not kill him. The widow placed a hand to her neck. If she had worn pearls, she would have clutched them. Angel never wore necklaces; she feared being hung by the pretty nooses.

"He never let me forget where I came from. Glacier insulted my ideas and called them blue-collar. Until they worked, of course. Then he claimed them as his and turned himself into a man of the people."

"Which one of those people wanted him dead?"

Vivian stopped, as if she had forgotten her husband's murder and had just been reminded of it. "Me. But I didn't do it."

Angel had not expected such honesty from a woman who might as well be a Capulet to her Montague, but she returned it in equal measure. "The police are blaming my father."

The news hit Vivian between the eyes. She looked up in shock. "Santos? He would never. We stopped being friends, but—"

It was Angel's turn to be surprised. "You were friends?" She did not remember such a time. She took another drink. In her mind, the men had been business associates, nothing more. Her father did not have the capital to start the globe alone and required partners to see his vision made real.

Vivian looked far away as if lost in a memory. "Until Glacier and he fought."

"What about?"

The woman looked down, afraid to meet Angel's eyes. A clock struck in the other room. "Glacier had this ridiculous idea your parents took a lopsided share of the profits."

Angel responded in a flash. "They would never. They built this place. Without them, it would be some sort of bland biosphere."

"I know. Glacier was paranoid about money and always thought other people wanted his. He wanted a prenup. Eventually, I caved, but I refused at first. I said if he didn't trust me, he had no business marrying me."

Angel agreed with the sentiment. She had no assets to protect and no interest in stealing someone else's, but why marry a person and keep wearing armor? Hedging the bet canceled it. A couple who entered matrimony fearfully would never survive the ordeal.

"You're no gold digger. You don't lunch with the ladies; the salon takes work."

Her hostess looked grateful, and her smile was genuine, if sad. These things aside, the woman loved her husband and lost him. "Glacier knew how hard I worked, but he took all the credit. He liked to tell people how he set me up and got all his friend's wives to support me."

"They would have never returned if you ruined their hair." Angel used a cheaper shop, but women did not allow a hairdresser a second mistake.

Vivian refilled her glass and offered Angel another pour. She refused. "It takes more than money, you know." Angel nodded. "A woman has to be smart."

Angel had never felt like she had any other choice. Men did not fall over her the way they did Vivian Harrison. People thought of her as the globe's princess, but she did not go into the family business. Education and hard work allowed her the meager success she had. "I know," she said.

"I saw you with Benny." The words did not indicate what Vivian thought of Angel's relationship with the man, and Angel steeled herself against unspoken judgment. The man came from outside the globe, and some people would forever consider him not one of them.

"We're getting to know each other," she said. Confidences, if held, could work both ways. "I'm not sure we have a future. He has a temper."

Vivian found it funny, or maybe the wine had gone to her head. "He's passionate. It's a different thing." Angel did not have any experience with life-altering loves. Her relationships had been tempered, not all-consuming. She bet Vivian had known the earth-shattering types found only in books.

Angel changed her mind, reached for the bottle, and helped herself to another. This was not as painful as she thought it might be. "How so?" She took advantage of the rare opportunity to ask questions she would never bring to friends or family.

"He's fighting to get something. Most men are just afraid to lose what they have."

"Did Glacier fear losing you?" The wine made Angel bold, and it offset her timidity. She loved being let in behind the curtain. What a bystander witnessed and assumed could mislead them.

Vivian found the idea amusing. "No. His mind didn't work that way. No one would walk away from the best thing they ever had, right?"

Angel wanted to ask how close Vivian was to leaving him when the man died, but the doorbell rang. The women looked at each other, and Vivian straightened her shoulders. Angel watched the professional mask slide back into place and knew their time here was finished. As she looked for her shoes, Angel heard a thump. A bird had slammed into the glass, trying to get at the feeder. The sound of crunching bone stayed with her the remainder of the day.

Eric, Etta's husband, stood at the door. He held a bunch of white lilies—funeral flowers. Angel said hello and nodded goodbye to Vivian; they did not hug.

Concerned about the bird, Angel skirted the building to the glass room. A cardinal lay dead on the ground. She rooted through her bag and found a stack of napkins. A messy eater, Angel kept emergency supplies. She leaned down to pick up the body and heard muted voices. Not wanting to be caught, Angel crouched behind a bush. Vivian said, "You shouldn't be here."

Eric—the man married to her best friend—said, "Don't say that. I had to come."

Were they having an affair? Angel thought about the fight she interrupted in the lighting store on Saturday. The day the police found Glacier's body.

Etta was her best friend. The woman did not dishonor Eric by talking about their marital issues, but what if Angel found out something horrible? She thought a wife would want to know if her husband cheated.

Angel knew no such thing, though. A kind man made a condolence call; she had done the same. His visit may have been altruistic, and Angel came with an agenda. She should not question other people's motives, but while she loved Eric, her loyalty lie with Etta.

Involving oneself in someone else's business never worked out well. If Angel told her Eric had gone outside their marriage, Etta may not believe her and would be heartbroken. If they split up and reunited, it would be challenging to maintain their friendship. Angel stood to lose either way. She would pray on it. Her sleeve snagged on an evergreen bush. The underground irrigation system must have come on last night because the ground was soft. Her heel slipped, and she fell.

Her sharp cry of surprise carried through the window. Vivian looked out to see Angel sitting in the dirt, a dead red bird in her hand. She dropped her head in shame. The beautiful woman turned and walked back into the room.

The Harrisons had created a striking indoor garden for their personal pleasure. When a creature from the outside attempted to enter, it died. She took the body with her to bury the kindred soul.

# CHAPTER 4

Angel reached work late because she had gone home, retrieved Prancer, and replaced the pair of muddied pants. Her boss had left a message asking to see her. It was a good thing she had come in yesterday and prepared today's lesson. Her boss was not a social person, and nerves caused her to sweat in the too-warm building.

The head of the music department reminded Angel of a scarecrow. His arm and leg joints dangled akimbo. He had wanted to be a conductor, but his movements proved too spasmodic for the orchestra.

"I stopped by your office at nine, and you weren't in." He did not waste effort on pleasantries. Nothing in his manner indicated he thought her worth the time.

Angel arrived early most days, though her job did not require a strict nine-to-five adherence. The college allowed professional staff flexibility, but he chose to ignore those lines in her contract.

"I worked from home, sir. It's the first day of class, and I needed a few extra minutes." Not true, but she had put in time this weekend. In the greater sense, Angel had met her obligations.

"In the future, I would prefer you handle lesson planning here. We supply computers for a reason."

"Yes, sir. What did you need? Is there something I can assist you with?" Angel hoped he did not assign her to another committee. She served on two already, and the time commitments ate into her day.

"The bookstore approved a rush order for you, and the shipping cost was exorbitant. Why do you need two sets of the same volume? I checked with the registrar, and there wasn't a last-minute rush to sit your class." He stared over the top of his rimless glasses, and Angel swallowed hard.

"I'm sorry, sir. I'll be glad to pay for the additional charge if you tell me how much it is." He handed her an invoice, and she gulped. It had cost two hundred dollars to express ship the books. Her Visa reached its limit with the half-price bottles of wine. She would need to find the money somewhere else, and fast.

Her boss's head snapped up, and he sniffed like a wolf who caught the scent of dinner. "What's that smell?" He sampled the air again and said with a tone of incredulity, "Have you been drinking?"

Angel's heart froze in her chest, and her hands clenched into wet fists. Homelessness scared the daylights out of her. If she lost her job, she would not be able to pay the landlord. No matter what, the rent check might be short due to the shipping charges. Her mind spiraled down a black hole. The wine had helped Vivian share her feelings, but getting tipsy before class had never been part of the plan. Angel's conscience castigated her overdrinking before work. She repented in full but allowed her fear to double down on mistakes.

"No, sir. I don't care much for alcohol; my college friends called me a teetotaler." She protested too much but could not stop. "Maybe a few on a Friday night—" Angel lied with an ease that bothered her. She counted two whoppers since arriving at work.

"Something is going on with you, and it needs to end. Connections aren't enough to ensure your slot." A picture of her bow-tied boss shaking hands with the deceased mayor sat on his desk. "Also, we are not bird babysitters." His voice dripped with scorn.

Her cheeks flared red, and Angel did not know if the wine caused the reaction but knew it could cause her to pop off at her boss. "He is a prop for my classes. It's helpful for the students to study a live specimen."

"You'll restrict his visits to class time, then?" Only the man's movements were random; he had sharpened his intellect to a wicked point. The buzzing in her head returned, and she worried about a brain tumor. Angel felt it growing while she defended her job. One she would not need if she were dead.

Her thoughts muddled, but she had worked hard to convince human resources to issue Prancer an ID badge. The parrot may deserve to be fired for his book eating stunt, but Angel would not let it happen without a fight. He had improved her life, and she owed him.

"Sir, no one has complained, and I'd lose too much research time if I had to run him back and forth. He's no problem, I assure you." She hoped her boss did not circle back to the question of what happened to the textbooks. Another lie would weigh heavily on her conscience. Besides, would she claim she shredded them? He already thought her a nutjob.

The department secretary knocked on the door, and Angel took the opportunity to run. "I'll drop this off to accounting right away."

Back in her office, Angel let out a breath. She must do better. Destroyed materials, tardiness, and drunkenness did not impress one's superiors. This one had not hired her, and she had a feeling he wanted to replace her with someone he chose. Angel would not give him the opportunity. Today's class must go so well the entire building heard about it.

She and Prancer greeted everyone as they arrived. Some she knew from previous classes, and Angel thrilled to see them. Returning students meant they had enjoyed her course and methods. The college used extensive feedback systems, and she feared negative reviews. Professors had lost their jobs over unhappy evaluations, and her boss did not need any further reason to question her employment.

Angel introduced herself to new faces and fed off their joy at meeting the delightful macaw. She helped a few brave souls hold him on their outstretched arms. Prancer worked as a secret weapon few could resist. To stoke the mounting enthusiasm, she played The Twelve Days of Christmas.

The bird knew most verses in the same way she knew radio songs. If the music played along, Angel could sing the words. Without it, she was hopeless in remembering them. Six of the first seven stanzas dealt with birds, and Prancer loved the swans the best. A ten on the looks scale himself, he had an eye for beauty. The new class members joined in the singing, and Angel beamed. The session had gotten off to a great start, and she hoped to redeem the morning's missteps.

"The song was written as a poem in 1780's England. Someone merged it with a folk song in 1909 as a forfeit game. If a person forgot a component, they had to provide a kiss or other favor."

"That's sexual harassment," said a young woman dressed in a mixture of paramilitary gear and baby doll clothing. Her painted face reminded Angel of an anime character, and she had died her hair cotton candy pink.

Angel did not take the bait. "The calling birds showed up around the same time. Earlier versions of the song listed them as collie birds—blackbirds or ravens."

"Who would give their love a crow? If my husband did, he'd soon be eating it."

The class chuckled, but Angel was mortified. Merry stood in the doorway and heckled her. "Please give me a minute, class." Angel grabbed a chubby arm and pulled the unwelcome interruption from the room. The woman wore a deep red dress studded with rhinestones and looked like a beauty pageant contestant.

"You can't be here," Angel said. She scanned the hallway to make sure her boss did not lurk within earshot. "I'm working." A colleague walked by, and she hoped her grimace passed as a smile. Two days ago, Merry had stranded her thirty feet in the air and walked away without a backward glance. Angel had not yet forgiven her, nor been asked.

"Me, too."

The woman looked so righteously innocent Angel braced for impact. Merry had worn the same expression the day she swore sparklers were harmless and set fire to Angel's dress. Thank goodness a fast-melting snowman had been close at hand. The kid who made it pummeled her for the stop, drop, and roll she executed on top of his contest entry.

"You don't work, and I don't have time for games." Merry got others to do her heavy lifting. Angel felt a surge of familiar envy and repented. She did not wish to be useless; God had created her for a purpose.

"That's why I signed up for your class. You're always bragging about having gone to college, so I'm following in your footsteps."

The only prescribed path Merry ever followed was down the aisle. The spoiled woman had no interest in music or ornithology. She did not believe the concept of self-improvement applied to her.

"The registration office can help you find something more interesting. This class doesn't have much to offer you."

Her cousin walked into the classroom and said, "I'm sure you wouldn't charge these good people for a worthless waste of their time."

"That's not what I said." Angel looked to see who overheard. They all had. "Guys, this is my cousin, Merry. She's new to school, so please welcome her." Everyone said hello, and Angel returned to the lesson. "People used to give live animals as gifts due to a lack of refrigeration. This way, the food lasted until they needed it."

"That's disgusting. They would also have to feed the thing. Labor-saving devices are bad enough as presents. Right, girls? Who wants a dishwasher instead of diamonds? But gifts you have to clean up after? Eww."

Merry had made her intent evident. Signing up for the course allowed her to torture Angel without the risk of public retaliation. Worse, as a student, she would have multiple opportunities to fill out evaluation sheets. Unemployment did not sound bad anymore. It beat giving her cousin a platform to mock her three times a week. Angel could confess to having killed a bottle of wine for breakfast, and her boss would set her free. No one would blame him.

Her unpaid bills and a starving parrot popped to mind, and Angel forced the rage bubble back down her throat. No job meant she must move home or marry. The prospect of a proposal looked dim. Prancer would eat his way through her cardboard box, and she could not live without him.

Angel fought her terror of humiliation and took control of the situation like the pro she was. "Comments are welcome but must remain constructive. Who can detail the life span and breeding cycle of the partridge?"

Merry smirked, "Birth to grave. Is this what they mean by higher learning?" She awaited the approval and love always given to the class clown.

Prancer said in perfect imitation of Angel's voice, "Sometimes, I just want to shoot you." The students looked around and calculated whether the professor or the bird had spoken. With all eyes on him, Prancer stage-whispered, "I see dead people."

Merry turned red when everyone laughed at her instead of with her, and she did not interrupt again. Angel vowed her teaching assistant would keep his job, and her cousin would drop the course.

Basil came to pick Merry up, and Angel had never been happier to see anyone. To her, he looked like a savior dressed in a stylish suit and shiny shoes. She found him handsome, and his large frame made her feel safe. He could handle whatever came at him. No one could explain what he saw in her cousin.

"Hi, ladies."

Angel wondered if he wore veneers on his teeth but doubted it. Everything about him appeared dependable and trustworthy. Magician-like, he pulled a bouquet of flowers from behind his back and handed them to Merry, who beamed—not at her husband, but at Angel. Another win for her. The two had met when Basil took a job with her father's company, North Pole Enterprises. He served as a vice-president in the entertainment branch, and her dad praised his work.

Angel assured the happy couple had left before she completed her business with the accounting department. Word of her predicament must not reach her parents. A coward to the core, Angel had texted them instead of phoning. An in-person assessment would have been fitting after their bizarre behavior, but she couldn't face it. Maybe tomorrow.

She wrote a check for the shipping charges and despaired at the account's remaining balance. The calendar informed Angel she had two weeks to replace the borrowed rent money. Returning the Christmas gifts had been hard, but now she had to cancel Thanksgiving plans as well.

The phone rang, and Angel flip-flopped over whether to answer it. She had not spoken to Benny since he had taken off like Don Quixote to avenge her honor. Cookie's bottle of wine remained undelivered in her golf cart, so Angel connected the call. She needed to know if it was going to be enough.

"I'm sorry." The guy knew how to start a conversation, but how often would he overstep and think a simple apology set things right?

Angel pressed her advantage. "For what? Treating me like I can't handle my own business or getting involved when I asked you not to?" Stating her grievances fanned the fire under them again. Even if they were married, which they weren't, he had no right to ignore her opinion and barge into her affairs uninvited.

"Both. It riled me up to see a harpy go after someone as sweet as you." Benny sounded contrite, but how practiced was he at begging forgiveness? Angel admitted to being terrible at apologies. She liked them fast and painless, while the people she offended tended to dwell on her misdeeds.

Warmth spread through Angel against her will, and she softened toward him and the woman who had hurt her feelings. "Cookie isn't a harpy. Glacier's death hit her harder than most, and I walked into the line of fire. I am sure she didn't mean it."

"Has she apologized?" His directness reminded Angel of her boss, and the comparison did him no favors.

She stared at her desk. Neither woman had made a move toward the other out of stubbornness or fear of rejection. Angel had bought a gift to smooth the waters, but it did not count as she had not yet given it to Cookie. "No, but I don't know what you said to her, either." Benny could have made it worse. He probably had.

"I told her she couldn't treat my girlfriend like that and get away with it."

Prancer made kissing noises, and Angel shot him a dirty look. Benny had told someone she was his girlfriend. Her heart clenched. Not knowing what to do with the information, she let it pass. "What did she say?"

"That your family was the local mob, extorting businesses and taking bribes."

Angel tried to breathe, but no air entered the collapsed passageways. Her vision blurred, and she thought she might blackout. Heart attacks were unusual at her age, but not impossible. Maybe it was a stroke. Or the tumor's growth had accelerated.

"Are you still there?" She banged her hand to indicate she was. The universal sign for choking would not work on a voice call. "What's going on?"

Prancer had stopped making suggestive noises and dropped from his perch onto her desk. He scurried to her and sang, "Yes, Jesus loves me," while staring at her face. Oxygen whooshed into her lungs, and she gulped in gratitude.

Angel's throat opened enough for her to say, "I'm okay. Sorry, I choked." She didn't tell Benny about the panic attack. The man would change his mind about dating her when he discovered how flawed she was. It did not have to be today.

Prancer climbed up Angel's arm and sat on her shoulder. Her heart filled with love for the bird. Like a seizure-sensing dog, he had helped avert disaster. The bird was brilliant and might sense the cancer growing in her brain. She would teach him to call 911

64

and say, "Help Angel." Practicing would be impractical, but she knew one of the operators. They would find a way.

"Did you hear what I said?"

She had. Cookie accused her father of running a crime syndicate. "It's crazy. You know that, right?" Benny hesitated, and Angel's blood pressure shot to a dangerous level. "Right?"

"She made some good points."

Angel fought the impulse to never speak to the man again. She kicked herself for being pathetic, but the only reason she did not hang up was because he had called her his girlfriend. The week had been a nightmare. Someone killed the mayor, her parents got drunk and mean, and Cookie accused them of being Cosa Nostra. Angel's messy mind had jumped the tracks and plunged her into a parallel universe where nothing made sense.

She grasped for an explanation. "You're new; you don't know all the good my parents have done." No one here longer than a minute would consider what he said to be true. The townspeople loved her family.

"I'm going to the city council meeting tonight. Come with me."

She had never attended one in her life. From all accounts, they were deadly dull. People showed up to complain about the neighbor's dog defecating on their lawn and trees overhanging fence lines. Pettiness caused Angel unreasonable dismay.

"The building is too hot. And small." Angel squirmed with the thought of being in an enclosed space with people who used cologne instead of a shower. She had a sensitive nose.

Benny laughed. "So?" He did not understand, and she could not explain without sounding a fool.

"I don't like tight spaces." She handed Prancer another nut, and he balanced on one foot to eat it. The shells landed in her hair. A lack of arms must be aggravating; Angel owned a set of them and still did not manage well. She prayed to never become paraplegic.

"I'll be with you, and it's not a rock concert. No one has ever died from crush injuries."

"Crowds aren't my thing, but thank you for asking me."

Benny let out a heavy breath, and Angel noted his frustration. She wrestled with the expectations of a new relationship. A person should not have to change for their partner but showing up for them was not unreasonable.

"I'm speaking against the tax on Lump of Coal, and your support would mean a lot to me." Would she be valuable to him because he liked her, or because of her family name? They had been an official couple for three minutes when her paranoia peeked out of its hiding place. "The guy with the prettiest girl in the room gets heard."

His words were utter nonsense, but she dove into them like a life raft. Benny did not seek some backseat alliance. He had taken her out in public and defended her to Cookie. In contrast, Angel had questioned his motives and ignored his calls. He may have overreached, but she had failed to commit.

"Promise me we can leave if it's too much." Angel needed an exit strategy at all times. Involving another person in her life required stating it out loud. It was only fair she warned him.

"Of course we can. I'm not going to let anything bad happen to you."

She believed him and wanted to prove it, so they agreed to meet in front of city hall a few minutes before 7 p.m. The hassles of the day receded, and Angel wondered what to wear. It was not a romantic date, but this one meant more. They were presenting themselves as a team, and it felt good.

Prancer picked up her excitement and ran back and forth on the branch. When he reached the end, he bobbed his head, spun around, and squatted. It was his version of the hokey pokey, a favorite.

"Silly bird. Want to go?"

"Jump!" he said and flexed his ankles as if to do so. Parrot knees sit much higher and are where people expect the thigh joint to be.

Angel got into the spirit. "One, two, three!"

Like a child on the side of a pool, Prancer bounced a few times and launched himself at her. He closed the gap without using his powerful wings, and Angel caught him on her forearm.

"Good bird!" he said. She agreed, and they headed home.

# CHAPTER 5

Angel chose a shimmery pink top and found earrings to match. Her hair clip allowed a few curls to escape, and the result was soft and feminine.

She walked to avoid having two carts if they grabbed a bite after the meeting. Evenings in the globe were magical. The engineers never let it get so cold one was uncomfortable, but the chill lent itself to snuggling and rosy cheeks. Twinkling lights covered every bush and doorway, and the corner carolers stepped fresh from a Dickens novel.

As Angel approached the hall, her nervousness increased. She grew warm, and her breath came faster. Large rooms where everyone sat and faced the front scared her. The last rows emptied first, blocking her exit. When she played the church organ, she sat alone and was grateful.

Benny stood in the light cast by a reproduction gas lamp and grinned when their eyes met. She did not hate the feeling of having a man excited to see her. He kissed Angel hello and reached for a mittened hand. Her heart made a pit-pat sound loud enough for him to hear. Sightseers passed on the sidewalk, exclaiming over the lovely sound of sleigh bells. She could have remained in the moment forever.

No tourists had ventured inside the stuffy municipal building as the square offered many more temptations for an evening on the town. Angel knew some of the attendees but not all. Had they worn name tags, a story about them would have sprung to mind. Gossip required no introduction.

The raised platform held a long table with a half dozen people chatting while they waited. Angel smiled at the familiar faces, but more than one turned their backs. They must not have noticed her. She did not frequent these gatherings. Angel tried to sit in the last row, but Benny shook his head and drug her to the middle. She took the aisle seat with the fastest escape route and hoped the fire marshal kept it clear.

The meeting began with half of the chairs still empty. Angel released her breath; it would not be as bad as she thought. No one wanted to attend one of these things, and she got points for doing so. Score!

Vivian Harrison entered the room, and Angel heard murmurs of pity. She felt defensive of the widow and wanted people to snap their gaping mouths shut. Someone said, "What's she doing here? He's not even buried yet."

Angel had no idea what one had to do with the other. Should widows remain cloistered until they saw their husbands nestled safely beneath the ground? She gave the speaker a withering look. The woman gave an uppity snort and averted her eyes.

The chairperson called the meeting to order, and Angel forgot the incident. The pastor opened with a prayer for the Harrisons, and she added an emphatic, "Amen," at the end. Someone read the notes from the last meeting, and a spirited discussion regarding a new stop sign took place. Angel stifled a yawn and daydreamed about food. She closed her eyes for a second and felt a sharp nudge from her boyfriend. It felt foreign to think the word.

When the chair asked for new business, Benny stood. Angel straightened in her chair but did not look at him. Her mouth had dried out, and she needed water, but it was too late. The room grew hot. Pinpricks of anticipation, shame, and fear ran through her body.

The speaker called on him, and Benny said, "Before his death, the mayor imposed an environmental tax. I would like you to rescind it."

"The man's not cold!" Outrage shot outward from the stage. The members of the council exchanged looks of astonishment. "Show some respect!"

"So?" Angel cringed, but Benny did not falter. "Why should we be stuck with poor policy because the guy who wrote it died?" She felt he made a good point, but worried his timing seemed uncaring. The issue could have waited another month until people had grieved.

"Sir, are you a member of this community?" Benny was new to town, and Angel did not blame them for checking. Re-writing statutes for outsiders would be a miscarriage of internal policy.

"A doubly taxed one. I sell freestanding stoves, and Glacier Harrison didn't like it. My business is legitimate, but unfair taxation is not."

"Does anyone know what this man is talking about?" the chairman asked. Members put their hands over their microphones and conferred. "We've agreed to address the matter. Leave your details, and we'll investigate your claim after the holidays. Is there any other new business?"

Angel felt snubbed by the committee's nonchalance. Benny had come to be heard, and the least they could do was listen. "Your great plan is to think about it two months from now? The holidays aren't for six weeks." She could not believe the outspoken voice belonged to her; this was not her fight.

"Things take time, Miss—" The chair looked over his glasses and started. "Angel, is that you?" She stood next to Benny, and her knees trembled with fright. A bathroom break would have been a Godsend.

"Yes, sir." She drew in a steadying breath. "It isn't smart to discourage new ventures in the globe." If the community wanted to grow more prosperous, they had to encourage new investors.

"Ha!" said the woman who had commented on Vivian Harrison's presence. "Your family has their hands in everyone's pockets and are just looking for more victims!"

Angel spun and stared in shock. The woman must struggle with mental health issues. "Frank," Angel said to the chief of police, "maybe your deputy could escort this woman home. She's unwell."

Voices around the room rose at once. It took Angel a moment to understand they shouted at her, not the crazy person.

"The police are on your payroll, too?"

"You should be the one to go home."

"Killing the mayor wasn't enough?"

"We've paid your toll."

"Extortionist!"

Angel staggered under the unexpected assault. Cookie had made the same claim, and she did not understand it in the least. "I had nothing to do with Glacier's death, and I have no idea what you're talking about!" She felt as if she had run a marathon. Her breath came out in short exhalations, and her pulse raced.

"He tried to stop you, and you killed him! Murderer!"

Vivian Harrison's face hardened, and Angel could not believe how things had changed. They had drinks this morning and shared secrets.

"Stop me from what? I haven't done anything." Panic flared in Angel's chest, and she needed to pee. She clenched and prayed for the best.

"Taking over! Your family wants it all, and with Glacier out of the way, there's nothing stopping you."

"Except us," said a burly man in a threatening baritone.

"It's our town, not yours," her first-grade teacher yelled. Angel stared at the woman. She had been the teacher's pet.

The dentist she had visited every six months since she got teeth said, "We won't let you get away with this." She would never again trust the man to come near her with a drill in his hand.

Her butcher glared, and Angel was happy he did not carry his meat cleaver. She felt dizzy. Why hadn't Benny listened to her? She had known this was a bad idea; her intuition had just listed the wrong reasons.

Benny put his arm around Angel and shoved her into the aisle. She had gone blind, and her feet stumbled. Jeers and applause ushered them from city hall. The cold air stung, but not as much as the words of life-long acquaintances had.

"I have no idea what just happened in there, but I promised to get you out if it got bad."

"That's not what I meant!" Angel had worried about claustrophobia and boredom, not a lynch mob. Benny moved them from the blast radius, though in Angel's mind, the debris still came down around her ears.

Two blocks away, he led them into a wine bar with muted lights and inflated prices. Angel had never been inside the place and looked around in confusion. It felt as foreign as a third world country. She spotted the ladies' room and ran. Inside a stall, she did not lock the door. The thought of having to crawl out when the mechanism failed proved too much. Angel voided and leaned her head on the cool stainless-steel wall. She felt raw, drained, and spent.

"Lord, please help me. I don't know what's happening here. I'm so lost. Please." The words turned to whimpers.

An unknown voice asked if she were alright, and if they could call someone to help. Angel thanked the woman and assured her she would be fine. It had to have been a kind tourist because the town hated her. Locals hung out in bars without signage. Most were unknown to the casual visitor but not blocked. Benny must not have found them yet, and no one had shown him. The globe should do a better job of welcoming new people.

At the table, Angel shrugged off her coat and stared at the patterned tablecloth. The meeting had numbed her mind as effectively as Novocaine. Benny ordered a bottle of white, and they sat without speaking while the alcohol thawed her emotions. Tears threatened but did not fall. Shame poured off Angel's hot skin in waves. She had been nervous Benny would embarrass her, and people would talk behind her back. Instead, the villagers came for her head-on, and it did not have anything to do with Benny.

"That was rough. No wonder you don't go." He looked at her in pity.

She stared at him. Did he think this was normal? The towns-people had lost their collective minds. Aliens had infiltrated their ranks. These were her friends and neighbors, and they did not act like this.

"You don't understand. We're the globe's first family. People love us."

Benny made a rueful noise that ended with a tongue click. He sounded sorry for her. "Not as much as you seem to think."

He was wrong. She had received special treatment every day of her life. It happened so often it made her uncomfortable. Angel needed him to admit something went haywire. The globe did not work this way. "Look, if I go into a flower shop, I walk out with a rose."

He looked at her like she was daft and refilled her drink. "So do I."

"But I don't pay for it. Candy from the store? A gift. People let me cut in line."

"You're cute, and folks like you. This place is known for its friendliness." He placed his hand over hers, but she found it con-descending, not romantic, and shrugged free.

The room vibrated, and she downed the second wine in one go. Her boss appeared tableside and stared at her in horror. "I just wanted to say hello." No one had told him about the better bars with cheaper drinks, either.

"Hello," she croaked. "This is my..." Why couldn't she think of what to say? She sounded like an idiot. "This is Benny." The night could not get any worse.

Her date's face tightened, and he said, "Pleased to meet you."

"Be sure she gets to work on time," her boss said. "It's import-ant." The loose-limbed marionette walked back to his table. He had some nerve assuming Benny was responsible for her, or that they would spend the night together. It was none of his business; neither was her drinking, though she had gotten drunk twice in a single day. It was a personal best.

"Let's go," Benny said, and his face had changed. The concerned boyfriend had disappeared, and an angry stranger took his place.

Angel tried to make her eyes cooperate. "We're not done." She did not want to go home. In public, the accusatory voices might leave her be. Alone in her apartment, she had no defense against the horde in her head.

"We are." He pushed against Angel, urging her to slide out of the booth. She did not move. For once, being a bigger girl worked to her advantage.

"What's wrong?"

"You didn't want to be seen with me at the meeting tonight, and you introduced me to that guy like we just met."

Pain flashed through her and brought with it a stab of regret. "He's my boss, and I'm sorry. It was lame. I care about you—"

Benny scooted the opposite direction. "But you don't want people to know you're my girlfriend. You've made it perfectly clear. I get it."

"That's not true!" The tears came now and would not stop. Angel felt abandoned and afraid. Glacier's death had ripped her ordinary life out from under her, and she dangled over a black hole in the universe. Pull-ups had never been her thing; Angel had almost failed gym class due to a lack of upper body strength.

"Hey, you don't need to get so worked up about it." Benny's tone softened, but she had embarrassed him twice this evening. He did not owe her kindness. "If you want to keep this more casual, we can do that. I really liked you, and I hoped you liked me, too." Through the dim, Benny looked sad.

"I do." Angel wiped her nose on the sparkly sleeve and regretted it. She regretted everything. "I stood up for you tonight. The time frame they offered was ridiculous." She was introverted, and it had taken moxie for her to open her mouth. Couldn't he see she put herself out there?

"You did," Benny admitted and dipped his head. Dark hair fell across one brown eye. "That was brave."

Angel thought so, too. She had used her power for good, only to find she had none. People had called her a murdering extortionist and told her to leave town. Something had gone very wrong, but she didn't know what or when.

"I don't like crowds, or speaking in public, but I did it. For you." She hiccupped. Angel fought to prove she had not disregarded him or his feelings. She did not know why the word "boyfriend" refused to cross her lips. It was a morsel she needed to taste a few more times before using it.

Benny moved back into the booth and held her hand. "I'm sorry I got mad. What happened to you tonight was terrible, and if not for me, you wouldn't have been there."

It was true, but it did not change things. Angel had gone, and she would never forget the fallout. The villagers kept torches and pitchforks in their pockets. Why had she never known before tonight?

"They hate me." The words hurt. She was not popular but had considered herself well-liked. It was a delusion. The blinders had come off and left her staring at the sun. She did not like the light.

Benny rubbed her shoulder. "They don't. Finish your wine, and we'll go."

"They do."

He smiled, and she felt better. "Well, maybe a little bit. What did you do to them?"

Angel needed an answer to his question, and she needed it now. It was late, but she did not care. She pulled out her cell phone and dialed. No answer. Her parents must be asleep, passed out drunk, or refusing her calls. They had to know what happened. Why hadn't they warned her? Something dark and slippery wormed its way around the back of her mind, but she could not grasp its tail.

They stayed for a while longer but did not speak much. Angel merged with the night and remembered no more.

She awoke with a start. Her limbs refused to respond. Angel had always feared being paralyzed but assumed it would require a traumatic accident. Finding it could come upon her spontaneously was much worse.

Something else felt wrong, but her foggy mind could not place it. The bed did not feel right. Dear God. It was not hers. Angel blinked to clear her eyes. She did not know where she was. Her hands flew to her face, and she realized they were not incapacitated.

Adrenaline spiked her bloodstream, but she held still and listened. No sound met her ears. Angel tallied the facts: her body suffered an impairment that fogged her brain and senses, she was not home where she belonged, and a crowd of people had threatened her last night.

Someone among them had abducted her against her will. They believed she had something to do with Glacier's murder, and maybe they wanted revenge. Or—her heart seized—she was next. They might have done the same to the mayor before they killed him. If they wanted information, Angel did not have any. Her captors did not yet know she was awake, and she planned to use surprise to her advantage. "Lord, help me. Please don't let me die here."

The globe did not allow kidnappings or murder. Angel's only exposure to the subject had been through library books and movies. In slow motion, she turned her head to survey the room.

Angel remembered nothing. Someone had obviously tranquilized her. She had a vague remembrance of sitting in a bar, but the trail ended there. Date rape drugs sprung to mind, but she pushed them from her thoughts. Survival came first.

The room held no clues; it appeared to be an ordinary bedroom. Angel's head hurt; she assumed it was a side effect from the knockout drops. There may be lasting brain damage, but she had no time to worry about it now. Angel breathed easier when she found herself alone and unobserved. The kidnappers must have cameras in place, but she did not look for them. She had no plans to be here long enough for the knowledge to make a difference.

She opened a door with as much stealth as she could muster, but found it was a closet. Men's activewear, tennis shoes, and a Santa suit gave her no clues to her location.

Another interior door led to a bathroom, and she used it without flushing. Eluding bad guys merited a breach of etiquette. With extreme care, Angel turned the faucet on a trickle. She could not leave without washing her hands. A quick inventory showed no harm had come to her so far. Angel's clothing had not been removed, and no bruises or other injuries marked her skin. God had protected her, and she believed He would get her home safely.

Prancer flashed across her mind. The bird had been left alone, and she did not know for how long. Had it been overnight, or several days? He must be worried she had deserted him. Angel would never abandon the macaw who meant so much to her. She would fight for both their lives.

Resolved to escape, Angel tip-toed back through the bedroom and tested the main door. To her immense surprise and thankfulness, it opened. God must have sent a team of angels with lockpicks, and she would forever glorify His name.

She cracked the door a quarter-inch at a time, and the hinges moved without making a sound. Angel peered through the opening, searching for danger in her path. Weaponless, she felt exposed and vulnerable.

The bedroom opened onto a standard living room. All was still. A form lay sleeping on the couch, and she could hear him snore. She had to be careful now; her life depended on it.

Angel's heart drummed so loudly it blocked out all sound. She crept inch by inch across the carpeted floor. Her mind clamored at her to run while she had the chance, but Angel fought the impulse with superhuman resolve. Only a single kidnapper kept watch over her. This was her best chance, and she must not blow it by moving too fast. Against the odds, she made it to the front door without being heard. She sent up a silent prayer of thankfulness and entreaty. Angel's hands shook as she disengaged the deadbolt.

Her heart pounding, she did not risk a glance at her sleeping guard. She pushed the door open and saw dawn light.

"Hey!" a man's voice called, and Angel took flight. The door banged closed behind her, and she flew as fast as her feet could go. "Stop! Come back!" Angel did not look back but fought for distance between her and the man who wanted her dead.

She had grown up in the globe, but her jumbled mind could not identify her location. Angel ran without thinking until she inhaled fire, and deadened legs refused to carry her bulk another step. She had gone three blocks. Out of breath and scared of being found, Angel huddled behind a stand of trees. Her chest heaved with the exertion, and she promised God to start an exercise program if He let her live.

"I'll do a better job, I promise. My body is a temple, and I will treat it as such." Sweat streamed down Angel's overheated face, and her lovely pink blouse looked a mess. She felt as if a giant had shaken the snow globe and scattered its contents willy-nilly.

Angel had neither her bag nor phone. The men must have taken them so she could not call for help. They had underestimated her, though. She had gotten free.

A brief feeling of pride flowed through her. It was the most unusual sensation, equal parts delight and dignity. Though crumpled on the ground and hidden behind a holly bush, she felt strong and capable. "Bring it on," the tiny spark within her thought. "I can take you." When Angel's ragged breath stilled, she risked a look around to find her bearings. No figure ran down the street in pursuit, and no golf carts roamed the streets this early. She wanted to run to the police station, but they would not open until 8 a.m. A childhood friend had lived in this neighborhood, and she charted her steps home. Angel's head and stomach both ached, not to mention her legs. She had survived a terrible ordeal but still stood.

Without her keys, getting in would not be easy. Angel did not leave a spare where just anyone could find it. The thought of burglars rifling through her underwear drawer made her cringe. She should update the stained and torn articles, but money was too tight for niceties.

She left the window to Prancer's room unlocked. The bird worked as a wireless warning system no intruder could hack, and he liked fresh air on warm days. Angel headed around the side of the duplex, not trying to be quiet. In the worst-case scenario, her neighbors would call the police and save her the trouble.

She jiggled the window frame and set off her avian alarm. "Prancer, it's me."

The bird clung to the wire just inside the window and stared at her. "Bad Angel."

"I know buddy, and I'm sorry." She gave the window another pull and managed to pry it open a few more inches. Angel made a mental note to add WD-40 to her shopping list.

Prancer did not like what he did not understand, and he screamed again. Explaining her stolen keys would be of no use. He wanted her to come through the door and feed her like she did every morning. The bird found comfort in routine.

"Give me a minute, and I'll help you."

"Help you," he said in a hopeful tone. Smarter than most animals, Prancer understood his total reliance on Angel. If she had not returned, he would have remained locked in a cage with no one to feed him. She tried not to think of it. Her parents or Etta would not forget about the bird, but she needed to make a long-term contingency plan for her best friend.

No. She was not going to die. Angel needed to get in the house and hurry them both away from here. Her kidnappers likely knew where she lived and would make another attempt to get what they wanted. She hoped the daylight would stall them. The window slid open the rest of the way, and Angel thanked God. It sat too high for her to hike a leg into, though. She needed something to climb on and went in search of anything useful. Prancer screamed when she left his sight.

Her next-door neighbor had welded a metal frame to fashion a poinsettia Christmas tree. It had four sturdy legs and three concentric bands going up to hold the plants. In full bloom, the deep reds were stunning.

Angel considered knocking and explaining her predicament,

but the sun had not risen, and the man did not care for Prancer's ear-splitting outbursts. He would be less than sympathetic. The top four poinsettias came down first, followed by the seven around the stand's middle, and Angel finished with the last ten from the base layer. She set all twenty-one flowers on the bird-hater's porch so no harm would come to them and drug the apparatus around the house.

Angel soon discovered the flaw in her plan. The base of the tree-shaped form sat only eight inches off the ground. It did not boost her high enough to reach the window, and her effort yielded nothing.

She would not give up now. Prancer needed her, and she had to rescue him. Angel grabbed the top steel circle with both hands and scaled the pyramid. Her weight caused the rack to lean toward the house. She rode it like Tarzan on a vine, complete with a yell—though fright caused hers.

Angel turned and caught the window at waist height. The metal track sliced into her mid-section, and she gasped. Using both arms, she grasped the wall and pulled. Her body advanced three inches. She felt the blood run into her head and exhaustion threatened to halt her progress.

The position was too uncomfortable to maintain, however. Necessity forced her to gather all reserve strength and try once more. She placed her palms flat on the wall and heaved. Angel's efforts tipped her center of gravity, and her torso headed for the floor in an unrestrained fall. She tucked her head so as not to break her neck. A loud "ommph" escaped as the wind left her lungs. Angel lay in a tangled heap for a second, trapped in the fifteen inches of space between Prancer's aviary and the wall.

Nothing seemed broken, but she remained unconvinced. Shock may have dulled her perception of pain. Angel closed her eyes and checked for internal bleeding. If she had sprung a leak, it was a slow one.

Prancer scurried down to her level and hung on the other side of the fencing. She must save them before someone arrived. If Angel lived, she would draft a will instructing her family to cremate the remains. No way could she spend eternity in a box underground.

"Are you alright?" Prancer asked. Using the fence weave for leverage, she untangled her limbs and pulled to an upright position.

"Good bird," Angel said and sidled around the cage's perimeter. If her stomach were any larger, she would not have fit. As it was, the fence imprinted a waffle weave on her mid-section. Prancer followed her with interest, wondering if they played a new game.

Her sense of urgency grew. She had no time to lose. Angel had disconnected the landline to save money, and the kidnappers had stolen her cell phone. They could show up here any minute.

Angel ran to the kitchen and rummaged through the junk drawer until she came up with the spare set of keys. She grabbed Prancer's carrier and loaded him into it.

# CHAPTER 6

The town had long ago removed the old payphones. Angel drove to work to call the cops from there. No one would look for her at the college this early, and later, other people would be around to protect her. Once she locked the office door, Angel let out a sigh of relief. Despite her fears and lack of physicality, she had rescued herself. She corrected the thought without delay. God had saved her. "Lord, thank You for saving my physical as well as eternal life. I'm grateful."

Frank, the chief of police, arrived ten minutes after she placed the call. He smelled of shaving cream and soap. Angel appreciated his tangible presence. With him in the room, no one dared come near her.

"Do you need an ambulance?" Frank stepped forward and grabbed her shoulders to assess her condition. Prancer screamed and flew at the man with an open beak. Angel heard the shriek and caught sight of the red blur as Frank covered his face. She spun and intercepted Prancer mid-air. His talons dug into her forearm flesh, and she let out an involuntary cry of pain.

Frank had retreated two steps and drawn his baton from his tool belt. He held it at an angle, ready to strike. "Put that down," Angel demanded and turned to shield the traumatized bird. This gave Prancer a view of the upraised weapon, and the macaw flapped his massive wings to mount another aerial assault.

The chief of police hesitated, and Angel repeated the order. With great reluctance, the man complied.

"Put that down!" This time Prancer gave the directive.

Angel's pulse pounded in her temples as she cradled the bird to her chest. Prancer considered Angel his mate. He would die to protect her.

"Why do you keep a pterodactyl in here?" Frank looked shaken. He remained poised to respond if necessary.

Angel waited until she regained breath control before answering. Inspiration and expiration required focus, but she forgot how to do it if she thought about it too much.

"Prancer is a macaw, not a flying dinosaur. He thought you meant to harm me." Angel had never seen the bird react as he had, and she was impressed and grateful. A parrot's beak could exert as much pressure as a pit bull's jaw. Hyacinth macaws cracked coconuts and broomsticks with equal ease.

She kissed Prancer and gave him a peanut reward. "Good bird." The bird's heart tapped out a furious rhythm. His typical pulse hit two hundred and seventy-five beats per minute, and fear had caused a significant swell in the number. Angel stroked his feathers and murmured to him until he calmed. The bird looked at Frank with suspicion and hatred.

Frank took a chair and eyed the creature with the same. His expression said he preferred his birds in nugget form. Angel ate chicken but had the good grace to feel guilty about it. She put Prancer on the stand and sat down at her desk.

"Are you sure you don't need a doctor?" Frank had asked Angel earlier, but she had declined. "Is your arm alright?"

Angel's nerves jangled, but she had no intention of seeking medical care. Hospital systems ran giant roach hotels; patients checked in, but they never checked out again.

"They didn't hurt me, and neither did Prancer." The kidnappers had not violated her in any way while unconscious. They must have wanted something else. Angel knew her dad would have paid a ransom for her safe return. Maybe they needed money.

"Tell me what happened."

"I told you on the phone." On television, the authorities made victims relive horrors numerous times as if they had done something wrong and needed to explain themselves.

"I need every detail you can think of; leave nothing out."

The man wasted time talking to her while bad men roamed the globe preying on other innocents. They must be stopped. "Do you have cars out looking for the perp?"

Frank blinked, and his eyes remained closed a fraction of a second longer than usual. She heard him exhale. "Looking for who? Can you give me a description of the men who held you? How many were there?"

Angel hesitated. "I can't. The one I saw was asleep, and the blankets covered his face." Did Frank think she should have woken him up to aid a sketch artist?

"What about when he took you? Was he wearing a mask then?"

"I don't remember." Angel did not remember anything, but someone had slipped her a mickey.

Frank stared, and she read the doubt in his face. Angel's anxiety increased. The village had never needed real detectives, but things had changed overnight. Now, when they needed an experienced lawman, they had none. If their chief of police could not do his job, the criminals would win. Cartels could soon run the globe.

"Tell me about your evening leading up to the abduction. What's the last thing you remember after leaving the meeting?"

Angel blanched. Frank had witnessed her shame. The townspeople had run her out of city hall, and he had done nothing to stop them. As far as she knew, he may have participated. She had no business trusting the man until she knew where his loyalties lie. Had he made any progress on Glacier's murder?

"Benny took me for a drink." She kept it simple enough for a mall cop to follow.

"Where'd you go?" The police chief watched her responses but kept half an eye on Prancer. Angel appreciated the bird's presence.

"A wine bar near the park. Vino's."

Frank wrote the information down in his notepad. "Did anyone see you there?"

Angel did not need an alibi; she had not abducted herself. "I'm sure a lot of people did, but it's a tourist trap. No one I know. I spoke to a lady in the bathroom—"

"Who was she?"

A memory flashed. "My boss. My boss was there. You can ask him when he gets here." Angel had managed to arrive on time despite a night of terror. What more could the man ask of a dedicated employee? The way she framed the narrative stretched things a little, but it remained indisputable.

"When did you leave?"

Angel hesitated. "Someone spiked my drink. I don't know when —or how—I left."

"What does Benny say happened?"

What would her so-called boyfriend have to say for himself? He allowed thugs to take her; she could have been tortured or killed. A sick thought knocked her feet out from under her. Had Benny played a part in the abduction? The idea made her ill, and she ran for the trashcan to vomit.

Frank stood to assist her but sat down when Prancer advanced. The two watched each other for any aggressive move. "We should take you to the ER."

"No." Angel did not suffer a concussion or a life-threatening condition. She had trusted the wrong man. Benny served her up to the meeting crowd and then handed her over to kidnappers. No bigger betrayal existed. The man was Judas. "Can you track my cell?"

"I'll ask for a warrant." Frank took out his phone and stared at the screen and up at her. He looked alarmed.

"Someone has broken into your house." Frank's eyes registered high alert and battle-readiness. "You need to tell me what the heck is going on here." The cop looked at Angel as if she held the answers.

All she had were questions. Why did everyone think she had changed overnight? Had Benny started their relationship to gain access to her or her family? Did he move to the globe as part of a larger plan? Whose?

Angel sat down with the poise of a hippo. She escaped her house mere minutes before the bad guys had come looking for her. "Thank You, Lord. Thank You." Angel offered the silent prayer with a full heart. It sunk in an instant. Where would she and Prancer go tonight? Her home was no longer safe.

"They know where I live." The break-in indicated Angel was not a random victim, and they were not done with her. Nausea crested in her stomach.

"It would seem you have enemies. Why did everyone turn on you last night?"

Frank's tone sounded cold, and his expression suggested Angel deserved the treatment she had received. She didn't. "I have no idea. I haven't hurt anyone."

She wanted to go home and crawl into her bed, but she couldn't. Someone had invaded her haven, and Angel would be forced to relocate. No point in paying rent, then. She would not be staying.

"Baloney. Too many people are angry at you for it to have been nothing. I can't protect you if you don't tell me what you've done."

Angel had been through hell and felt like it. Her eyes, head, and tummy all ached. Nerve endings misfired all over her body, and she felt like someone had taken a cheese grater to her skin. Tears threatened, but she would not let Frank see her cry. Any sympathy from him would be fake.

"I'm the victim, remember? What did the thieves take?" Her belongings would not entice a common burglar. Any reasonable thief would donate a thing or two when they learned how she lived. Had someone planted something in her house without her knowledge?

Frank answered his phone and listened for a moment. "Call in everyone, cordon off the area, and get me a list of the kids who went missing statewide in the last year." He looked at Angel in fear-tinged amazement, and he placed a hand on his nightstick. Fear spiked in her bloodstream.

"You're the kidnapper, aren't you?" She asked, but her heart knew. The police were in on it the whole time. No one could be trusted.

"Child exploitation is a serious offense." Frank positioned his chair to block the office door—and her exit. No matter how hard she tried, Angel could not fight her way free from this nightmare.

She was innocent: her only crime was failing to recognize evil had moved in and taken over the globe. When someone murdered the mayor, she naively believed life would return to normal. Nothing could have prepared her for recent events.

"I have no idea what you are talking about, but I'm leaving." Angel's instincts told her to flee. The oxygen in the room had run out, as had her options. She reached for Prancer's carrier.

"The only place you're going is with me. You're under arrest."

Angel's heart wanted to explode, but the blood vessels in her brain threatened to burst first. "You can't arrest me. I haven't done anything." Innocent people did not go to jail. The globe didn't even have a correctional center. Angel panicked when she realized Frank would deliver her to outside authorities.

"My men found a steel cage inside your second bedroom—outfitted like a playground with climbing ropes and kid's toys. How sick are you?" His look communicated pure disgust for her.

Angel's breath whooshed out of her lungs, and she laughed. Once she started, she could not stop.

"It's why you killed Glacier, isn't it? The mayor found out you snatch children and sell them to the highest bidder." His face reddened to a dangerous level, and Angel was glad no one allowed Frank to carry a gun.

The hysteria abated in an instant, and Angel composed herself. "It's not a holding pen for child sex slaves. It's Prancer's aviary."

Frank looked to her from the bird who chose this moment to sing, "Root, root, root for the home team."

"What about the ropes and toys?" He looked dubious. Angel explained the macaw's needs and how she had gone about meeting them. "I'm going to have to see for myself." His cell buzzed with another text. "It seems your neighbor has had some trouble, too. Someone unloaded the poinsettias from his display and used the frame to get into your house."

Angel lowered her chin. "That was me." Frank gave her a curious look, and she explained. "The kidnappers have my phone and keys."

"So, you broke into your own house? Why?" His excitement over having nabbed an evil child molester had turned to irritation at a wasted morning.

"I had to make sure Prancer was safe."

Frank sighed. "No one is going to mess with that bird." He gave the macaw a dirty look. "I'll start the trace on the phone. Where were you when you woke up this morning?" The policeman in him perked back up; he still had a kidnapping and a murder to solve.

Angel described the neighborhood and how she had come to know it. She told him about running down the street and collapsing in a bush before making her way home.

"Where were you the night the mayor died?"

The man was lazy. If he couldn't nail her for running a child prostitution ring, he would charge her with an unsolved murder. "Benny and I went bowling, then I went home."

Angel did not bring up overhearing the man's telephone call with his wife. Vivian had lost her husband, and the police chief would investigate the shortfalls of their marriage.

Frank studied her face. "Alone?"

Heat rose in her cheeks. Her sex life was not this man's business, though he had a singular focus on it. Maybe he had perverted secrets to hide. "Yes, alone."

"Can anyone verify your story? Angel wished she had never called him. The town's top cop had no interest in the criminals who targeted her and instead questioned her as if she were the bad guy.

"Prancer," she said.

"Good bird," the macaw said when he heard his name. He did not like Angel to ignore him for this amount of time.

Her boss poked his head in the door, probably to make sure she had arrived on time. He wrinkled his nose when he saw she wore the same top she had worn last night, only now it was stained and torn.

"I see the party continued all night, and the police caught up with you this morning. We do have a dress code. It's in your handbook." His voice dripped with sarcasm, and he looked for Frank's amusement at his wit.

"A killer took me captive." She had no proof, but he had not been a rapist. The educated man recoiled. One of his disjointed hands flapped like an injured bird. He stepped back as if her ordeal were contagious.

"Who would kidnap you?" He looked at her in revulsion. Angel had not known a worthiness threshold existed for forceable abductions. It was the single most insulting question she had ever been asked.

Frank said, "Did you see Angel at Vino's last night?"

Her boss's mouth turned into a thin, bloodless line. "Yes. She was guzzling white wine." He surveyed her and added, "I think she may have an alcohol problem. I swore I smelled it on her yesterday morning."

The policeman made another note. "What time did she leave?"

"Her—" her boss hesitated over his word choice, "gentleman friend escorted her out around 11. I went home shortly thereafter." If Angel was found in the bar at 11 p.m., she was an alcoholic. If her boss left later, he had ended the evening at a reasonable hour.

Wait. Benny? Benny had led her out of Vino's? Angel's mouth went dry, and her heart sank. He had been in on it. The guy had never liked her; he had only pretended he did to get close. But why— because of her famous family? No one without an agenda would ever want her. Angel's mind shut down, and she heard no more.

A piece of trash hit her shoulder, and she looked up into Frank's expectant face. Her boss had left, and the policeman threw a paper snowball instead of approaching her. He did not trust Prancer, and with good reason. "Where can I find Benny? I need to talk to him."

They had not gone out long. The man's number was in her phone; Angel did not know it by heart. She had never been to his house, either. The relationship was over, and she felt numb. The man had betrayed her. She had been a fool to think she interested him.

"Try his store, Lump of Coal. I'll press charges." The story would make the news, and Angel would be humiliated, but she could not let the man get away with what he had done. She wondered how much he had gotten paid. "Find out who his partner is. The guy's still out there."

Frank got up to leave. "Where will I find you?"

Angel had nowhere to go. The thought of telling her father what a mess she had made of her life depleted her. "I'll be here. The orchestra practices the Christmas cantata today, and I must attend. Am I still under arrest?"

"Not unless your neighbor wants to press charges."

The real crimes remained unsolved, but Frank had time for misdemeanor borrowing. People had grown too complacent if they worried about their poinsettias in a week of kidnapping and murder.

"For what? Illegal flower arranging? Harassing a Christmas tree stand? I'll wash and return it."

Frank left, and Angel locked the door behind him. Her boss was right—she smelled. The college had a workout center for students and employees. She found a T-shirt from an old charity event and headed for the gym.

Once out of the shower, Angel felt better. No stranger had broken into her house; she might be able to go home. She needed to talk to her parents. They would know what to do. The line rang several times and went to voicemail. She left one but felt uneasy not reaching them. The town had turned on her, and then a mad man snatched her from a public place. Maybe someone had gotten to them. Her mother called most every day, but she had not heard from her since dropping in on them the other night. An attempt to reach their cell yielded the same results. Angel's stomach churned.

Desperate, she phoned Merry and wasted no time with small

talk. "Have you seen or heard from my folks?" The brown-noser spent half her life buttering up Angel's parents and visited them more often than she did.

"They said you hadn't bothered to check on them after the tragedy. You treat the bird better than you do the most important people in your life. You should—"

Angel had no wish to hear what Merry thought she should do with her relationships. All her cousin ever did was take. "So, you've seen them." She breathed a little easier and felt foolish. Her parents ran the globe; they wouldn't run out on it. They were getting older, and the mayor's death had unsettled them, that's all.

"I'm just their niece, but I care more about them than you do. It's scandalous, really. People talk about it all the time." Once Merry got started, it was difficult to break back into a conversation.

"Your selfishness forced us to fill in for you and your husband." She made an irritating gasp of fake surprise. "Oh, I forgot. You don't have one of those either. No one will have you."

Angel fumed but had no energy to engage with Merry on the subject yet again. Choosing her own future never meant she disrespected her parents, and being unmarried did not make her sub-human. Basil was God's compensation to Merry for saddling her with so many character defects.

"Tell them I'm looking for them, will you?" Angel disconnected before Merry had a chance to answer.

She called Etta. Angel had suffered through a harrowing night, and no one she loved knew yet. "Don't tell me you're canceling," her friend said.

"I would never," Angel said and wracked her brain to figure out what she had promised to do. Today was Tuesday. The information clicked. She had agreed to help install the sculptures in the park tonight. Angel had forgotten about The Twelve Days of Christmas and the town's attempt to win the tree topper award.

"Five o'clock, okay? No later—I mean it." Etta's tone underlined her seriousness about Angel's timeliness. "I asked the guys to let it get dark later tonight, but you know how they are about these things. You'd think they had to stop the actual sun from setting."

"Orchestra finishes at 3 p.m., so I'll be there. I just wanted to—" Angel did not know how to begin. Etta was no fan of Benny's. She had witnessed him lose his temper at Cookie's last week, and the mayor turned up dead the next morning. "There was a scene at the city council meeting last night." She pushed the words out in a rush of air.

"I know," Etta said. "I've received three calls so far this morning, and I'm sure there'll be more." Angel had known it wouldn't take long for word to spread. "I'm so sorry that happened to you."

Etta's sympathy felt like salve on a burn, and Angel choked up in gratitude. Before last night, she had always felt loved and admired in the globe. It was her town, and people greeted her with a hug everywhere she went. The rabid crowd had turned on her with snarls and bared teeth. If she had stayed, they would have torn her apart, and Angel still had no idea why. Her wounds bled, and she felt sorry for herself.

"They need something better to do with their time."

"They could help tonight," Etta said. "We're going to need it."

It didn't seem right to tell her about the kidnapping over the phone. She would fly into overprotective mode and show up at the college foaming at the mouth. Angel's boss resented her taking the time to report a felony; he would not welcome a visit from a friend.

"I'll see you in the park." They said their goodbyes and ended the call.

Angel felt guilty for not being forthcoming with the news, but Etta would drag her parents into the matter. The people who loved Angel the most would hijack her future and commit her to a nuthatch or an arranged marriage no matter what she wanted. She would not let them. Angel desired a real partner, someone she could share a life with and rely on to help parent their children. The problem was the ideal man did not exist.

She saw the doorknob turn, and her blood ran cold. If she

died now, it would be as an unpopular spinster. "Go away," Angel shouted in fear before realizing it could be her boss. Fine, he could get lost, too.

"Come in," Prancer said in Angel's voice. She wished the bird would be silent for once. He had no business inviting people into the office. The kidnappers could be standing there, wanting to accost her.

"Prancer, be quiet. Go away, whoever you are." Her tone sounded shrill at the end, and her heartbeat increased.

"It's me," Benny said, and the words filled Angel with dread. Panic bloomed. She needed a way out, but the windowless room had no back door.

"Quiet as a mouse," Prancer said, and made a shushing noise.

Benny stood on the other side of the hollow-core door. She had escaped to trap herself in a corner. Angel's heart seized, and she searched for something with which to defend herself.

"Go away! I'm calling security!" She picked up the phone and dialed it. The seconds passed.

"Why? I don't understand. I brought you coffee." He sounded boyish and a little hurt.

Coffee? He helped kidnap her and thought a warm beverage would buy forgiveness? He was as dense as a fruitcake. "Security, there's an emergency. Room 218. Hurry." She hung up the phone and stared at the door, praying to God it would hold.

"They're on their way, so you better leave. The sheriff is looking for you." How long could it take security to get here? They did not do anything all day. Angel watched them getting paid to play cards.

"Why? I just wanted to return your keys and cell phone. You took off so fast this morning, I couldn't catch up with you."

Benny's words bounced off her ears and ricocheted around the room. *He* couldn't catch up with her? It had been him on the sofa? The snake. The man was arrogant and beyond devious. She had underestimated his cleverness. He had dreamed up the perfect pretext to come to the college. All he had to do was pretend she had forgotten her belongings at his house. It would be his word against hers. Except she was the town's darling, and Benny was a newcomer. People would side with her. She hoped.

"Leave them and go!" Her voice cracked. What if he did? How would she know he had really left? Whenever she opened the door, the waiting man would grab her.

"What's wrong? I know those people were rough on you, but I thought we had a good time afterward."

"You kidnapped me, you monster!" Angel stood to the side of the door; a hole punch raised over her head.

Prancer screamed in a child's voice, "Monsters! Monsters!" Angel had not known the bird ever lived with a child, but it was impossible to know his full history. The mimicry of a scared little girl sent shivers down her spine.

Benny sounded incredulous. "Kidnapped you? I took you home to keep you safe." He lowered his voice and said, "You had too much to drink. Don't you remember?"

Angel was confused, and her arms had gotten tired. She set the hole punch on her desk. "I remember waking up in a strange apartment I never agreed to visit." No matter how much someone had to drink, people had no right to take them somewhere against their will.

"That's my place. You wouldn't tell me where you lived, so I had no choice but to take you home."

She took a second to congratulate herself. All her years of refusing personal information to strangers paid off when she needed it. "Why was I in your bed?"

Angel heard Benny's sigh through the wood. "You were knackered, and I wanted you to be comfortable. I took the couch and never touched you." He sounded sincere. Had she misinterpreted the entire episode? A wave of shame built within her, but Angel held out hope she had not alerted the police over nothing.

"Why didn't you take me to the North Pole Complex?" Anyone else would have; they would not have kept her. It was suspicious.

"You told me your parents were super stressed after Glacier's death. Your mom called, and you refused to talk to her. I didn't think you wanted them to see you so drunk." He hesitated, "I was trying to save you trouble."

Angel's actions were shameful, not his. Benny had tried to protect her from the fallout of her own bad decisions. She wrestled with the knowledge and tried to say something in her defense but found no words.

"Sir, you have no business being here. You need to leave." The deep voice sounded threatening, and Angel flung the door to find two security guards and Benny flat up against the wall. He had raised his hands in surrender.

Prancer's vantage point gave him a clear view of the scene, and he said, "Bang. Bang. You're dead." It was a game they played, though now it did not seem as funny.

"Your macaw, I assume?" Benny asked in a dry tone, but he did not lower his arms.

"It's okay, guys. I made a mistake." Angel's face felt as if she had sunburned it. The worst thing that ever happened to her had happened only in her imagination. She felt as if she had murdered someone based on a dream.

The security officers did not seem willing to take her word for it. Both stood where they were and eyed Benny. The globe offered little in the way of excitement, and Angel believed they wanted a chance to throw their weight around a little.

"Totally my fault, my apologies." Angel grabbed Benny's arm and pulled him into the office. She closed the door and put her back to it. After a moment, she heard reluctant bootheels click down the corridor.

"So, you didn't kidnap me." She stared at the tile, unable to look at him after the commotion she caused.

Benny looked stricken. "Of course not. I didn't know what else to do, so I took you home and put you to bed."

Angel searched his face for any sign of deceit. She found none

95

and crumpled. Constant worry exhausted her. She might freeze to death in a meat locker, find a worm in her apple, have peanut butter glue her mouth shut, or be kidnapped.

"I'm sorry," she said and walked around her desk to sit. Benny handed her one of the coffees, and she drank it. "This is Prancer. I believe you've just met."

"How could I forget?"

She pointed a gun finger at the bird and repeated the line. Prancer wobbled from side to side and said, "I'm hit." With a dramatic flourish, he flopped onto his side on a flat platform.

Benny grinned like a child. "That's amazing! What else can he do?"

Angel loved Prancer because of who he was, not his ability to mimic. She enjoyed playing games with him and found the bird endlessly amusing, but she did not want to exploit him for her entertainment.

"Be the best friend I ever had."

Benny stepped closer to her and said, "I was hoping to work my way up into the position." Angel's heart melted.

"I'm sorry I called the police. I'll tell them it was my fault." Angel was embarrassed and ashamed, but Benny did not seem bothered.

"It'll add to my bad-boy image," and he winked. She fell, hard.

# CHAPTER 7

Orchestra practice soothed Angel's spirit. She read the score, and her hands translated it to the keyboard. Sacred music gifted her soul stillness she could not get anywhere else, even in prayer.

Angel wanted to hang onto the assurance as she traveled to the North Pole Complex, but it melted like snow. Her father was not on his platform in the plaza when she arrived. Another couple heard the children's wishes. She loved family time, but the last visit made her anxious about future ones. The Halloween version of Mom and Dad had scared the daylights out of her, and she feared a nightmarish repeat.

A light tap notified them of her presence. Her mother answered the door and said, "Think you're company now? Do you want me to wait on you, too? What will it be then, your highness? A drink? Lobster in cream sauce?" Knocking had been a bad idea; maybe visiting was as well.

How had Merry not noticed anything wrong here? Her mother, the globe's benevolent queen, oozed hatred from every pore. Maybe her cousin had lied about stopping by; it wouldn't have been the first time. She claimed to dote on her aunt and uncle, but Merry only did what served her purposes.

"I didn't want to disturb you," Angel said, and it sounded lame. More than a security door stood between her and the imposters who inhabited her parents' bodies.

Someone had turned off the holiday displays, or they had plunged into hopelessness and gone out one by one. No roman candles, entertaining bubble lights, or strings of winking garland lit the darkness. Angel shivered.

"Then, why are you here?" Her father had taken off the top to his Santa suit but still wore the pants. A plain white T-shirt covered his torso, and he used the orthotic boot on his injured leg. His other foot wore a filthy sock with a hole in it.

Angel swallowed and ordered her rising fear back into the corner. "I came to check on you. Do you need help? I could start some laundry—or make some food."

Her mother plopped into the worn chintz chair Angel had always loved. In the dim light, it looked dingy and sad. "You're too late. Several years too late."

She got defensive. "I've been right here. You call me all the time. If you had said you needed me for anything, I would've come."

Angel had opened with a half-truth, and her father lifted his injured leg to dispute it. "It took you three months to paint a bunch of doves. If you can't be trusted with the small stuff, don't ask for the big." Angel felt terrible; he was right. He made a trivial request, and she blew it off for a serious amount of time.

He buried the lead, though. A couple of dull doves did not create this tension. "This isn't about taking out the trash. Something much bigger is going on here."

Her mother burped, something Angel had never heard the woman do. A small, natural sound, but it agitated her. Politeness used to be a hallmark of their home. "What was your first clue? A murder?" Her mother laughed, and Angel noticed she had not brushed her hair in days. The gray, tangled mass lay around her shoulders in knots.

"Things got out of hand at the city council meeting, too, and I think you know what's happening." She searched their faces for a clue. The world had turned into a stunt plane, and Angel had not strapped in for the ride.

"You want to know what's happening. That's a good one." Avoidance was not her mother's style. Problems got placed on the to-do list, and she dealt with them in order.

"That's not what you said when you left for college," her father said. His sadness broke Angel's heart. He felt discarded by her, and she never knew it. "You should've stayed gone."

Angel and her father had fought about her career goals and the cost of higher education, but he had never been this vicious. She sucked in her breath. "I'm not you; I can't run this place. No matter how progressive the world gets, people insist on a male Santa." Biology won out every time, and she lacked the necessary equipment. Not that she desired a role in the globe's endless Christmas parade.

"And being a wife is beneath you, isn't it?" Her mother had also been hurt by Angel's decision to branch out and make her life elsewhere. At the time, she had hidden it and voiced mild approval of independent women.

Angel regretted coming, but she had already stepped in it and wanted answers. "People think we're crooks who killed Glacier. Why?"

"Not us," snapped her mother. "You. You did this to us." It was clear she believed her guilty; Angel just wanted to know what they thought she did.

Her temples throbbed, and she worried for her sanity. "What did I do?" Hysteria had crept into her voice. Why wouldn't they just tell her? How bad was this? She thought she might puke.

Her father ignored her question and said, "Had you just done what we asked, none of this would have happened. You would've had plenty of money."

Did her parents know she dipped into the rent to pay the bookstore? How? When she was growing up, they instructed her to seek solutions, not someone to blame. These were not the same people.

Her mother looked at her with open antagonism. "Your father accomplished what no one else could. He built a world of harmony, and like a selfish brat, you shattered it. You don't get to cry if the glass cuts you."

Angel had never been more unhappy in her life. Finding herself too homely to be a snowflake or too fearful to start a family paled in comparison.

"I haven't done anything!" She felt like a child, explaining yet again why Merry deserved the punishment, not her.

"Exactly," said her father. "Not one blasted thing. Decent children help their parents, but not you. You took advantage of the system, and the results are on your head." The harsh words struck her like blows, and the room spun. Up until now, her parents had given her unlimited love and support. She wanted to run, but the experience was so out of character it felt hallucinatory. Had she believed any of it was real, Angel would have fled.

"I wish to God we'd had a son. At the very least, a daughter capable of marrying," her mom said and refilled her glass. Fingerprints smudged the rim as if she had not washed it in days.

"What did you do?" Angel looked from one to the other but met a concrete wall of resistance. They had locked her out like a backyard dog. Good thing Benny had not brought her here last night; this was no longer her home.

"Only what we were forced to," her mother said. "You left us with no other option. You've ruined everything!" The woman shouted now, and anger made her tremble.

Her father had asked her to paint, nothing more. He had never requested a ride or die co-conspirator. Turning him down would have never crossed her mind if he had asked. If her parents were in crisis, they should have told her. Angel had yet to discover a boundary for her love. She would have done whatever was necessary—illegal, or not.

"Tell me what's going on so I can try and fix it. Did you kill Glacier?" She hated the words as they came from her mouth. Angel stood frozen, delaying the next heartbeat until she knew. What would she do if they admitted to murder? Turn them in to the police? Smuggle them out of the country on a cargo ship? She had no idea what the proper response was but knew it would impact her future and possibly her freedom.

Her parents looked at one another, and Angel witnessed a silent conversation she could not interpret. The pair had been married for forty years and needed no words between them. Would they make her an accessory after the fact? A jury might think she had been in on it all along. Angel could go to prison for something she had not done. Her parents had warned her about keeping low company, but associating with them posed the biggest danger.

Their telepathic conversation ended, and her mother said, "We've lived without your help this long. What makes you think we need it now?" They again chose to exclude her. Profound disappointment mingled with momentous relief. These people had raised her. When they were healthy, they provided everything she ever needed. Angel owed them her devotion, no matter their current state or behavior. The mounting evidence of their need slapped her in the face. Her parents had not left their home in days. They had not showered or eaten but had drunk themselves into a stupor.

"You're both tired. Let me pitch in for a while." It was what they said they wanted. Etta would have to understand some things were more important than the town's wish to win a prize.

Her father sat as if awaiting a scheduled execution. His mind and body decayed prior to the state throwing the switch. "Back then, we begged you. Begged." A deep sadness etched lines in his face. "But you had grand plans and couldn't be bothered."

"That's not true! I went to school to build a life, but I never shut you out the way you're doing to me."

"You play a church organ and talk about birds, while your family suffers. It's time you left. I won't let you upset your mother anymore."

"I—" she did not know what to say. They refused her help and presence. Angel considered calling in professional help but feared it would make things worse. Some quack could lock her parents away and deny her access. She felt orphaned and alone.

Angel sat in her golf cart and sobbed. A tornado might dip down any second and remove her from the earth, or a tsunami could rush through the globe and drown them all. She did not know which direction trouble would come from, but the barometer had changed, and the emergency alarms sounded high alert. She had zero interest in putting up the sculptures but had promised Etta. At an impasse with her parents, she could not lose her best friend, too. The woman would be busy, but maybe afterward, they could have a drink and talk.

Booze might be a bad idea. Her boss thought she was a lush and waited for her to screw up again. Most of the town was angry with her as well. She was running out of places to seek understanding.

Prancer had not wanted her to leave. Angel told Alexa to play his favorite documentary on Costa Rican birds, and he shouted, "Home! Home!" Angel hoped the macaw missed her and not the rainforest.

After composing herself, she drove the bucket truck to the park. It was the only private vehicle capable of accomplishing the work they needed to do. At the last moment, she threw in Cookie's gift but vowed not to drink it. Angel had not told Etta or her parents about her fake kidnapping, and she thanked God for small favors. Her legendary ledger of embarrassments did not need another entry. It weighed on her personal tally, but she would have to live with it.

Vivian Harrison had arranged a welcome tent for the volunteers. Hot chocolate, coffee, and sodas stood ready for thirsty workers. Angel counted fifty villagers in attendance, not a bad showing. A few people whispered when she walked by but most ignored her. She preferred invisibility.

The grieving widow greeted everyone and thanked them for their concern. "Have the police found anything yet?" Someone asked. Angel wondered how many people had shown up for the chance to walk the crime scene and quiz the bereaved. Ghouls.

"We'll know more tomorrow when the autopsy results are made available," she said. Angel admired her poise. In Vivian's shoes, Angel would have worn slippers. How the woman got out of bed, much less visited the park where they found her husband's body was beyond her. "In the meantime, we'll bring Glacier's biggest wish to life." She attempted a smile and failed.

Some people cheered; others looked uncomfortable. No one knew the appropriate response in such an awkward situation.

Eric and Etta had delivered the sculptures to their specific locations earlier in the day. Tonight's teams would work together to secure them in place and string miles of smaller lights. Wind and weather would not be an issue, but extra care needed to be taken with the breakable works of art.

Vivian handed out the duties she and Etta had devised. They assigned Angel the first exhibit, the partridge in a pear tree, because she brought the vehicle capable of doing the work. The mayor's wife tasked Basil with assisting her in the bucket and asked Merry to run things from the ground.

Angel had not thought the day could get any worse. "Why don't I stay in the truck, and the newlyweds can work up top?" She had good cause not to trust her cousin at the controls.

Merry pouted. "Vivian said I could do it. Anyhoo, you know I'm afraid of heights, silly." Baby talk made Angel insane.

Basil beamed at his wife as if her insipidness made her more irresistible. "Don't you worry, hon. Angel and I will manage. You stay down here where it's safe."

Angel was afraid of everything from ketchup to bubble wrap, yet no one worried about her dangling a glass bird thirty feet in the spot she had found a dead body. Merry's fear of step stools, however, needed accommodation. If Vivian could stomach being here, Angel could too. It was just a tree. She wanted her cousin's sensitivities catered to somewhere far across town. Still, with her husband in the bucket, Merry would not risk any shenanigans. It would destroy Basil's image of his perfect wife.

Angel loaded up her crew and moved the truck to station one. She looked around and shuddered. No yellow tape remained, but she saw it in her mind. Why had Glacier ended up here? Had someone sent a coded message? If so, they should have supplied the key, as well. Angel pushed the thought from her mind. Dwelling on it would make tonight's undertaking impossible.

She hissed a stern warning to Merry, "If you screw around with us up there, I swear I'll push him overboard." Angel would never do it, of course, but her cousin's gasp made the threat worthwhile.

As it was the only installation with a single item, Etta had built a partridge the size of a house. Its creator arrived by cart, and they all stared at the glass maker's giant creation. "I may have overshot," Etta said. "This bird could dwarf its roost." Her long blonde hair formed snowballs on each side of her head, and she looked like an adorable toddler.

"How're we going to get the thing up there?" Basil asked, and his handsome face looked doubtful. He had uttered Angel's question word for word.

Etta ignored the fact her husband stood next to her and ramped up the charm. "Don't worry; it's light. No problem at all for a strong guy like you."

She turned on her megawatt smile, and Angel watched her cousin-in-in-law expand into a superhero. He straightened his shoulders, flexed his chest muscles, and widened his stance. Even married men sought Etta's admiration. Merry narrowed her eyes and placed a possessive hand on Basil's bicep. Angel smiled at her discomfort. Her immature cousin simpered while Etta wielded blow torches, electrical current, and gasses pulled from the periodic table of elements. There was no contest.

"You guys get in, and I'll hand it to you," Eric said. Angel did not want to do this. She would make a mistake and cause a disaster.

As Eric picked up the piece, Angel saw another way out and grabbed for it. "Why don't you ride up there with him? I'll stay down here and tell you if it's straight."

"There's not enough room for two men. I'm sorry; it's got to be you."

For the first time ever, Angel wished her bathroom scale read five hundred pounds. Every brownie sundae she hadn't eaten could have saved her this fate. Heights bothered Angel but sharing such a small suspended space brought on palpitations.

Merry climbed into the truck, and Basil sprung into the bucket without effort. He extended a hand to Angel. She took a shuddering breath and put one leg over the side rail. Basil grabbed her shoulder and hauled her in like a tuna. He claimed the position closest to Eric, and Etta's husband handed him the neon partridge. The globe's electricians had run a cable up the center of the trunk in preparedness for today. All they needed to do was suspend the sculpture from the hook already in place and connect it.

Basil leaned his head over the side of the bucket, and Angel did not envy him. His arm muscles strained against tight shirt sleeves. "Don't let it hit the side!" Etta said.

Angel heard the nervousness in her voice. She had put countless hours into the art, and the idea of it being ruined terrified her. Angel's heart went out to her friend, and she said a quick prayer for their success.

Basil yelled to his wife, "Take us up slow, hon. I don't want to break this thing." Merry did not jerk the mechanism, and they ascended at a controlled pace.

Angel held her breath and lent a hand to make sure the glass did not connect with the metal bucket. She watched the earth recede and was glad she had not yet eaten.

"Partridges nest in the dirt," she said. "Whoever wrote the song got it wrong." By all rights, Angel and the big bird ought to stay grounded.

Basil smiled and said, "And hundreds of years later, we're paying the price. Doesn't seem fair, does it?"

"Nothing does these days." If only the murder turned out to be a mistake, the way her kidnapping had. Angel would give anything to go back to when she did not know how easy her life had been. She felt ungrateful for all her thoughtless moments of contentment.

Basil looked toward the tree where Glacier's body had rested in the branches. "I know what you mean." As they neared the hook, he motioned for Merry to slow their ascent.

They spent a few minutes aligning the bucket to reach it without overextending their arms. No matter what Angel had said to the contrary, she did not wish either of them to take a header. Merry did a competent job guiding the arm, and they stopped in the proper location. Workers had placed a golden cuff around a thick branch, and a three-inch bolt assured it would not move.

Angel and Basil looked at each other in nervousness, and her partner said, "Here we go. On my count. One, two, three—" His voice crescendoed on the last word, and they lifted the neon tubing into place. Basil held the bird while she maneuvered around him to attach the fastener. The position felt too intimate, and her body trembled. While threading the nut to secure the apparatus, Angel's sweaty hands lost their grip. The integral part fell to the ground, and she groaned in mortification.

Basil sucked in his breath, but instead of cursing her, he laughed. Merry was indeed a fortunate woman. Men with tempers scared her, and Angel did not want to be suspended above the ground with one. She thought of Benny. He had chuckled when she told him about calling the sheriff. Angel was lucky, too.

Basil yelled down to Eric. "Sorry, I fumbled the ball. Can you find it for me?" The chivalrous man covered for her to boot. She gave him a grateful smile.

"Can you steady this for a minute?" He asked, indicating the overgrown partridge.

The thought terrified her. She had just proven she had no business touching anything. Etta should have come up and done it. Angel's irritation flared. Etta had taken off to oversee the other installations when she should have waited until they completed this one. Angel nodded in misery and held onto the giant bird in penance for her fumble fingers. She stared at tree bark and prayed nothing else went wrong. What if she dropped the thing on someone's head?

Behind her, Eric flung the nut upward. Basil bumped into her backside trying to get it but missed. Both men laughed. She wanted them to hurry. No one should have put Angel in charge of the bird, but she lacked the coordination to hang onto, much less retrieve, the dropped nut. The guys goofed around and enjoyed their game of catch while she sweated. They made another two tosses without success, raising Angel's anxiety. Basil reached out too far the second time, and she worried he would fall.

"One more time. Then we go down and get it." She sounded like someone's mother, and Basil looked like she had asked him to put his marbles away for dinner.

Angel's perspiring hands grew slippery, and one at a time, she dried them on her pants. Her breath quickened as the time expanded without end. She stared at a knothole. The wood had grown a round, protective bubble around something the way an oyster forms a pearl. Angel wondered what irritation had caused the growth. She yearned to poke a finger into the crevice but could not let loose of her breakable charge. Something about it tickled a childhood memory deep in her mind.

"Good one!" The guys cheered as Basil caught the nut and did a victory dance. The bucket jumped with his movements. He noticed the terror on her face and ceased the party. "I'm so sorry!"

Angel let out a steadying breath and forgot about the tree's malformation. She desired only to be on the blessed ground. "Let's get this done. I've got a hold on it, so you thread it through this time."

"Sure thing," Basil said. It was his turn to lean over her. He smelled of the woods. It matched his Paul Bunyan physique, and Angel approved.

"What the heck is Rudolph doing way over there?" Basil stopped work and stared off in the distance. "The idiot's supposed to be on Fifth Street." He was talking about one of his roving entertainers dressed as the famous reindeer. His face turned dark, and Angel sensed heat coming off him. She felt uncomfortable but held her position.

"You know everyone's assignment?" He was a vice-president, a much more important job than scheduler. "I would've thought your secretary handled the details."

Basil clenched his fists, and Angel grew concerned. "These guys think they can wander wherever they want. When are they going to take me seriously?" The man's irritation occupied their tiny enclosure. He took personal offense at his employee's actions. Angel's dad had said Basil excelled at his job, but his response to a minor infraction seemed overblown.

She wanted out of the bucket. "Hey, my arms are getting tired." Angel tried to make her voice sound light.

"Oh, geez, I'm so sorry." Basil completed the task in ten seconds and grinned. The brief storm had passed, and Angel's breathing calmed.

They checked their handiwork and called to the ground for confirmation. "Looks good," Eric said and gave them a thumbs-up.

"Moment of truth," Angel said and held up the electrical connection. She wriggled her eyebrows. Basil grinned and steadied the partridge. The power flowed, and the sculpture flickered then sprang to life. The ground crew cheered. It was magic, and Angel felt honored to have played a small part.

Merry brought the bucket down, and Basil leaped out to assist Angel. "We did it!" he said, and they fist-pumped in triumph. "Good work, hon!" he said and hugged Merry, who had gotten out of the truck to join them.

"You're all monsters," said a distraught voice. Angel turned to see Cookie standing to one side. "How dare you celebrate at a great man's grave?" The truth stung. Glee seemed inappropriate, and Angel's stomach churned. She had earned two consecutive strikes with Cookie and would never get to try a pah-rum-pum-pum-pum.

"I'm sorry. We meant no disrespect," Basil said in a humble tone full of apology. She nodded her sincere agreement and felt terrible for not honoring what a huge tragedy took place here.

The café owner ignored Basil and spoke to Angel. "You'll never be satisfied, will you? Killing him wasn't enough? You want to bring tourists to the spot?"

The insensitivity of their actions floored Angel. The committee had discussed whether to re-route the display, but no viable alternatives existed. Vivian Harrison had blessed the continued project and chose to see it as a memorial to her deceased husband.

Angel flushed, all eyes upon her. Merry smirked a little at her discomfort though she had participated in the desecration. "I'm so sorry. The theme was Glacier's idea, and Vivian wanted to go ahead with it. We're all devastated by his death."

"Sure, you are. Did you kill him yourself, or send your boyfriend to do your dirty work?" Angel remembered Benny's outburst in the café. He did not mean to threaten the mayor. He only wanted a fair shot at a successful business, free of onerous regulations.

"Neither of us had anything to do with it, and you need to stop saying we did." Angel glared at Cookie. Maybe she was the one who had incited the townspeople to hatred.

"You can't silence me. I want you to pay for what you did."

Angel worried events might spin out of her control. She tried another tactic. "I never meant to offend you in any way. To show there are no hard feelings, I got you a gift."

She was glad she thought to toss the wine in her bag. Angel retrieved the bottle and handed it to Cookie. "I'm sorry you lost a friend. So did I. The whole town misses him."

Cookie accepted the bottle, and for a second, Angel held out hope the public scene would end well. The woman smiled as if all were forgiven, lifted it above her head, and smashed it to the ground. Angel feared a glass sliver would pierce her skin and find its way into her bloodstream. From there, it would follow the river and lodge in her heart, killing her. She jumped away, but dark purple liquid splashed across her cheeks like tears.

"I'm an alcoholic, you moron, and so was Glacier. It's something his friends knew." Angel wondered if Cookie had been a happy drunk. All signs indicated no.

"I didn't realize you two were so close," Basil said, and Angel was glad of his assistance. Merry would find a way to use tonight's events against her, but she had married a decent human being. Etta had no luck convincing engineering to alter the sundown schedule, so Angel couldn't be sure but thought she saw fear in Cookie's eyes. The growing darkness made it difficult to tell.

"My relationships are none of your business. Keep your polar bears dancing, and we won't have any problems," Cookie said to Basil.

The two stared at each other until Merry stepped into the middle. "I'm starved, and you promised me dinner." She used her long eyelashes and a swish of her skirt to convince him to follow. Unable to make his wife unhappy, Basil allowed himself to be drug off by Merry. Angel's cousin had removed the only person who protected her. She tensed for another round.

Cookie surveyed the broken glass on the ground and said, "Clean up your messes, girl. They're piling up everywhere." Her opponent left, and the fight whooshed out of Angel. She took a seat in the truck to regain her equilibrium.

Eric approached with a sheepish smile. "I'm sorry she went after you. I've never seen her so bothered. I stopped by her shop earlier, and she bit off my head."

"Been there, done that." She sighed. Eric had not stepped up the way Basil had to defend her. Angel guessed he must have lost his encounter with the crazed baker.

"Can you give me a lift to number nine? Etta took the cart."

Angel wanted the day over with but still hoped for a chance to talk with her best friend. "Sure."

They drove the route visitors would experience Friday night when the exhibits opened. The Twelve Days of Christmas portion provided a strong opening, followed by an undersea section, fairytale characters, and an entire zoo of exotic animals. Cart drivers would end their journey in a winter wonderland. The tech guys had synchronized music to the choreographed light shows. Once finished, guests could join a sing-a-long while enjoying spiced cider and donuts. Benny had donated the use of the propane burners for the gathering tent, and Angel felt a surge of gratefulness toward him.

She dropped off Eric at the nine ladies dancing, but Etta was not there. Angel called and found her helping the twelve drummers drumming. She waved goodbye and went to meet her.

Instead of reproducing a dozen identical pieces, Etta had given each drummer his own unique facial features and body proportions. A toddler sat cross-legged with an overturned pot, while a fat man stood behind a tremendous kettle drum. A lithe dancer lifted a tambourine and mallet, and a member of the first nations played a leather-topped hollow log.

Angel stopped, enraptured. Etta spotted her and came over for a quick hug. "It's the most beautiful thing I've ever seen," Angel said. Her friend had brought the drummers to life, and each personality shone.

"Thank you. I wanted people to see themselves as part of the tableau. We each have our part to do."

"You've covered yours for the next ten years," she said. Etta had created a lasting attraction the globe would use for many years to come. The effort and love she put into it humbled Angel.

"Don't short me. I am covered for a minimum of twelve."

Only a few of the globe's hundred shops lent serious help to the project. Etta spent the year laboring, but she persevered. The people closest to Angel sacrificed so much; her efforts seemed insufficient. Doubt built within her. Were Angel's parents right? She had accepted the safety and love the village extended without replenishing it. Now others resented her selfishness.

Angel started her rehearsed tirade about how unfair it all was but stopped when she noticed her friend's weary eyes. The woman ran on willpower and fumes. "Can I bring you anything? Snacks?"

Etta's face lit up at the mention of food, and Angel smiled. The petite powerhouse burned calories faster than a piranha cleaned a carcass. To bring the universe back into balance, every calorie Angel ingested stayed with her for life.

"A cupcake isn't going to cut it. I could eat a side of beef."

Angel knew the feeling. "Burgers it is then. I'll be back in a few."

Etta gave her a grateful smile and yelled, "Don't forget the fries!"

as she drove away in the truck. The globe did not have drive-thru fast food, so she called in a restaurant order to go. Angel decided to return the bucket truck as well since they had finished with it.

She parked the oversized vehicle in the garage and replaced the keys without incident. Fifteen feet from her golf cart, she stopped. A shadow moved in the front seat. Her heartbeat increased, and she looked for the nearest nutcracker. None were to be seen. Angel considered going back to the plaza where people congregated. She had never feared bodily harm in the globe until this morning, and her imagination had run away with her then. Movement didn't indicate sinister intent. The village was still home, and Angel knew it to be safe.

"Hey! What are you doing?" she called. Villagers recognized her customized cart with its "Santa Jr." logo. Her parents gave it to her when they still held out hope she would take over North Pole Enterprises. The figure stiffened then escaped through the far side door. She saw a crouched runner dressed in black, nothing more. Angel approached with caution, though she could see no danger remained.

The wine had met a bad end, and she kept nothing of value inside the vehicle. Angel made a quick inventory and found no vandalism or theft. The intruder left no clue as to their identity or purpose. Fear flowed through her, and she wanted distance from the complex. The cart accelerated, and she checked the mirror for any sign someone followed her but found none. She picked up the burgers and headed back to the park.

As they ate, Angel told Etta about the thief.

"Are you sure it was a man? It could have been a cat."

"No. It was a person."

Etta tore off a massive hunk of meat and chewed. Angel was impressed with her friend's appetite, but more so with her metabolism. "Could it have been a woman?"

Angel had assumed the robber, or whoever they were, was male. Still, thinking back, she had no reliable indication of the person's sex. "Maybe," she said. "Why?"

"Eric told me about Cookie. It could have been her." She deposited a half dozen french fries into her open mouth. Strangers assumed such a dainty woman would avoid trouble, but they were wrong. Etta jumped into fights faster than most men.

Angel thought about it. "It could have been anyone, I suppose. I thought it was a teenager looking for beer money. Why would Cookie be in my golf cart?"

"Better check for dog poo under the seats. What'd you do to make her so angry?" The two women knew each other's faults, and Angel was capable of tactless behavior. She never acted with malice but was sometimes thoughtless.

"Nothing. I stopped in the other day, and Cookie went off on me. She said my family ran a crime syndicate, and we snuffed out Glacier."

Etta did not explode with indignation the way Angel had expected. She took a drink of her triple-thick shake before speaking. "I've heard whispers."

Angel's blood pressure skyrocketed. Middle school had never been this bad, and it was the worst. "I'm done with whatever is going on around here. People accuse me of crimes without explaining what it is they think I did. Even my parents won't come clean with me."

Etta wiped her lips with a napkin, and Angel noticed the delicate bone structure of her hands. They belonged to an artist. "I've been busy, but I haven't seen your dad around at all. Usually, he's everywhere."

"No one has, and believe me, it's a good thing."

They had been friends since childhood and knew each other's parents as well as they did their own. "What do you mean?"

"Blackout day drinking."

Etta looked alarmed. "Since when?" She held the burger in her hand but no longer brought it to her mouth. Angel noticed the lights in the park had shut down except for those lining the paths.

"The morning they found Glacier." The day the world changed.

"Did he have something to do with it?" Etta's directness knocked the wind out of her. The air refused to inflate her lungs, and she feared asphyxiation. The idea of her father murdering someone was far-fetched, so her mind had scrapped the information. The reasoning behind her parents' behavior dropped back into her consciousness with a click.

"The police have a video of dad driving the bucket truck near the park at 2 a.m. Frank may arrest him." The words caused Angel to lose control of her hands. Her dinner fell to the ground.

Etta picked it up and threw it into the bin. "There must be an explanation. Your dad didn't kill anyone."

Angel knew it, too, but her stomach filled with dread. Prison terrified her. She had nightmares of causing a cart accident and being put away for it. Movies involving courtroom dramas affected her for days. Unable to cage her macaw, she could not see her father locked up like an animal.

"But he acts like he did." The drinking, lack of hygiene, not going to work—it all fit. Angel had to consider her father had done something unspeakable.

"What about your mom?"

"Good question. She's worse than him if that's possible. Blames me."

Etta finished the last of her shake with a loud slurp and tossed the cup. "How's it your fault?"

Angel wished she knew. "They keep talking about stuff from the years before I went to college."

Her friend looked at her in confusion. "What would it have to do with someone killing the mayor?"

"I don't know." Angel felt heavy. The energy to fight had vanished.

Etta smiled from somewhere far away; everything receded. "I hate to break it to you, but your career path did not alter the planet's orbit. None of us are that important. You going to school did not change the course of history."

# Chapter 8

Angel set her alarm twenty minutes earlier than usual to spend a few extra minutes with Prancer. It went off ten minutes sooner than she expected, and her sleep-deprived fingers could not make it stop. She pushed the button numerous times, then unplugged it. Still, it rang.

"Darn battery back-ups," she fussed and fumbled to pull the offensive AAAs free from the device. When she held them in her hand, Angel realized the clock had never made a sound.

"Prancer, you rat." There had been a time when she answered the doorbell a dozen times a day. The bird had learned the chime and fooled her every time. She posted a sign telling people it was broken and to please knock. Prancer imitated the microwave ding, the tea kettle, and her cell phone, too. Angel had changed her ringtone to a song snippet to prevent his continued harassment. She did not know if he derived joy from sending her running or liked electronic noises.

This morning, the bird's message came through loud and clear. Prancer wanted her up and paying attention to him, but he ruined his surprise party by demanding one. Beak-boy loved music above all things, so they staged a dance-off. Angel asked Alexa for disco tunes, and the pair boogied until breakfast. She had more fun than at any Zumba class. So did Prancer. The joy of letting go helped dispel the demons who had followed her home.

Benny sent a good morning text asking if she recognized her surroundings. She typed, "2 soon 4 that joke," and got ready for work.

Angel was not drunk, hungover, traumatized, or late to work. All systems were a go, and she determined to make it a good day. Whenever thoughts intruded on her bliss, she blocked them. Memories of Cookie received the same brisk brush-off as those of her parents. Her encounter with Glacier refused banishment.

She and Prancer spent the morning working in her office and shared a brown-bagged salad for lunch. It was not much, but she had a budget deficit to overcome. The macaw sat on Angel's desk and picked out the tastiest elements: sunflower seeds, dried cranberries, and almonds. Prancer's selfishness left her with a pile of lettuce and lingering hunger. Her thoughts turned to cheeseburgers.

"Mmmm," he said. "More," and rooted through the dish looking for anything not green. Angel would not have minded finding a fry or two at the bottom.

"You have food," she said and set him back on his stand. The ornery bird picked up his stainless-steel bowl and emptied its contents onto the floor.

"Oops." He placed the metal dish back in its spot and said, "More."

Prancer did not like the nutritionally complete pellets she had given him. He preferred Angel to cook his meals. A blend of oats, seeds, peas, beans, and fruit was his favorite. She made the mixture every couple days, but they had danced their time away this morning, which left him with the equivalent of avian puppy chow.

Class started soon, so she prepared her belongings. "Ready to go?"

Letting him perch on her shoulder proved the easiest way to carry him hands-free. Prancer maintained excellent balance and did not dig into her skin. He did mess with her hair in an amorous display of love.

"Aye, matey." Angel had not taught him the pirate lingo, but he knew quite a bit. His previous owners had not been too creative. The bird knew no Shakespeare or Maya Angelou but recited a dirty limerick or two.

She opened the door and stood still, unable to advance. Someone had booby-trapped the long corridor leading away from her office.

116

The fiend had not used razor wire or claymore mines; he was far more diabolical in his methods. Angel's body shook, and Prancer said, "Aaarrrgggghhh. Blow me down."

Gnomes lined both sides of the hallway. One rode a pink flamingo while another bare-bottomed monster mooned her with a grin. Some of the bearded dwarfs sat in wheelbarrows, others on toadstools. Angel counted at least fifty of the cunning creatures blocking her path.

Someone must have spent their night stealing from every garden in town. Angel looked for the culprit, sure they waited nearby to witness her reaction to the prank.

"Very funny. Now, move them, so I can get going." She received no response. Angel tried again, but no smirking face appeared to mock her. The tiny little men and women leered, some from under flower petals, others around tree trunks.

"Lousy buggers," Prancer said. Angel agreed. Their plaster smiles hid sharp teeth and evil hearts. She could not walk between the two ranks of the tiny terrorists. Did whoever placed them want Angel fired? The department head looked for a reason to dump her, and this would suffice. Maybe he had done it.

The clock read seventeen minutes to the hour, and Angel did not know what to do. "Hello," she called to the row of closed doors. "Is anyone around?" She hated the labyrinth of hallways. Closed doors provided no view of the dangers lurking within, but open ones offered no protection from the threat.

No one came to her defense. She wondered if a scream would bring them running.

Angel called security and asked them to come. "After yesterday? You made us come all the way up there and then told us it was a joke." Angel heard the rattle of a chip bag, one of her favorite sounds, and knew she interrupted the man's lunch.

"I'll buy you a pizza." She did not have any money, but she had not promised to deliver today.

"I've got food."

These guys were on call. It's how the system worked. Security sat around and played games until someone needed them. They did not get to say no to employees in distress. "Please. I'm trapped in my office, and I have to teach." Angel wished they were more prone to action than talk. What if her life had been in danger?

"Trapped how?" The man sounded dubious. It was obvious he had never been flanked by a squad of spade-wielding evil fairies.

Angel fidgeted, then blurted out, "Gnomes, okay? A battalion of them—an army."

"Stop screwing with us, or I'll report you to the dean," he said and disconnected the line. Angel heard the plaster-of-paris conspirators whispering, forming a plot.

Desperate to not be late, she called Benny. "I need you; it's an emergency. Can you come?"

To her relief, he did not ask any questions other than if she were safe and said he would be five minutes. "Thank you, Lord," she said.

Prancer said, "Amen, me hearty." Angel took the bird off her shoulder to deactivate pirate mode. They played basketball with a Ping-Pong ball and a miniature hoop until Benny ran down the hall toward her.

He skidded to a stop and looked confused. "You needed a third? Is that why you called?"

"Yes," Angel said with heavy sarcasm in her voice. "He's outscoring me." Benny did not appear amused. "I have class, and I can't leave."

Benny looked for danger and back to her. "Why not?"

"Them." She pointed to the ranks of blue and red marauders spread out along her path.

"You're kidding me." He looked for confirmation this was a practical joke at his expense.

Angel turned red. "This is a longer conversation, and I'm glad to have it, but right now, I just really need your help. Please?" It was bound to have happened sooner or later. She had hoped to log a little more time together before he found out how stunted she was.

Angel had provided him a big clue yesterday with the kidnapping fiasco, but he still answered her call. She held out hope this would not be their last meeting.

His face softened, and he exhaled. "Sure. What can I do?"

"Move them." Angel thought the answer obvious. The man was cuter than he was smart, but it was a trade-off she was willing to make. She could think for him. "Please."

Benny spun the first two, so they faced away from her. "Not enough," she said. He sighed, picked up several in his arms, and asked, "Where to?"

Angel thought about it. The owners would want their gnomes back, but that was up to the person who stole them. It was not her problem. She needed them out of the way to reach class on time.

"There's a supply closet on the left, end of the hall."

He took off in the right direction, and Angel breathed easier. She was going to make it. Benny's next load included a bearded woman who creeped her out more than the others combined. Five minutes later, he had completed the task.

Angel hugged him, and Prancer said, "Love you." She had no control over the bird's vocalizations and hoped her boyfriend understood.

Benny laughed with delight and said, "Love you too, dude." He winked at Angel. "I'm back to it. Want to grab something to eat later?" She did. She really did.

Angel arrived in her classroom with two minutes to spare and found her boss waiting at the door. "How's it going?" she asked in a cheerful voice. "Want to sit in with us?"

He did not answer, so she continued, "Did you know turtle doves don't tip their heads back to drink? They suck up water like a straw. Fascinating birds."

The man looked constipated at the best of times, but now he appeared impacted. His expression wavered between disgust and disappointment. Angel held a strong suspicion he expected her to be a no-show for class, and her appearance ruined his day. She would have to be vigilant.

"I have business elsewhere," he said and puffed out his chest. It did not make him appear more important.

Having defeated her plaster persecutors, Angel felt devilish. "Are you sure? Doves sleep with their heads between their shoulder blades instead of tucking them into their breasts. So cute!"

Her boss rejected her a second time and left, his long arms jangling. She giggled and felt victorious. The students had taken their places, and Angel spotted Merry. Her cousin wore the same look of defeat as her boss.

Inspiration struck, and Angel moved Prancer's stand closer to the woman's seat. "Lucky day," she said. "He wants to hang out with you." She gave her brightest smile.

Merry blanched but did not want to embarrass herself in front of her classmates. A decade older than the group, she needed to be twice as cool. While her cousin stared at the macaw, Angel made a hand-sign behind her head. Prancer leaned forward, spread his tremendous wings, and said, "Boo!" Everyone laughed, and the class continued without incident. Merry remained quiet for the next fifty minutes.

Angel met Benny at a local's restaurant and promised to show him a few more of the hidden gems around town. "I feel like an insider, now," he said and held her hand.

A pleasant shiver went up her arm. They ordered toasted ravioli and eggplant parmesan. "Want to share?" Angel suggested when the food arrived. She loved the intimacy of communal plates.

"No, it's all yours." Benny looked at her, and his eyes smiled their approval. She had worn her favorite blue dress and let her hair remain loose.

"Don't dare me." She said a silent blessing and picked up her fork.

Benny leaned closer and said, "Can we pray first?" They had yet to speak of many things: her phobias, their religious beliefs, and any serious hopes for the future. Up until tonight, they had kept all encounters casual.

"Please." Angel's insides tingled. A true partner must also be a believer. She knew too many women at church who shouldered the spiritual burden for their families, and she did not desire the role.

He said grace. They both dug in and raced each other for the savory morsels. It was her kind of competition. They chose tiramisu for dessert and ordered coffee to go with it.

A musician unpacked his speakers, microphone, and instrument. Nothing beat live music; she wished the bar allowed birds. Prancer had only heard the portable keyboard she used for practice. Maybe Angel would learn to play the guitar.

"Tell me about the gnomes," Benny said. His voice sounded compassionate, and his facial expression indicated curiosity, not judgment. He was a good sport who had closed his business down to rescue her. She owed him an explanation.

Angel leaned back in her chair and let her muscles relax. Benny would accept her as she was, or he wouldn't. Either way, Angel did not have a say in the matter. No longer a teenager, she knew pretense only carried a person so far, and love based on fakery never succeeded.

"When I was little, someone told me vengeful sprites lived in the figurines." Merry told many untrue tales, and Angel had taken her word as gospel. She wished she had been more discerning.

Benny squeezed her hand. "What an awful thing to say to a kid." He would be a good dad; she was sure of it. Patience and kindness toward children were non-negotiable in Angel's book.

"Merry said they moved and blamed them for her tricks. She sent me on errands or waited until I was involved in a game, then rearranged the gnomes and stole my toys."

"I would've smashed the little beasts so they couldn't sneak up on me again." Angel wondered if gender or personality accounted for their differing reactions. Benny's method sounded more straightforward.

Angel grew up in a fantasy snow globe but felt foolish for her naiveté. "Merry said if I broke them, the sprite would shoot up my nose and use me like a puppet." A shiver ran through her at the thought of inhaling evil.

Benny laughed but said, "Your cousin is a monster." Angel agreed. The years of torment had scarred her in a meaningful way. Merry did not cause Angel's fears, but she exploited them for sick entertainment.

"You have no idea. I woke up one morning with gnomes all around my bed, staring at me." Angel plowed ahead with the most embarrassing part. "I wet my pants."

The kind man put his arm around her and swore he would have done the same. "Was it her at it again today?" A shadow crossed his face. It was one thing to be a cruel child, another to carry the trait into adulthood.

Angel took a sip of the coffee. She loved restaurant brews; hers at home never came out anywhere near as good.

"Who else? I have a condition. It's called panphobia." Angel watched to see which direction Benny would run. She bet to the door. He seemed too direct to crawl out the restroom window.

"Shouldn't it be gnomeophobia? An entirely reasonable fear of tiny gardeners?" Benny smiled and spooned up some of the dessert. His butt remained firm in the seat, and her heart broke a little. He was a good man.

Angel took a deep breath and explained the thing that would kill their relationship before it ever got off the ground. "I'm afraid of everything. It can be debilitating."

"Spiders? Dirty socks? The cap being left off the toothpaste?" He teased, but the disease was no joke. Once he understood the ramifications, he would be gone. Angel felt the sadness grow inside of her; she had really come to like him.

"A dozen varieties are venomous; they cause trench foot, which can lead to amputation, and germs could crawl into the tube." Angel shuddered at the thought. Most things she could not control, but those under her discretion got dealt with appropriately.

Benny did not realize the seriousness of the situation and what it meant to them as a couple. "We all have things that make us uncomfortable. It's alright." He sounded reassuring as if it were no big deal.

People who had never been terrified of refrigerated biscuit rolls discounted her experiences. They saw nothing sinister in how the inanimate dough sprang from the container and didn't know why she should.

"It's more of a filtering disorder. Sidewalk cracks could open fissures in the earth and swallow me whole. A porcupine might drop from a tree and impale me. Everything is a death threat."

The man with the acoustic guitar began his set. He played word-less tunes, mournful of lost love.

"That's a blessing," Benny said. He pushed the empty tiramisu plate away from him and took a sip of coffee. "It forces you to use other criteria to rank your priorities."

"What do you mean?" His theory sounded cockeyed and a way to dismiss her reality. She felt defective and inferior. Other people did not struggle to pick up a pencil because they worried about graphite poisoning.

"Fear gives you a base—a pedestal in your case." His smile indi-cated she deserved a gilded one. "If all things are equally scary, then nothing is."

"But I couldn't leave my office." Angel wanted to believe his pretty words, but the jitters had won. She risked losing her job over molded plastic characters painted red and blue.

"What other things frighten you about the hallway?" Benny's face looked intent, and she could tell he had an agenda, so Angel played along for the moment.

"There's too much wax. I'll slip and crack my head open like a melon." She also feared the mirror-like surface reflected her undergarments but didn't mention the fact.

"Good. What else?" Benny watched her, and she could tell he wanted to know. Most men brushed off her plight as ridiculous, then ran the first time she embarrassed them in front of family or friends.

"Those fluorescent light assemblies. One day, they'll fall and crush my skull." As far she could tell, the flimsiest of screws held them into the ceiling. They were the commercial equivalent of her apartment's weak curtain and towel rods.

"Anything else?"

She thought of a dozen more items but didn't want to be locked up in a looney bin. "Everyone exhales their germs, and there's nowhere for them to go. Years' worth of them have accumulated there, waiting."

Benny smiled. "You're the bravest person I know."

Angel's heart plummeted. She had trusted him and opened up about her situation, and he ridiculed her. Letting her guard down had been a significant mistake. Benny would share this conversation the moment he could, and people would pity her for a fool.

She pushed her chair back, ready to walk away from the relationship. Angel had enjoyed their time, had even dared to hope they could make a future together, but she couldn't be with someone who mocked her. Prancer excluded, of course, but he was a special case.

"There's no reason to be mean. You can say it. I'm too broken." She stood up, and Benny grabbed her hand. Angel tried to shake him loose.

"Please sit; I didn't mean to upset you. It's true." He looked sincere, but Angel wanted to go before she cried in tune with the sad guitar. Benny gave her wrist a gentle tug, and she sat to avoid a scene.

"Every day, you face the floor wax, lighting brackets, and deadly disease. They're all still there, but you conquer them. Every day. It's extraordinary."

She stared at him and listened for any insincerity in his tone. None existed. Angel ducked her head and made another confession. "I wear non-skid shoes, walk to one side, and hold my breath."

Benny beamed at her, and she stared at him in confusion. "It's brilliant! Most people don't have anywhere near the level of anxiety you do and don't manage half as well." He had not let go of her hand, and she hoped he never would. It soothed and excited her. Angel had spent her life tallying what the limitations cost her. Benny thought of her as accomplished.

"I'm sure to embarrass you." She felt at once buoyed and miserable.

"I promise to return the favor." Benny possessed remarkable empathy and called her heroic, but their relationship would end regardless of his intentions. The constant grind would exhaust him; it did her.

"I can't imagine," she said. She would be proud to be with the man.

"What about my public outbursts?" Angel remembered him confronting Glacier in Cookie's bakery, and her gut tightened. The waiter came by to check if they needed anything else. It allowed her to give the question serious consideration. She hated being the center of attention. Her introversion had restricted her from taking over the family business and broken her parents' hearts.

"I can't stand them," she said, "but I will manage. How do you feel about a date who runs out of dinner parties because the host served a whole fish?"

Benny smiled, "Unacceptable, except in your case." They would both need to make allowances if they wanted to be a couple. Angel could not believe their conversation had gotten so deep. They had established a wish to try and to honor each other's absolutes. Overwhelmed, she changed the subject.

"What animal would you choose in a tag-team match?"

The question surprised him, and his face brightened. "Change the topic much?" He seemed a little relieved. Neither wanted to swim out over their head.

Angel waved for a refill of her coffee. It was delicious. She wondered if Benny knew the only thing she cooked was bird food, and if it would be a deal-breaker. "Just tell me."

"A shark." The guy was sweet but dim.

She shook her head. "Useless on land." A woman with her inhibitions needed to maximize every advantage. Angel would go with a goose every time. They were plain mean.

"Look, it's Frank, the chief of police," she said as the man walked in the door. "Did they release Glacier's cause of death today? If so, I didn't hear it."

Important news passed like wildfire inside the globe. It would have been discussed in every home and shop. She had not spoken to people other than her students, so maybe she missed it. Her mother had not called, and Angel had not yet built up the courage to reach out to her.

"Not that I heard," Benny said. A newcomer, he did not seem too interested. Outside of the globe, murder was commonplace.

The man walked by, and Angel stopped him. "Did you release the autopsy results today?" The mayor's death had tilted the globe off its axis. Solving the case would right it. A person could count on physics.

"Gunshot wound to the head." Frank's face remained closed, and she read nothing in it. He would be an excellent poker player.

"You're holding something back, aren't you? Something only the killer knows." Police withheld vital information to weed-out crazies who took responsibility for crimes they had not committed. Investigative news reporters sometimes broke such stories, but she did not hold out the hope the local daily employed any.

The top cop looked at her with a fortuneteller's gaze. "Do you have knowledge of the crime you would like to share?"

The man irritated her. Delving into the facts was his job, not hers. She handled birds and organ music, neither of which were consequential in this situation. "Of course not. I don't know anything about it."

"Your parents have refused to see me. Twice." Angel was happy to hear it. No one except a psychiatrist should visit them in their current state. "You might want to explain cooperating is in their best interest. The same goes for you." What did he mean, her? Angel had less information on the topic than anyone. People acted as if she were somehow involved, and gossip ran wild, but she knew nothing.

Benny interjected, "You're just looking for someone to pin it on, and no one with half a brain is going to step into your trap."

Frank turned on him. "Does that include you? I have a sworn statement you threatened Glacier Harrison the day before his body

126

turned up in a tree, and you haven't returned any of my calls. There's also the matter of a kidnapping charge." The cop's gaze was stony.

Angel's heart beat faster, and she wished curiosity had not prompted her to waylay Frank en route to his dinner. The hangry man needed food and a stiff drink. "I withdrew the complaint, and you know it."

"Don't you watch television? The state brings charges, not victims. Crimes are committed against us all." Angel did not find his smirk appealing.

"You'll lose," said Benny, "because I didn't do anything wrong." Frank's entire fictitious case rested on her testimony. They could not make Angel testify. If compelled, she would tell the court the humiliating truth of her drunken misconceptions. Frank did not alter his expression, and Angel noticed the room had quieted. The musician had gone on break, making their conversation easy to overhear.

"Maybe so," the police chief said in a careful tone meant to intimidate, "but defending it's going to be costly. It'd be a shame if you lost your livelihood to attorney's fees."

Anger ignited Angel's sense of justice. The globe did not bully its residents into false confessions or run businesses out of town. "He's done nothing wrong," she asserted.

"It's not how a jury will see it. An outsider shows up, threatens the mayor, and kidnaps Santa's daughter. They'll believe what I tell them to believe." Frank was evil, and Angel recoiled at how far he would go to get what he wanted.

"Forget you, man. Go ahead, take your best shot." Benny had solidified into a larger man. The easy-going guy had disappeared, and a fighter took his place. Panic bloomed in Angel's chest.

Frank said, "I've got all the time in the world. People talk, and I'm listening."

"Do you have anyone willing to testify? Written statements?" Benny asked. Frank's face darkened. "I didn't think so. Have a good evening."

The police of chief walked away, and Angel said, "I'm so sorry. I had no idea he would act like this." Frank had been understanding with her about the break-in and overnight misunderstanding. Something had changed.

"Do you think he'll go after your folks? It's a gutsy move."

Angel had observed her parents' reaction to Glacier's death. Instinct said if they weren't involved, they knew who was. Frank was not much of a cop, but a moron could tell guilt ate away at them. She felt ill.

"I know he is." If Angel's family would not confide in her, she needed to find another way to get at the truth.

On Friday, the opening day of the drive-thru exhibit, Angel received a frantic call from Etta. "I need you. Two of the exhibits aren't lighting."

"I'm not an electrician." Her fix-it skills came in handy around the house, but she never went near live power.

"We need the truck." Angel had driven the bucket vehicle more in the last few weeks than in the previous year. "Will your folks let you borrow it again?"

She had tried to speak to her mother, but the attempt was unfruitful. When Angel offered to come over and bring dinner, the woman told her not to bother because Merry had it covered. Even during the worst of times, the family had never been so estranged from one another. She felt orphaned.

"Sure," she said, though Angel did not plan to ask. The truck was not in use, and no one would stop her. She was not a thief, and the display was for the village's greater good. "We need to do it this morning, though. I have class later." Her boss would have to get over it.

They arranged to meet at the park. Teams had worked all week on the final preparations, and Etta's emotions ran high in the final stretch. Angel hugged her friend and felt the woman vibrate.

"Will you be here tonight?" A snowflake had caught on one of

Etta's lashes, and Angel thought she had never been more beautiful. A pang of love seized her heart. People did not need to be related to be family.

"I'm on the committee, aren't I? I wouldn't miss it." Angel and the others would supervise traffic flow, concessions, and trash removal. A successful event required a concerted effort of volunteers and people hired to help. The globe expected hundreds of visitors and had imported extra golf carts to accommodate them all. She planned to walk to avoid a parking nightmare. "Which sculptures are malfunctioning?"

"Number one and number five." Angel felt terrible when the one she had connected landed on Etta's list of headaches. Everything she touched turned into a disaster these days.

Last night while cleaning her apartment, Angel had sucked up one of Prancer's playthings. She had broken the vacuum and his favorite squeaky toy in a single movement. The poor guy brought the injured eagle to her and said, "Not working."

"The five rings are everyone's favorite. Let's start there." The symbol of love and commitment, the golden bands, gave people hope. The recent bad press regarding the murder had some concerned tourists would shun them this year. After the expense and work the town had invested, it would be a devastating blow.

Angel believed the opposite. The notoriety would bring in gawkers. The killing did not appear random, so there was more morbid curiosity than fear surrounding Glacier's death.

She was taken with how marvelous everything looked. Angel grinned at Etta and found her proud as a mother hen. "It came together nicely, didn't it?"

"Smashing," Angel said. "You're going to get contracts from across the country. Europe will call. Do you speak any other languages?"

"Only what I remember from high school French." As teenagers, Angel and Etta had spent summers dreaming of Paris and the shabby chic flat they would call home.

"Then I will need to translate." She affected a terrible accent and recited one of the old memorizations. Both women laughed. Angel had been too fearful of joining the class trip to France, and Etta claimed a summer internship to stay behind at home.

"Wouldn't it be great to bring people this much happiness?" Etta had run her lighting store, took care of her husband, and pulled off a full-sized miracle in her spare time. Angel admired her more than anyone she knew. The woman was a marvel.

"You already do." The pair linked arms like six-year-olds, and Angel felt good. Etta's neon legacy would burn for decades. Every business owner in town owed her a debt of gratitude and a slice of their future profits.

The famous rings formed an archway over the cart path, a tunnel of love. The fourth in the series did not shine like the rest, and they could not have marriage's legacy tarnished. No one wanted a reminder not all unions lasted. "Ready for me to run you up?" Angel asked.

"I'm sure something just jiggled loose. If you can't figure it out, I'll give it a shot."

Etta had pulled the entire exhibit together. It was time someone else helped. Angel felt more comfortable twelve feet off the ground than she had at the greater heights.

Instead of plain gold bands, Etta had fashioned intricate braids to simulate her wedding ring's woven pattern. Details set Etta's work apart from other craftsmen. She was not satisfied with meeting the standard; she wanted to establish a new one. The effort cost time and money but made her creations memorable. The concept of beauty enthralled the artist, and it showed in her work.

Angel choked up while looking at the masterpiece. She yearned for the love represented in the endless circles. The trick lay in finding the person willing to go round after round with her.

She checked the connections and found one to be loose. Etta had provided a toolbox, and Angel dug around for a Philips head screwdriver. The bag held everything but a tuna sandwich. Her friend had come prepared.

In a sane world, Angel's parents would have hosted the community drive-thru. The townspeople expected them to wave hello to tourists as they arrived or hold court in the warming tent. The globe existed for Santa, and Santa for the globe. No one could have guessed the bond would be so easily broken. This year, they would not officiate. Strangers would neither know nor care about the use of stand-ins, but the locals would, and pressure would mount for a leadership change. What would happen to her parents then? She could not let them take over Prancer's room and get drunk in her living room.

Angel tightened the connection and asked Etta to throw the switch. The resulting brightness made her turn away, but she wore a big smile. If only her relationships were so easy. Angel knew she could no longer put off a visit home. She would go tomorrow.

"Bring me down," she said, and Etta did. They sat for a minute and admired the work. "What will you do with all your spare time?" she asked her friend.

"Eric and I have a plan." Her best friend since childhood looked and sounded mysterious. Would she drop the retail work and specialize in large commercial projects?

"Spill. Will you take a long vacation? Hawaii?" Her friend had always dreamed of spending time in a tropical paradise, the antithesis of the globe.

A slight smile curled the edges of Etta's mouth, and Angel understood. "No way."

Etta nodded, and Angel wondered why she had not noticed before now. Winter clothes hid the tiny tummy, but the glow was unmistakable. She was going to be an auntie.

"It's true."

Happiness and a tinge of jealousy flowed through Angel. "When?" "In June."

The timing was perfect. Almost too perfect. It would be off-season, and Etta would have time for proper maternity leave.

"I hope it's a girl," Angel said. She hugged Etta and remembered the tea parties and fun they shared as children. "We can dress her up in little outfits."

Etta laughed. "You hated dresses. Remember the little lace socks your mom made you wear? I thought she'd rip her hair out when you turned them into slingshots."

"It was my hair she pulled. She could never deal with the curls. I'm so happy for you."

The two chatted about bassinets and Binkies as Angel drove them through the course. The undersea portion featured floating pink jellyfish and a large blue whale, but Angel's favorites were the flamingos she found in the zoo animal collection. They rewound their way to the beginning. The pear tree's branches stretched majestic against the backdrop of the dome. The bird itself shown full of life, but the round perch he swung from remained dark.

Angel climbed back into the bucket. No wonder a pregnant woman had not wanted to go up; she didn't blame her. No one wanted a dizzy baby. They could toss the post-womb child when she wouldn't bang her head on Etta's bladder.

After maneuvering her enclosure close enough to the neon sculpture, Angel remembered the curious knothole. The magic bag of tools held a pair of long-nosed pliers, and she grabbed them. Curiosity had stayed with her all week, and she wondered what could have caused the blemish in the trunk.

The wood had formed a tunnel, and Angel inserted the pinchers into the hole. Four inches in, she felt something. Not being able to see, she worked by feel. The object seemed solid. Several times, she withdrew her tool but brought back only splinters.

"Everything OK up there?" Etta yelled. This was the first stop on the route; it had to function. Her friend leaned toward perfectionism. She never gave in near the end or considered skimping.

Angel had not yet investigated the source of the power outage but answered, "Doing fine, it's just going to take me a few minutes."

She felt guilty for damaging the tree, but her mind would not rest until it understood why the knothole formed. Questions of origin always plagued her, and evolution explained a lot of oddities.

Angel pulled a slender blade from the bag and used it to carve more space around the object. With added effort, she felt it give way. Renewed determination led to more digging. At last, she had the unknown mass in her grasp. The grippers held a bullet. She turned it in her fingers and stared. Had this small hunk of metal killed Glacier? No blood coated it. This slug had spent years in the tree, but how had it gotten here?

"Do you need help?" Etta shouted again. Several long minutes had passed while Angel probed the knothole.

She put the projectile into her pocket and investigated the partridge's problem. "No, almost done," she said. Angel deployed her no-fail method of fixing electronics. She unplugged the connector and reattached it. "Try it now."

"Whoop! Whoop!" Etta said.

Angel grinned and looked a final time at the tree, wondering. She brought the boom down to ground level and hoisted herself into the truck cab.

"It's perfect," Etta said. She looked like Angel at her college graduation. Ongoing hard work and struggle had manifested into a soul-satisfying achievement. Neither desired to do it again, but its completion meant the world.

"Want to grab a bite before I've got to get to class?" Angel thought of her unhappy boss. She would deduct the morning as personal time. It would not improve his mood, but it legitimized her excursion to the park.

Etta's cherubic face turned to her, and she said in all innocence, "Cookie's?"

Angel pushed her friend's shoulder and drove them to the deli. They split a Reuben, and each added a cup of pea soup to go with it. The sandwich came piled two-inches thick with corned beef. After an appropriate poison-testing interval, Angel moaned at its divine saltiness.

"I found something in the tree," she said and reached into her pocket. The metal felt cool and slick in her palm as she handed it to Etta.

Confusion passed over her friend's face. "A bullet? In the tree?" She stopped eating her soup to rotate the object between her fingers. The waitress refilled their iced tea, and Angel waited for her to leave before she explained.

"Tuesday night, I dropped the nut, and it took Eric and Basil a minute to toss it back up to us. I was holding the sculpture and staring at this knothole when I realized there was something in there. This is it."

Etta's demeanor changed. The pinkness drained from her cheeks, and she glanced around as if expecting an enemy. "Where did you get the tree? Did you take the one at the old Franklin place?"

"Yes, I told you." She had no idea why her friend looked distraught, but Angel caught anxiety faster than a cold. "The city owns the property, and Glacier signed off on it." She had followed the rules, and it was the largest pear tree in the globe. No one went to the farm these days, anyway. Angel did not understand the big deal.

Etta's excitement about opening the Twelve Days of Christmas display had vanished. She looked as if she had seen a ghost. "Do you remember playing out there when we were kids?"

Angel remembered marrying her best friend in a pretend wedding. Etta played the bride and wore a gunnysack veil. For flowers, she used a gorgeous head of cauliflower. Twenty years later, Angel realized traditional bouquets did not look much different than their childhood version.

"Sure, we rode our bikes out there to feed the horses and play with the goats." She had always loved animals. For years, Angel planned to be a veterinarian, but she could not abide seeing pets or livestock in pain.

"I lied to you." Etta looked stricken. Her face was white, and her hands shook. She fidgeted in her seat, lunch forgotten.

Angel tilted her head as if a better angle could help her make sense of the words. She and Etta had been friends for decades. Of course they had lied to each other.

"It's okay. It happens. Really, I forgive you." Once, Angel had ruined Etta's school project by accident and pretended she knew nothing about it as her friend cried. The guilt made her sick to this day, but shame kept her from using it as an example. Etta's expression did not change, and Angel got scared. Her blood chilled, and her fingers dropped the sandwich. Food had never taken second place in her consciousness, but it did now. Cookie, the town hall attendees, her parents, and now Etta had transformed into strangers. Angel could not trust any of them.

She clung to the edge of the earth, and eternal darkness lay below her. Angel knew whatever confession Etta intended to make was not kid stuff.

"I'm so sorry. I never meant to hurt you." Her head spun, and she wondered why friends and lovers always said the same thing. People never meant to destroy lives, but still did. They came in like wrecking balls and laid someone's existence to waste.

"What did you do?" Angel's voice sounded foreign and cold, and she tensed for an incoming blow. She found it unspeakably unfair how easy it was to lose everything. Innocents suffered by other's hands; it was a significant design flaw in God's plan.

"You were so scared. You couldn't sleep, and you cried all the time." Etta broke down, tears streaming down her cheeks, but Angel sat unmoved. She was a granite block, incapable of warmth or voluntary movement.

The lie was not recent, then. Angel had night terrors as a child, but those resolved before she was a teenager. "When?"

"The summer we were nine." Etta had worked herself into such a state the words came out garbled, half-drowned in misery. Deli customers had noticed, but for once, Angel did not care what they thought. She felt removed from the moment as if she observed it from a distance.

At times, her memory blazed with absolute clarity, and at others, it swam through murk. The year in question bogged down in thick, protective mud.

Angel struggled but failed to bring back any definitive events from the time frame. "What happened?" She feared the answer more than the rickety bookshelf behind Etta, which she expected to fall and crush her at any moment.

Her best friend shook with terror. The substitution of roles threw Angel for a minute. Etta stood up to things. She did not quiver, nor did she hide. The woman's strength and doggedness had abandoned her, and Angel could tell the woman would rather flee than finish this conversation. Phobias had taught her how to navigate looming tragedies; they abounded everywhere. Straight through provided the best chance of survival and was often the shortest route.

"You have to tell me. I won't hate you; I promise." Angel prayed she did not lie. She would not know until Etta told her. What happened after was anyone's guess, but she needed to know. Etta looked at her, unsure of whether to speak. She thought their friendship lay in the balance and gave Angel no reason to believe otherwise.

"Are you sure you don't remember?"

The continued avoidance rankled her, and paranoia clawed at her gut. It seemed everyone in the globe knew a secret she did not, and Angel had grown tired of being treated like an outsider.

"Etta. Tell me now." Maybe the build-up was worse than the news. Good movies never lived up to their hype. The same might be true for uncomfortable truths. It could be something Angel had come to grips with years ago, and Etta only assumed she did not know.

"We saw Glacier try to kill your father."

The deli had gone still, and she shook her head to clear the fuzz. Angel worried she had suffered hysterical deafness. Customers' mouths moved, but she could not hear them. Etta's face looked at her with expectation, as if she expected a reaction, but Angel did not know which one. The buzzing returned, as loud as a swarm of cicadas. She held her hands over her ears to block the awful noise. Without warning, the hum halted as if by unseen cue.

136

"That's ridiculous." The information had shocked her, but Angel knew these people. They had banded together and built a marvel; they didn't bludgeon each other, and Angel had certainly not watched them do it. The idea was comical. She giggled in relief. "You scared the snot out of me. Good one." Who knew Etta was such a good actress? She took a deep, calming breath. Her friend did not smile or accept Angel's congratulations on a prank well played. She shut her eyes.

"You were there." The syllables hung heavy in the air and landed with a thud. Angel believed she could brush them to the floor and step on them.

She let her growing anger loose. People needed to stop messing with her because she had reached her limit. "You're lying. Again. Why would he do such a thing? They were friends." Vivian had said so.

Glacier had made someone mad enough to kill him, but her father never had. He helped people. Every person meant to support her had done the opposite. Crushing loneliness hit, and she wanted to go home and be with Prancer. He loved her. She knew he did.

"I'm not, but I did, and for a very long time." Etta sighed and went on, though Angel no longer wanted to know. She desired nothing more than for the woman to shut up and never speak to her again. Ever.

"Don't." Her throat had closed off, limiting air and speech. She held up a hand to ward off injury.

Etta did not listen to her plea. "We went to the farm when we were told not to. You wanted to pet the goats." It did not sound implausible. The globe was the safest place in the world, and she its princess. The villagers watched out for each other, and her parents believed in a free-range style of children rearing. She could come to no harm.

"Two carts drove up, and your parents were in one, so we hid in the barn. We thought they had come looking for us, and we would be punished." Etta waited. If she hoped any of this sounded familiar, it did not. Still, Angel believed the words, and they filled her with dread.

"I don't want to hear anymore. Please." If Glacier had tried to kill her father, maybe he waited twenty years and returned the favor. Angel begged Etta to quit, but she refused. Once the determined woman had decided on a course of action, she could not be swayed.

"They were fighting, and we were trapped. If we came out, they would have seen us." Vague memories swam around Angel's ankles like unseen alligators, ready to latch on and drag her under the water. She felt sick.

"Your dad was mean—really mean. He yelled about how Glacier had screwed them, and they would lose everything. I'd never seen him like that, and neither had you. You cried and wanted to make him stop."

Angel had never been brave but could not abide shows of anger. To her, each felt as if it could end in death. This incident might have solidified the idea.

"You broke away and were near the door when we heard the gunshot."

# CHAPTER 9

Asound as loud as gunfire rang through Angel's head, and she rocked back as if struck. She had to leave. Her feet stumbled blind, and she banged out the door into the chill, midday air. Etta followed and called her name. Angel paid no attention to her. She ran, and the truth she did not want to acknowledge followed. The square's hub-and-spoke pattern led to the North Pole Complex, the last place Angel would ever want to be. Several blocks away, her lungs burned with cold and exertion. She stopped. Etta placed a hand on her arm, but she flung it off and ordered her to leave.

"Let me take you home." She wanted nothing else, so she allowed Etta to lead her in the proper direction.

Angel wanted to slam the door in her friend's face but didn't. She could not trust her emotions. The hatred within her toward the people she loved made her question her mental state.

To prove her coherency, she said, "I left the truck." It was not the most pressing consideration Angel had, but it was a detail she could put right.

"I'll take care of it after I leave. Give me the keys." Angel handed them to Etta without another thought. Mission accomplished.

Prancer greeted her as he always did, his voice full of excitement at her return. The poor creature had no choice but to wait for her. God had assigned pets a fate over which they had no control. The powerlessness of his situation saddened her.

"Hi!" His tone was so bright it hurt. "I love you."

Angel smiled, but tears filled her eyes. "I love you, too." She opened his enclosure and brought him with her to the living room. The bird bobbed his head and whistled. She laughed. He knew joy because they were together, and it was enough.

"Hey, birdy," said Etta. Prancer crawled from Angel's lap to Etta's and let her stroke him. The two had an understanding. Macaws could be very territorial, but he allowed Etta into the family circle. They played tug-of-war with a dog toy for a few minutes. After being alone, Prancer required Angel's unbroken attention before he settled.

"Do you remember the week we spent in the igloos?" Etta asked while Prancer preened his feathers free of the oil their hands had deposited there.

Townspeople never stayed in the globe's various resorts. They enjoyed all the village had to offer and returned to their snug homes. Angel did remember the igloos, though, as a special treat they once shared. Outsiders always filled them to capacity. Her parents must have made the reservations far in advance.

"I do. We watched the northern lights from the round bed." The remarkable streaks of color had enchanted her, and they stayed up late, mesmerized by the show. The Aurora Borealis beat any low-level fireworks set off on a holiday. "I'd love to go back there."

The glass enclosures were a luxury she could never afford now. Angel needed to consider the shortfall in her rent, and soon, or she would have nowhere to stay. Living at her parents' had ceased to be an option, and it was too early to consider Benny's. She had only seen him once since the gnome encounter, and then only for an hour.

Etta shuddered. "Not me, not ever." She cringed and writhed as if creepy crawlies made their way across her skin. It was the same wiggle of disgust she used for fishing worms or maggots.

Angel was confused as to how they had such different memories of the remarkable place. "It was the best week ever." Her parents had not said no to anything. The nature of her father's job made time off impossible, and it was the only vacation she had ever had.

"It was meant to shut us up about what we saw. Your parents kept us captive until we promised to never speak about it. Ever." Etta clutched her stomach as if it pained her. A spike of fear went through Angel, and she prayed the stress had not hurt the baby.

"No. That can't be right." She shook her head in disagreement. Her mom and dad had indulged her as a child, but they never bought her compliance. Duty and honor topped the list of motivators, not bribes.

"You screamed when the gun went off, and they turned and saw us." If Glacier had attempted to murder her father, Angel was sure she would have screamed; anyone would have.

"If it had happened, I'd still be screaming." She felt like doing so now, twenty years later. "You're lying—or an accessory after the fact."

The words struck Etta across the face, and her head jerked back from the force. Angel felt no guilt.

Tears glistened in her friend's eyes. She had cut her deeply. "We were both there, so the same is true of you." Angel could not dispute the logic but gritted her teeth instead of admitting it. She wanted Etta to leave and never return. Angel could not believe anything she said.

"It was horrible." Etta shook her head as if to rid herself of the memory. "They went crazy and acted as if he had shot you instead of the tree. They cried and held on for dear life."

Memories lurked, but Angel did not allow them any closer. Her best friend was a liar. She had admitted it. "You're jealous because your parents got divorced, and mine loved each other and me. We had a real family." Angel needed Etta to stop talking, and whatever she did to make it happen was fair.

Etta's beautiful, kind face looked sad. "I was; you're right. My mom worked two jobs, and your family lived in a castle."

Angel felt a pang of guilt. Everyone wanted to be her; she was a fairytale princess. "My parents let you live there, too." Years passed where no one ever asked if Etta was staying to dinner; she was

expected. She slept over, even on school nights. Angel much preferred her company to Merry's, who barged in whenever she could.

"They took us to the igloos to keep us from telling."

Etta repeated herself, and the pain in Angel's heart verified
the story was true. No matter how much she hated it, something
deep within her remembered. Angel hoped her suspected brain
tumor would complete its work soon. She had decided not to seek
treatment but would accept God's will in the matter.

"When I die, will you take care of Prancer?"

Etta startled as if Angel had zapped her with a cattle prod. "What
are you talking about? You're not going to die." She looked panicked.

"If I do, will you promise to keep him?" Her intensity forced
Etta to answer.

"Of course, I will. But nothing's going to happen to you." Her
friend hesitated. "You're not—" She let the rest of the sentence
hang between them.

Angel would not commit hari-kari on the spot. "No. Don't worry.
I could never harm myself." It was true. Cowards did not take the
coward's way out; they were too afraid. It was a terrible irony.

Etta calmed down but kept an eye on her for any sudden moves.
"We spent a week in the igloos eating s'mores and drinking hot
chocolate," she tucked her chin into her chest, "and convincing
you it hadn't happened."

Angel felt sick as she remembered the illegal number of sweets
they consumed. No parent had ever indulged their child the way they
had her. Presents appeared daily, and every minute was spent pursu-
ing fun. Whatever she wanted, she got. She felt greedy and shallow.

"What about you?" A little ice cream and a few trinkets bought
Angel's silence, but what about Etta's?

"Your dad was Santa, for gosh sake, and I was a kid." Etta's face
hardened. "He threatened to cut me off forever and fire my mom
if I ever said a word. No one would've hired her if he said not to;
it meant moving out of the globe."

Angel thought she would puke. Her father was a powerful man, but up until now, she had believed him benevolent. The truth was he had threatened to banish Etta's family to protect his awful secret. No child could take a stand against the guy with the naughty list.

Etta stared at the couch. "I pretended it was a dream, but I never forgot. I'm so sorry." She looked up, seeking forgiveness. "You couldn't live with the memory, so we made you think you were crazy and had dreamed the whole thing."

Angel's family and best friend had gaslighted her. The ramifications boggled her mind. She felt like a fool and hated them all for putting her in this situation. Who were they to say what she could or could not handle? Any response she had to such a wild scenario would have been valid. It was they who acted inappropriately, not her.

"Why didn't you call the police?" She demanded. If Glacier had done this terrible thing, her father should have never hidden the fact. Nothing made sense, and her head pounded. Angel closed her eyes to block the painful sunlight and yearned to return to darkness.

"I was nine, and it's not like we had cell phones. Your parents called my mom and told her I was going on vacation with you. Then they trapped us in an igloo until we agreed it was all a nightmare."

Her dad must have muscled his way into the igloos and pulled strings to get the northern lights. He had influence, and unlike Angel, he was not afraid to use it. His elaborate ploys worked; Angel had no memory of the event. She had suffered nightmares for years. Loud noises still frightened her, but so did everything else.

"What about Glacier? What happened to him?"

"Nothing, as far as I know. Your parents may have held it over his head, but we'll never know." Etta looked sad. "One of them stayed with us every minute for the rest of the summer. We weren't allowed out alone until school started."

Angel felt gut-punched. She moved to the floor where the earth could swallow her without taking the couch. Her parents had victimized them both. Misery filled her as if she had been an empty vase.

"Why did Mom play along with them?" Out of all the unthinkable things Etta claimed happened, this felt wrong. Her mother set the pace, not her father. She called the tune, and he danced. "How could she let Glacier get away with it?"

Etta shook her head. "Thinking about it now, it seems obvious she should have called the police. Who gives a murderer a second chance at killing their husband? But back then, I never considered it, and I don't think she did either."

Maybe her mother had seen the events as an opportunity to gain power. Had she blackmailed Glacier into relinquishing control? Angel felt random and inconsequential in her own life as if she were an unnecessary component.

Etta leaned toward her, and Prancer waddled over to see if she was alright. "Good bird," he said but sounded unsure.

"You're a good bird," she said and kissed his beak. Her tears fell on his neck, and it convulsed. Prancer regurgitated to feed Angel like a baby bird, the only way he knew to soothe her. "Stop that," she said, and he did.

The bird's instinct led him to provide for and protect her. He had risked his life against Frank, the chief of police. Angel was neither his chick nor mate, but Prancer put her first. Her parents' love fell far short of the mark set by a parrot. They convinced a child she imagined a real-life happening, and when adult Angel did not do as they instructed, they cut her loose. Had they ever wanted her, or was she a means to an end?

"Why did he never try again?" If a man set out to murder another, why did he not complete the task? It would not have been something one did on a whim. What had changed?

Etta looked confused. "I don't think Glacier had some elaborate plan. Your screams broke whatever spell drove him to madness."

"Did you tell anyone? Your mom?" The globe knew when someone stole their neighbor's paper or ran over a bush with a golf cart. A shooting could not have gone undetected. An odd lunch order could spin-off rumors of pregnancy, divorce, or terminal illness. Townspeople commented on everything.

Etta hung her head in what Angel interpreted as shame. "No. I couldn't risk it." She looked miserable, and Angel wondered about the toll her father's secret had taken on her friend.

"Dad was wrong for threatening you. I'm so sorry." Apologizing for someone else felt inadequate, but it was all she could do.

Angel returned to the sofa to hug her, and the remorseful woman burst into tears.

"Jesus loves you," Prancer said.

"You're so smart," she said. He knew how to make them feel better.

"Peanut." He was also an opportunist. Angel gave him several; Prancer had never lied to her.

Her parents did not care about Angel's short or long-term mental health; they wanted to keep her quiet about Glacier's misdeeds. Probably so they could leverage the man. She cut Etta more slack because her friend was a child at the time, but anger prevented total forgiveness. The woman lied and withheld crucial information for two decades, making her feel stupid. Angel did not know if she could trust her again.

"Aren't you late for school?" Etta said and looked at her watch.

Angel uttered a little cry and did the same. Class started in ten minutes, and there was no way she could make it. She pulled out her cell phone and dialed.

"Where are you?" Her boss said without preamble.

She had no planned excuse, so Angel played it straight. "I can't make it. Things came up, and the day got away from me." She was in crisis and unable to function. Claiming to be sick would not have stretched the truth.

"It's unacceptable. You've left me no time to bring in a substitute. Get here, or I'll let you go for unprofessional behavior. Emergencies require twenty-four-hour notice."

"That's not how emergencies work." She would gift him a dictionary. Did the man have nothing else going on in his life but work? Was there no Mrs. Bowtie with flappy arms? If the man wasn't so mean, she might have felt sorry for him.

"Time is ticking." He hung up on her, and Angel sat, looking at the phone for answers it could not give.

She told Etta what her boss had said. "He's a jerk. If he fires you, you can fight it."

Angel knew an appeal process could drag out for months, and she might not win. In the meantime, she would be unemployed. Homelessness was not a current option. "I can't risk it." Her words echoed Etta's. They had both been pressed into uncomfortable situations by powerful males. She hated the circumstances and the men.

"Will I still see you tonight?" Etta looked anxious. The unasked question was whether their friendship would survive this, and she did not know. They had shared enough pain today. Angel loaded Prancer into his carrier and headed for the golf cart.

"I'll be there." When Etta turned, she whispered, "If I can," low enough her friend could not hear. Angel did not want to lie but could make no promises. Her drive to work endangered the lives of several pedestrians, but she arrived only five minutes late. Once again, her boss stood in the doorway. Angel brushed past without stopping or acknowledging his presence.

"Hey guys, sorry I'm late. It's an exciting day. We're getting hands-on with our geese skeletons." A few people moaned, and she smiled at their discomfort. "They're cleaned. The taxidermy class meets on Saturday mornings for those interested in a more authentic experience."

Angel removed Prancer from his crate and placed him on his stand. She unloaded her supplies while still talking. The moment her bodyweight hit the seat, a high-decibel air raid siren sounded. The unthinkable had happened, and enemies had taken aim at the globe.

Prancer screamed, as did several female students. Males stood, ready to fight or flee. Angel startled so violently her chair flipped over, and she landed on her back. Later, she was glad there had been no time to change into a skirt before coming to work. Thoughts of nuclear war raced through her head. She worried about her

146

parents and Prancer. Her pantry contained military rations and bottled water in case of natural disasters. Angel had long dreamed of a bunker but would die in an unprotected classroom.

With her weight off the rolling chair, the horrible wailing halted. She looked around to assess the situation. Two foreign exchange students lie prone with their hands covering their heads. A couple of kind people rushed to Angel's assistance, but Merry was not among them. Her cousin sat in the front row, non-plussed by the unholy shriek or resultant excitement.

Her boss walked away without checking to see if she had suffered a fractured skull or other lawsuit-inducing injuries. The two had joined forces against her, but she did not understand their end game. What did they hope to achieve? Merry could not fill her job; she had no education. From her vantage point on the tile, Angel understood the anatomy of the joke. Someone had positioned the airhorn's handle to depress when she sat. Angel pulled the canister free to avoid a repeat humiliation. A helpful student took it before she could pitch the thing at Merry's smug face.

A graceless flip brought Angel to her knees and then feet. She dusted off her clothing. "The goose is unhappy about today's lab, but he's already plucked, so let's get to work."

Angel struggled throughout the lesson to maintain enthusiasm and impart knowledge. Her day had become a write-off the moment Etta explained the bullet's history; the best she could do was fake it. Things refused to return to normal, and Angel came to the slow realization her innocence died the day Glacier did. She could never reclaim it.

"Round and round the cobbler's bench," the voice belonged to her, but she had not broken out in song. Angel looked at Prancer, who continued. She took a breath and joined him. "The monkey chased the weasel. The monkey thought 'twas all in fun; POP goes the weasel." The bird made a solid point. Two could play at this game, and it was time Angel went on the offensive. She had tired of being fate's punching bag and intended to take a few swings.

After class, she planned to fill out a timesheet and claim personal leave for the morning hours. Angel did not wish any further confrontations with her boss. The man had conspired with her cousin to strip Angel of her dignity. She needed a plan sure to keep him in his corner and out of her business.

Paperwork sat on her desk, but not the kind she sought. The scarecrow had penned a formal reprimand citing Angel's tardiness and lack of presence on campus. The document brought her tenure into question. Rage boiled the acid already present in her stomach. She could have used it to dissolve his bones.

"Can you believe this?" she said to Prancer and remembered the man did not want the bird here, either. Angel felt persecuted. Her work was exemplary. She created special courses and did not rely on the canned curriculum devoid of effort. Her students would leave their studies with a better understanding of birds, biology, music, and history.

Quitting the thankless job crossed Angel's mind, but the globe only contained one college. She refused to be driven from her home, even if she did not recognize it anymore. Angel stayed until 5 p.m. and wanted the heartless administrator to witness her exit. When she arrived at his office with the form, she learned he had left early for the day. She took a selfie with his wall clock and emailed it to him.

Emboldened by her rebellious act, she looked around for anything incriminating. Nothing jumped out at her. He had a golfing trophy and a plaque that read: "Save time and admit I'm right." To Angel, it perfectly summed up his management style. On her way out, she checked his secretary's desk. Angel liked the long-suffering woman and felt a little guilty, but her affection did not hinder her quest. The department head wanted her gone, and she needed ammo to hold her ground and position. She took pictures of the man's calendar and hoped they yielded something useful.

After dropping Prancer off at home, Angel walked to the park. They scheduled the official opening for 6 p.m., but a golf cart line waited at the entry. It did not appear the tourists shunned the town on account of the mayor's death. If anything, the publicity may have reminded people to make the trip.

She spotted Vivian Harrison, Glacier's widow, surrounded by a crowd of people. When she approached, the woman pulled her to one side and said, "Thanks for coming. Etta said you had a rough day."

"What else did she say?" Had the woman kept a secret for twenty years to shatter Glacier's widow with the news her husband had been a would-be murderer?

Vivian looked shocked and hurried to say, "Nothing. She was just concerned about you, that's all." The deceased mayor's wife stared at her as if Etta had been right to worry. Maybe she was.

Etta had overstepped by withholding vital information, but her intentions had been good, and the lie had cost her. It wasn't Etta's fault Angel was so eager to deceive herself. They had seen the same thing; she had only herself to blame for choosing a fantasy memory.

"It's probably best I don't stay home," Angel said. Left alone with her anger, she might act in haste and regret at leisure.

Vivian's smile was sad. "I know exactly what you mean." Gossips had judged her for not staying hidden until the priest threw the first shovel of dirt yesterday. Angel found them cruel. Human beings were fragile, and she believed they should be treated as such. Most did their best to get through the day, and outside interference turned bad things into worse by exerting pressure when it could least be tolerated.

"Yes, you do." People repeatedly asked the bereaved how they were doing, and it made them insane. They appreciated the concern behind the question but tired of reassuring everyone else, so Angel did not ask. "Will you occupy Glacier's seat until the next election?" Someone had to step up, and Angel did not want it to be Merry. The woman would make her life unbearable if given any power.

"Yes, I intend to." Vivian lowered her voice, and her eyes scoured the area for spies, "Do you think I can do it? Will they listen to me?"

Glacier's death had diminished the dynamic woman's confidence, and Angel was sorry to see it.

"Of course you can. You were the brains behind the operation, anyway. Don't let them intimidate you. Trust your gut."

Vivian looked at her in gratitude. "Want to have a drink sometime? Maybe tomorrow afternoon?"

Angel did not know if alcohol was a smart move. Still, it was the weekend, and the suddenly single woman needed company. "I'd love to."

"I'm going to have you handle the first-aid tent. It should be quiet in there. All you have to do is call for help should someone need it."

It was Angel's turn to be grateful. Vivian had assigned her a vital role requiring minimal effort; she could not have hoped for anything better. The medical tent was enclosed for patient privacy. Angel could hide inside all evening and not be forced to smile. It was perfect. She had brought a water bottle, but not much else. As part of the committee, Angel had planned to be working the front lines. A book would have provided a much-needed escape, but she had not packed one.

No one visited her in the first hour, and the canvas walls moved in closer. She felt hundreds of unseen eyes taking note of her position and felt exposed. Others could scout Angel's location without her knowledge. She needed outside cameras and inside monitors. Angel tried to distract herself, but social media failed to stimulate anything but envy. Strangers who spent money on lavish entertainments depressed her, and someone's two-thousand-dollar bar tab made her sick when she couldn't afford rent.

She had grown up thinking her family was happy. Every photo on the mantle showed them smiling, yet it was a mirage, like the snow globe itself. Her parents were illusionists. Angel could not wrap her head around Glacier firing at her dad. She felt guilty for wondering what the man had done to deserve it. Vivian had said Glacier thought him a thief, but no answer justified the action. The audacity of deciding to take another's life boggled her mind.

Etta said her dad worried about losing everything, but it never happened. Her parents held the same jobs they had then, and still lived in the North Pole Complex. Dad's company, North Pole Enterprises, continued to grow. Angel was unaware of any financial difficulties. If there had been a problem, they had found a way to fix it.

The tent flap opened, and Angel jumped up, ready to fight. She grinned when she saw it was Benny. He carried two hot chocolates and a tray of midway food. Her stomach greeted the sight of funnel cake as warmly as her heart did the man.

"You busy?" he asked and sat down his load to hug her. His jacket smelled of campfires and comfort. The embrace lasted a full minute.

Angel released him and assumed a professional role. She ran her hands over Benny's limbs to assess his health. "Have you been injured? Are you having a stroke?" Her hands cupped his face, and she looked deep into his eyes.

He made a suggestive growl. "I will if you keep touching me like that."

Angel snatched her fingers back in a hurry. This was not that kind of tent. "How's the shop?" she asked.

"Business? You want to talk business? I'm wounded." Benny clutched his heart and staggered to a chair. "Things are slower than I had hoped," he said with a slight frown. "This is a tough town to crack."

"That's where you went wrong. The globe's shatterproof."

He smiled, and his hair fell over one eye. She wanted to push it back but restrained herself from touching him. "People come by, but it's more to snoop than buy."

"It must be a hard sell, though. A family only needs one stove." Maybe he should expand his line to include hot tubs, or better yet, puppies.

He grabbed Angel and pulled her onto his lap. She giggled and fought, but not much. "Spreading propaganda like that will ruin me. You have the nerve to sit under my heat lamp and tell me there are no uses for my products?"

Benny had a point. The lovely glass cylinder with the blue gas flame kept the space toasty warm, as did his arms. A cold current cut across the room, and Angel looked up to see Cookie standing in the entryway.

She made a sound of disgust. "It's what I should have expected." Angel hopped off Benny's lap and apologized, her face red.

"I'm sorry. Do you need medical assistance?" Cookie walked with a slight limp Angel had never notice before now.

"Darn tourists let their kids drive, and one ran over my foot, but don't trouble yourself. I see you have your hands full with your felon."

Angel remembered liking the woman but could not recall why. "You mean fellow." Insults would never allow the rift between them to heal, and she hated being at odds with anyone.

Cookie snorted. "I said what I meant." Her face held a look of superiority and knowledge of clandestine meetings Angel would never be invited to join. She imagined her dancing in a moonlight gathering to summon demons.

"Here, sit down, and I'll call the EMTs to have a look at your foot." Angel let the rude comment slide. The woman looked to stir up trouble, and she already had a bushel.

"No, thanks. I'll find Doc on my own. You and your thug can go back to what you were doing." Her tone made it clear what she thought was happening in the tent. Angel did not block her exit.

"What was all that about?" she asked. The first time Cookie insulted Angel, Benny went to have words with her. This time, he kept silent.

His face darkened. "We should talk." Those words had never indicated a lottery win. People reserved them for affairs, bankruptcies, and jail terms. Angel teetered on the edge of losing her job, her best friend, and her parents. Benny had been her only remaining hope, and he seemed intent on taking it from her.

"Not now," she said and moved across the room. "I'm on duty, and there are a thousand people out there who might need my assistance." Angel stood looking out, hoping tragedy befell a stranger.

152

Benny crossed the distance and touched her arm. "Until they come, there's something I want to tell you."

Angel stepped outside, but Vivian had gifted her this Christmas plum of an assignment, and she couldn't abandon it. "I think you should go." She couldn't leave, but Benny could. One more blow would snap Angel's frayed tether.

He met her eyes in defiance. "I'm not going to. I need you to listen to me." His tone was serious, and he intended to force another piece of unwanted awareness on her. She wouldn't let him; she had her fill for one day.

Angel whirled, guns blazing. "When did everyone stop caring what I want? I tell people. I beg, but no one listens. Everyone thinks their agenda is far more important than mine. Let me clue you in, it's not."

Benny did not flinch. "I don't know about the others, but I'm trying to save us future problems."

"Feel free to blast all problems to the future! I've had enough for today!" She screamed, not caring about her loss of decorum or that only a piece of tent material stood between her and a crowd. "My parents murdered Glacier, my best friend has been lying to me for twenty years, I'm going to lose my job, and the town has turned against me. What fresh hell do you have in store?"

Angel had forced herself to function when everything within her ordered a spiritual and physical rest. She had worked, attended organ practice, visited her parents, volunteered on the lighting display, and cared for Prancer as the world crumbled. No energy remained. Her exhaustion increased, and she wavered in place.

Benny led her to a chair and helped her sit. "It's okay. We're alright. We don't have to do this now. I just didn't want anything to come between us."

"There is no us. I'm alone and always will be." Her sobs formed words, but Angel had no idea if Benny understood them. The people she relied upon had betrayed her, and she would not put her trust in anyone again.

If a person looked after themselves, others could not disappoint them. What skills she lacked she would do without. Prancer was the only relationship she needed. All others ended in pain.

# Chapter 10

Angel turned off her phone and alarms before sleep. She could not think of a single reason to get out of bed ever again. Prancer called to her several times during the morning, but for the first time ever, she ignored him. Maybe he would think the house was empty.

"Alexa, turn on Prancer's playlist," she heard him say. Angel had not known the bird could do it alone. It made sense; artificial intelligence could not decipher the difference between her voice and his. She reminded herself to order his treats through the app and never out loud to avoid surprise visa bills.

The music lulled her back to sleep, where she dreamed Benny whispered in her ear. "I love you," he said and stroked her hair. Angel had told the man to get lost; he was not in her bed and never had been. Her tired mind must have conjured him for comfort. She regretted giving him the brush off last night, but she had been overwhelmed.

"I love you," came the words again. Angel started when she felt a slight brush along her arm. A lifelong fear of cockroaches brought her upright in the bed. No giant bug crawled on her; it was Prancer.

When she restarted her heart, she said, "Holy heck. You scared me." She stared at the bird and wondered how he managed to get out of his enclosure. Her father used the same pen for reindeer, which weighed two hundred times what Prancer did.

The macaw laughed like an evil scientist, which disturbed her even more. His brain weighed ounces but computed in pounds. He had not believed she left the house and insisted she get up and

take care of him. "Rise and shine and give God the glory, glory..."
he sang, trying to start the day in the usual way.

Today was not typical. Most mornings brought a smile to Angel's
lips and a bounce to her step. The nighttime frightened her, and
she was always thrilled to watch the sun send it scurrying. Angel
looked at the clock. It was 12:05 p.m. Her limbs felt sluggish, and
her head hung too heavy for her neck. She had not drunk anything
last night but felt hungover, nonetheless.

"How did you get in here?" She took him with her to the shower.
Prancer loved the water. He perched on a towel bar as she turned
on a fine mist, and sang a *Sesame Street* song about how his rubber
ducky made bath time fun. He bobbed his head and did a little
dance while they sang. "All clean," Prancer said as they finished. He
ran his beak along each feather shaft to wring it out and extended
his wings to dry them as she dressed.

When they walked down the hall, Angel found evidence of the
jailbreak. The enclosure's lock had been dismantled piece by piece.
Unless he had burglary tools, Prancer had used his beak, tongue,
and toes to unscrew the assembly. She looked at him in amazement.

"What did you do?" What looked to her like standard bird body
parts had morphed into lock picks. It must have taken hours of
concerted effort for him to manage the disassembly.

Prancer looked contrite. "Oops," he said. "I dropped it." He
dipped his head in submission. The bird knew when he did things
she would find upsetting, but he rarely cared. The quality made him
almost human. Angel had to laugh. She took a picture with her
phone to show people how smart he was. Who would she send it to,
though? Her parents? Etta? Benny? The most important relationships in her life lay as broken as the lock. She put the phone back
in her pocket and headed for the coffee pot. It never disappointed.

She had determined to verify Etta's story and find out why it
took place. To do so, she would need to visit her parents. They
deserved an opportunity to defend their actions. Would they
lie? Angel had never known them to be dishonest but could not

imagine a scenario in which her father confessed to brainwashing. What would she do if they stonewalled her yet again?

She fingered the bullet and wondered about statutes of limitations. Adults who blamed their upbringing for their current jerkitude made her nuts. People needed to own their behaviors and stop blaming everything on their childhoods. Had they left the slug for leverage against Glacier? Did they use it as silent incrimination or blackmail? Why didn't the mayor remove it, then? An errant bullet did not prove anything. Anyone may have taken illegal target practice; it wasn't traceable to him.

Angel made Prancer an oatmeal breakfast bowl and ate an edited version of the same. She diced the fruit into small pieces, worried because she did not know how to Heimlich a bird.

The macaw's enjoyment tickled her. He gave dramatic moans of pleasure and said, "Mmmm. Finger-licking good." She had taught him the advertisement to amuse herself as the bird did not have fingers to lick.

Angel remained present in the morning, and every time thoughts of the past or future imposed themselves, she ignored them. They played, sang, cleaned, and pretended the outside world did not exist. It took longer than expected to fix the broken lock.

It was one of the most delightful afternoons they had ever spent until she ruined it with a trip to the North Pole Complex. Angel did not bring Prancer, as what she wanted to say did not bear repeating. Not seeing her parents on stage no longer surprised her. She expected to see an alternate wear the big guy's suit, but the pair seated in the red velvet thrones today were thieves, not substitutes.

She stood in shock, mouth open, and watched Merry and Basil hold court in her parents' place. The scene brought bile to her throat. It was if Lucifer appointed himself to play Joseph and leaned over the helpless Christ child. Angel lost all equilibrium. Merry had no business playing Mrs. Claus. Her pudgy form fit into the dress, but she had no right to wear it. Angel wanted to strip her cousin down to the petticoats and expose her for the fraud she was.

Outraged, she stormed the platform. Two nutcracker security officers stepped forward to block her, but the look on her face and recognition of who she was made them retreat.

"What in the heck are you doing up here?" Angel demanded, her gaze traveling back and forth between the padded performers imitating her parents. Degenerates in Santa suits were still degenerates.

Merry gave a self-satisfied smile and said, "You'll need to stand in line, dear. All of these children are in front of you." Angel wanted to strike her. She did not care if she ruined Christmas for an entire elementary school or a busload of orphans.

Basil said, "Ho, ho, ho. Don't worry, kids, I've got gifts for all of you." He lifted his red sack brimming with bright packages and beamed. His large frame and friendly demeanor lent itself to the role, though Angel would never admit it.

"Get off of this stage, or I'll drag you off by your wig." She heard the hysteria in her voice and knew the bubbling rage to be unhealthy, but Angel could not stop herself.

The nutcrackers, concerned about a brewing scene, took tentative steps toward her. Angel held them off with her eyes. She was the princess, the heir apparent, and they had no wish to anger her father. Angel could not have articulated why seeing Merry and Basil commanding the platform bothered her so much. Fill-ins had worked all week, and Angel had never had a problem with any of them. Those couples wanted a paycheck; this pair wanted the crown.

Basil waved at a couple of performers. They stepped up their acts, drawing the attention of as many children as possible. A team member started a sing-along, while another juggled glass ornaments. An elf on stilts teetered wildly while the children gulped in fear he would fall into the Christmas tree.

The distraction worked for a few minutes, but Angel did not care who saw or overheard her. Merry had tried to get her fired, and now she wanted to put her parents out of work as well.

"We're not going anywhere," her cousin said. The infuriating smirk remained, and Angel wanted to violently dislodge it. She had never hit another person but was confident she could do so.

In frustration, Angel sent Mrs. Claus's table of sugar cookies flying. Merry gasped, and Angel widened her stance, ready for a fight. A small boy burst into tears at the destruction of dessert.

"I said get out!" She did not care where they went, but it should be far from her and the family's legacy. Merry had always desired the spotlight. Sheer cussedness was enough reason for Angel to prevent her from getting it.

Basil looked uncomfortable and got to his feet. He approached Angel and touched her arm. "This is not the place," he said. "The children are watching." The man had aligned himself with an unscrupulous opportunist, and choices had consequences. Angel pushed him.

"Let go of me." Angel knew Merry was unfamiliar with the concept of boundaries but thought she had married a man with sense. Basil wore a full fake beard, so she could not tell but thought he looked chagrined.

"We're just helping," Basil said. Her cousin had found a man willing to do anything she asked. So had Angel, but she told Benny to get lost, and he did. The memory of him walking out of the first-aid tent would haunt her for the rest of her days.

"Helping yourselves, you mean," Angel said. Merry stayed seated and played the dignified queen to Angel's out-of-control jester.

"You need to leave," one of the nutcrackers said. They had come from behind to escort her off the platform. She did not intend to go until the imposters did. This was her father's domain, and these two charlatans had no business anywhere near it.

With sudden clarity, Angel understood what angered her. Seeing Merry and Basil playing her parents' parts made her think they were dead. It was as if her cousin had buried them alive. Someday, the pair would grow old and retire, but not today. Merry could not behave as if they had never existed. Angel would not let her.

The nutcrackers each took an arm and led Angel from the set. She imitated protesters on television and let her body go slack. If they wanted to be rid of her, it would cost them a herniated disk.

"Angel, stand up; don't make us drag you," one of the guys said. They had gone to high school together. He looked ridiculous in his shiny red vest and false mustache, and she told him so.

A few people in the crowd filmed her exit with their cameras. Basil addressed the children. "Ho, ho, ho. Who's next?"

Merry motioned for someone to bring a broom for the crumbled cookies. Colorful sprinkles littered the platform and shone in the lights. She was too good to do any cleaning herself. Servants suited her; she had undoubtedly married one.

Angel's arms hurt from being drug. Her bulk worked against the men, but it weighed on her as well. When they reached the outer circle, she stood.

"Thanks for the lift, guys." She gave them her brightest smile.

Her friend from school shook his head in exasperation. "What's up with you? Why'd you upset the kids?" He looked disappointed. She had broken the globe's primary directive to "never ruin the illusion." Interchangeable children had taken priority over Angel her entire life. Her parents had cited them every time they broke a promise. The kids needed them; they were sorry. The brats were strangers with wish lists—nothing more than tiny beggars. She had tip-toed around them long enough.

"Life is harsh. It's not all candy canes and stocking stuffers." She walked away with her head held high. It was a good thing she did not care for social media; Angel had a feeling the video would go viral.

She skirted the edge of the plaza and approached again from the back, this time with a plan. Merry and Basil had caught her unawares the first time, but they should have listened and done as she said. She would make sure they never played pretend on the big stage again. Angel was glad she had not forced the nutcrackers to call for back-up. The guys guarding the rear said cheery hellos, and she waved and smiled. They would not learn about her escapades until break time when it would be too late.

She walked with purpose toward the key box. Instead of the boom truck she drove so often, Angel selected the set for the front-end loader. They seldom used the massive piece of equipment and parked it a block away from the North Pole Complex. She pocketed the keys and headed to the garage. No one monitored the storage facility. They did not store anything of value here except large vehicles, and it wasn't as if someone could steal them and leave the globe. Teenagers had once taken Santa's sleigh for a joy ride, but six months of shoveling reindeer poop had cured them of such impulses.

Angel opened the tall bay door in readiness to exit and climbed into the cab. The vehicle's wheels stood as tall as her shoulders. She settled in the operator's seat and surveyed the controls. Due to the framework of the loader, she had no view behind her. That was okay; Angel only planned on going forward.

A roll bar restraint loomed over her head, and she snapped it into place as if on an amusement park ride. Her father always made a point of safety first. She wondered if he came up with the rule after having live rounds fired at his head. The engine started, and she adjusted the throttle to keep it running. Angel knew the basics but had not spent much time behind the wheel. How hard could it be?

She practiced with the joysticks, moving the bucket up and down and extending its arms. Signs warned her of roll-over risks. Merry was chunky, but not heavy enough to unbalance the machinery. Angel grinned in excitement. It was her cousin's turn to be afraid. The twit had challenged her one too many times, and now she would pay. Diesel exhaust built up within the enclosed space and made Angel cough. She moved the lever into position and drove toward the doorway.

The machine lumbered and shook. The power vibrated through the vehicle's frame and hers. There was no steering wheel, only right and left controls, which moved the carryall in the opposite direction. Angel did not judge the aperture well, and the rig's right side struck the door frame. The flimsy metal crumpled but did not slow her. She entered the street without stopping to close the bay door or inspect the damage. Niceties seemed silly after she had made a commitment to destruction.

A right turn took her toward the plaza. Angel drove in the middle of the street, careful to miss parked golf carts. People driving pulled to one side and let her pass. Size mattered.

When she reached the North Pole Complex, Angel increased her speed. She depressed the horn. The blast equaled or excelled the air siren horn Merry had used to humiliate her. It seemed appropriate, and Angel took it as a good sign.

Mothers pulled their children from the walkways. Several small boys grew excited, and one shouted, "Look, it's Bob the Builder!" Angel smiled and kept going.

She steered around the eggnog stand and waved at its owner. The man stared at her with incomprehension. A costumed ginger-bread man leaped out of her path, and she laughed, remembering the story.

"Run, run, run, as fast as you can! You can't catch me, I'm the gingerbread man!" Angel called after him. She had not had this much fun in years.

The loader drove like a tank and made her invincible. Nothing could stand in her way. When she drew close enough, she saw the fear in Merry's face. The woman gripped the arms of her stolen throne and looked to Basil for help.

"Being married won't help you now," Angel said. In the end, everyone stood alone, and she had a lifetime of practice. Why had she never seen it as an advantage before now?

Policemen called such stunts a joyride, and she understood why. Euphoria flowed like a sugar rush, and she enjoyed a clear-headed drunkenness. Thousands of Christmas lights dazzled her eyes, and Angel experienced colors in a new way. The smell of fudge filled her nostrils, and she promised herself a hunk of chocolate walnut when she completed the mission.

Angel had found a purpose larger than herself; she was a super-hero. The globe had gotten off track when someone murdered the mayor and needed someone to purge it from the evil. She steered hard left and brought the bucket around to face the ramp. Designed for much smaller vehicles like the boom truck, Angel did not know if it would hold a front-end loader's weight, but she was willing to try.

"Hey!" yelled her friend, the nutcracker. He looked lame and inef-fectual dressed in his formal jacket while she drove an assault vehicle. "What do you think you're doing? Stop it. You're scaring people."

Angel gunned it. For a moment, the incline focused her eyes on the wooden doves she had painted a lifetime ago. They looked good. Then the front wheels grasped the platform, and she came to level. Merry and Basil stood looking at her. Angel depressed the lever and lowered the bucket; a bulldozer would have been better suited to the job, but she did not have access to one.

She had never experienced a thrill anywhere near this. Roller coasters could never compete. The adventure intoxicated her, and she felt high. Forget academia, she wanted a job running an earth-mover. Heavy equipment left a mark on the world.

"You can't do this. It's our special day." Merry's voice squeaked with indignation at having her moment in the sun ruined. She had waited years for the opportunity to take center stage. Angel's cousin needed to be adored, and Mrs. Claus's role gave her a legion of followers yearning for her wisdom.

When her parents balked, Merry had encouraged Angel to go to college and move away from the globe. She may have instilled the idea in the first place. Angel's cousin needed her gone so she could assume the title role.

"Basil, make her stop! She's ruining everything." Tears fell from Merry's eyes, and she pouted.

"Move," Angel said and revved the engine. A few little girls cried in confusion, but their parents did not remove them from the plaza. They wanted to see the show. Everyone held up a phone, taping the confrontation.

"Angel, shut off your engine," yelled a nutcracker over the din. He took a step toward her, and Angel pivoted the machinery, so the upraised bucket faced him.

"Back off, or I won't be responsible." The man left the platform and raised his radio to his mouth. She did not have much time.

Basil blocked Merry's body with his. Angel found it endearing and was sorry she had no one who would endanger themselves for her. "You don't have to do this. We mean no harm. If you want us to go—"

Angel had asked the pair to leave. Then she told them. She felt by the time heavy equipment showed up, they should have gotten the hint.

"We're not going anywhere," Merry said, coming around from behind her husband. She set her mouth and stout legs. "You never wanted any of this. You just don't want me to have it."

Her cousin spoke the truth. If the facts made her shallow, so be it. She would see her boss or Cookie take over as the globe's spiritual leader before she allowed Merry to assume the position. The time to get her out was now before her plump rump indented the chair, and people grew accustomed to her role.

"You're a greedy, selfish, little woman with bad manners. You'd make a terrible Mrs. Claus, and I'll never let you do it." Angel put the loader back into gear and drove toward them.

"Don't do it." Basil grabbed Merry and pulled her back with him, but Angel did not stop. She lined the bucket up with the matching velvet chairs and pushed. The splintering of the wood caused several screams in the gallery and a wallop of pleasure in Angel.

The sumptuous furniture disintegrated and proved to be particleboard. It was all part of the globe's illusion. Merry and Basil fled the stage, and Angel rejoiced. She had won.

Frank, the chief of police, leaned up against a pillar. Angel did not know how long he had stood there, nor did she care. He was allowed on the stage, and Merry never would be.

"I forgot this thing existed. Haven't seen it used in years." He did not seem upset by her antics, and she breathed a sigh of relief.

Angel smiled. "Drives like a dream." She wondered again about a different career field. Being a crane operator could be amazing if she got over her fear of heights. Did they allow birds on construction sites? Prancer would need a custom hard hat.

Frank approached the loader and extended his hand. Angel shut down the engine and unlocked her restraint. She was sorry the ride was over; she had a blast.

"You're under arrest. You have the right to be silent. Anything you say can and will be used against you in a court of law. You have the right to an attorney, and if you cannot afford one, one will be appointed to you. Do you understand these rights as I have explained them to you?"

"I do, but I haven't broken any laws." Angel had been consumed with hatred when she set out to dethrone Merry. Still, ever practical, she had also considered the ramifications. Prancer could not fend for himself.

Frank considered her with wonder. He held a set of handcuffs in his hand but made no move to clamp them on her wrists. The idea of having her hands tethered cause tingles of fear in her spine.

Angel had not done as well expelling her cousin as she hoped, because Merry reappeared from behind the stage and said, "I'm pressing charges, you nutcase. You're going to jail for a very long time." The thought excited her; Angel could see the color in her cheeks. She clung to Basil's hand and looked up at him for reinforcement. "Tell her."

"I need you two to go to the station and fill out a statement," Frank said. Angel did not see the need for a paperwork trail that culminated in a dead-end, but if it got the woman away from her, she would take it.

Merry drew her shoulders back and said, "I'll be glad to. Things like this don't happen here." Her imitation of a concerned citizen played as weak as her version of Mrs. Claus. "We can't have a lunatic running around town smashing things with a tractor." She put a hand to her chest, and with a tremor in her voice, said, "I could have been killed!"

Angel laughed, then applauded. "Bravo! Bravo!" Merry gave her a dirty look.

Basil pulled her close to comfort the not-distraught woman. "Angel would never hurt you. You're family."

"Whose side are you on?" Merry turned her fury on her husband. "You just stood there! You should have jumped in the thingy and made her stop! She threatened your wife!"

"But—" Basil's handsome face looked confused and crestfallen. He hated to disappoint Merry, but it was apparent he had not seen the situation as life-threatening.

A competent doctor would have worried about her cousin having a stroke, but Angel was not a physician. Cockroaches lived for two weeks without heads, and Merry would be fine.

"But nothing. Take me to the station. I want her locked up for good." She marched her husband off the stage, and they were gone. Angel smiled in victory.

"You were saying?" Frank asked. The man did not appear eager to haul her in, and she took advantage of his hesitation. Her family's name still meant something in the village.

Angel looked for a place to sit, but she had broken all the furniture. Nutcrackers worked dispersing the crowd and asking them to return the next day. The photographer's assistants handed out discount coupons for the kids' disappointment.

"I've broken no laws."

The cop pointed at the yellow monstrosity parked in an unusual place and said, "What about grand theft?"

She snorted. "I'm an employee of my father's corporation; I use the equipment all the time." It was true. Angel's position allowed her access to the inventory owned by North Pole Enterprises. She had not stolen this or anything else.

"And the property damage?" He waved his hand toward the broken thrones, tables, and Christmas tree littering the stage.

"Scheduled demolition and remodeling." Angel had begged her parents to update the set. Now, if they wanted to resume business, they would have to.

Frank laughed. "I'm sure you can produce the calendar to back it up." She could do so with a few keystrokes. Technology was marvelous.

"Merry claims you threatened her life." His look remained steady, but Angel's instinct said he thought it hooey. Maybe he had seen the entire encounter, or he had met her cousin. The woman was a champion whiner unable to handle her own affairs. It stood to reason Merry had filed formal complaints against other people in the globe.

Angel did her best to look taken aback by the policeman's unfair accusation. "I saved her life by warning her to vacate the premises. It's not my fault she did not heed basic safety protocol."

One of the nutcrackers had hung around, relishing the excitement in his otherwise dull job. Most days, the best entertainment he could hope for was some kid barfing on Santa. "She did. I heard her."

Frank looked from her friend to her and back again. "Angel never threatened to harm anyone?"

The nutcracker scoffed. "Of course not. Angel works here; Merry doesn't. She had no business being on the platform. Angel told her that and asked her to leave. The woman refused."

"Did you cause damage to any property not wholly-owned by North Pole Enterprises?" Frank looked serious, but Angel noticed the amused light in his eyes and slight twitch of his mouth.

She smiled. "I did not." She had been cautious not to. No golf cart, pedestrian, or street had suffered due to her actions. Her parents might be upset with her, but they would not send her to jail.

"I'll have my guys take statements." His demeanor changed, and Angel's heart fluttered. She was not off the hook just yet. "You'll need to come with me in the meantime."

Chills ran through her. The globe police did not detain people overnight; he must release her or send her to an outside law agency. "No. Give me a ticket. I promise to show up for my court date." She was not a flight risk.

"As I've said, you're under arrest." Frank held the handcuffs out in front of him. The nutcracker stared but did not intervene. He probably hoped to get a job with the police department so he could stop wearing a velvet jacket with gold buttons the size of dinner plates.

"Those aren't necessary," she said. Every fear she had fired at once. What would happen if she fell into a pond while restrained? She would drown. Her leg strength was not up to par, but she vowed to work on it as soon as possible. If a stork tried to peck out her eyes, Angel could not defend herself except with her elbows, and hers were padded, not pointed. Scenarios of doom scrolled endlessly through her mind. Her least favorite involved an alligator.

Some visitors had not cleared the area when asked to, and Angel saw phone cameras tracking her every move. "I'm not going to run. Let's just take your cart and go."

Her cell rang, and Benny's face lit up the screen. She wondered if it was nutcrackers dragging her off the plaza or her spin behind the wheel that had gotten his attention. Angel ignored the call and turned off the ringer.

The top cop assessed her for signs of deceit or a latent ability to sprint. Angel assumed an innocent demeanor, but as she had just committed her first set of felonies, she failed. "You come with us," Frank said to the security guard.

The man snapped to attention, more tin soldier than nutcracker. "Yes, sir!" He beamed at Angel in thanks for screwing up so badly a real cop required his assistance. Never mind the recruit had failed to control her on two separate occasions in the last hour; she was happy for him.

The nutcracker drove but watched to make sure she stayed put, and Frank sat next to her with the same goal in mind. Angel's superpowers had abandoned her outside of the earthmover. In the golf cart, her ample thighs overflowed the seat, and her cowardice blossomed. She also really wanted the fudge she had promised herself.

God had designed Angel for comfort, not prison. She could not eat food prepared in vats, nor shower with other people in the room. High school had been a nightmare on both accounts. She took calming breaths and assured herself everything would be alright. Her parents would secure her release. This was still their town, even though they had been absent of late.

They entered the small station designed to reassure tourists, not intimidate criminals. Merry smirked from across the room, where she dramatized her near-death experience. Basil kept a concerned arm around her. Angel was thankful Frank had not insisted on the handcuffs. She did not want her cousin to derive any more satisfaction from this than she already had. A weight settled in her chest, and she wanted the punishment phase of the day to end.

Frank escorted her to his private office. "Are you sending me to town?" She asked. Angel had not left the globe in years and saw no reason to change. The world outside provided none of the village's protection. Weather and humans alike could attack a person with impunity. Poinsettia Point gave Angel everything she needed without exposing her to unknown dangers.

The man looked surprised, then calculated, at her evident concern about prisoner transport and housing. He had no idea about her views on open toilets and orange jumpsuits. "It depends. While I have you in custody, I thought we could talk about your parents."

She could not believe it. Outside police departments had reputations for strong-arming information from suspects, but Angel never thought she would be one of their victims. By skirting the law, she had opened herself to extortion.

"I've nothing to say." Her relationship with her parents had changed, but it did not mean she would never be disloyal to them. The commandment said to honor thy father and thy mother. It provided no exclusionary clause if they lost their minds.

"That's too bad. It's the weekend. They'll hold you until Monday when the judge arrives. If he's not on a bender. I hear the man drinks." Frank did not appear the least bit sorry for the timing or state of the judiciary.

Angel was supposed to share a drink with Vivian tonight, not a cage with unwashed criminals. She wondered how many incarcerated women's hair carried lice. Her pulse rate spiked, and Angel calculated the odds of a fatal cardiac event. Betraying her family was impossible because she knew nothing. All she had were suspicions, and Frank possessed a set of his own. "What do you want to know?" She asked in a tentative voice.

Frank's eyes shot up; the move had tipped her hand and exposed her as a snitch. It was not her proudest moment. Angel hated her faintheartedness. If enemy captors threatened to delay her lunch, she would spill national secrets.

Frank looked at her and knew he held the upper hand. "Where are they?"

She shook her head, not understanding. Maybe stress had caused a hearing loss. Deafness did not look fun, and Angel hoped it was not permanent. Her hand coordination was sub-par, and she could never learn American Sign Language.

"What do you mean?" Angel's eyes searched Frank's small office as if it held clues as to what he was getting at. She learned he liked to enter BBQ competitions.

The cop's face turned dark. He probably thought she played for time. "You're under arrest on multiple charges, and I'll have you remanded into custody if you don't cooperate."

Angel clutched the arms of her chair and gazed with longing at the door. She was not fast on her feet. "Where are they?" He repeated and glowered at her.

The question made no earthly sense. Was it an advanced interrogation technique like waterboarding? She hoped the local police force who reunited lost children with their families did not practice such methods.

Panic restricted her lungs, and her voice squeaked. "I don't know what you mean. They're home. They're always home." Her parents lived, worked, ate, and inhabited the North Pole Complex. Anything they needed came to them. They rarely left the plaza.

Frank pushed back from his desk, and Angel feared he meant to hurt her. She no longer wanted to be a common criminal subject to the man's aggressive tactics. Angel repented to God with her whole heart, "I'm sorry, Lord. I knew it was wrong, I'll never do anything so stupid again. Please help me."

"What are you mumbling about? I know they're not home. I went to speak to them, and while I was there, you went on a rampage." Angel thought he overstated the situation. She had thrown a tantrum, but the word rampage implied indiscriminate violence. "They've cleared out."

Angel's vision swam. Her parents had not fled. "They would never leave without telling me. You've got to send out search teams. Someone must have kidnapped them. Have there been any ransom requests?"

Frank's look pitied her lack of reasoning power. "You think there've been two abductions in the globe this month?" His tone accused her of being an imbecile though he never said the word.

Angel's face grew hot and uncomfortable. She did not need to be reminded of her drunken misunderstanding. "I'm sorry about the first time. Truly, I am. But this is different."

She pleaded with him, but the man had no mercy. "Let me call them." He had not confiscated her phone. She saw eleven missed calls and figured word about her exploits had circulated around the globe. People she had not spoken to in months had left messages. Three were from Benny, but she ignored them all.

Angel speed-dialed her father's line but got no answer. The same thing happened when she called her mother. "It won't work," Frank said. "They left their phones on the kitchen counter."

The news punched her in the gut. "It's proof they didn't leave voluntarily! Can't you see that?"

"It shows they don't intend to be found," Frank said. "Where would they go? To a vacation home? Some special place?"

Angel had no idea. They had no friends outside of the globe. Her parents had established this community, and in doing so, lost contact with distant family members. The undertaking had absorbed all their energy.

"We don't have any other homes. Everything my parents own is here."

Frank did not believe her, but Angel knew he would check statewide real estate deeds and come up empty-handed. "Relatives?"

Angel came from the smallest family she knew. "Neither had a sibling, and their parents are dead." She had wanted a sister, but Etta became her shadow. Too bad her twin had not trusted Angel enough to tell her the truth. Their friendship was more one-sided than she had known.

"Convenient." He flipped through his notebook and made notes. "Does your father do business outside the globe?"

"No." She thought a minute. "I mean, he has suppliers, but that's it. The tinsel has to come from somewhere." The globe only employed artisan craftsmen. Mass production took place off-site. She had always considered it a selling point, but it kept the villagers dependent. Shunning industry had been a mistake. They could all be held hostage to their needs. Someone should address the matter.

Frank sighed. "The man is a murder suspect. I need you to tell me everything."

Angel got angry. "He's in trouble and needs your help. For all we know, he is the murderer's next victim. You've lost control of the situation."

The man did not receive her words with warmth. He narrowed his eyes at her and picked up the desk phone. Angel's heart froze. She had overstepped, and now she would be drug off to jail.

The office door opened, and both heads swiveled. Vivian Harrison entered without knocking. "Let her go, Frank." She looked lovely in a classic sweater set and a pair of dark jeans. Angel believed

172

the woman woke up looking glamorous, something she could not achieve without professional help.

The chief of police opened his mouth and closed it again. He hung up the receiver without dialing. "I'm trying to solve your husband's murder. You, of all people, ought to respect that." It was clear he wanted to be sensitive to the victim's family but did not appreciate unsolicited interference.

"Is that why you arrested her?" Vivian remained nonplussed as if the event had nothing to do with her.

Frank looked defiant. "She drove a dump truck across the plaza and smashed all the furniture on her father's set." He put his feet up on the desk, and Angel assumed his body language was meant to convey control. It made him look off-balance. She doubted the chief ever tilted backward in the thing.

"Front-end loader," Angel said, though she should have kept her mouth shut. It made no difference what she drove.

"Is that against the law? It's all her stuff." Frank did not look pleased to have the stand-in mayor echo Angel's point. "Do you suspect she had anything to do with Glacier's death?"

Vivian kept her cool, even in tense situations. She would never jump into three tons of machinery and mow down a city. Someone had killed her husband, and the woman pressed forward to assume his duties. Angel admired her tenacity.

Frank looked uncomfortable. "Her father is my prime suspect." He removed his feet from the desk and shuffled through file folders. The murder was the only recent crime committed in the globe; the reports must have detailed parking tickets and littering offenses. Prospective occupants underwent rigorous background checks and psychological testing before allowed to move here. The board passed the resolution after the village experienced a horrible domestic violence incident no one wished to see repeated.

"Then grill him instead of his daughter. I'm taking Angel home." Angel stood up, more than ready to leave and grateful to her pearl-wearing savior.

"She's under arrest." The police chief did not want his limited authority undermined by the wealthy politician's widow and the daughter of the town's most influential person.

Vivian softened her facial features and tone. "I'll take full responsibility. Should I post bail?"

She opened her handbag and extracted a checkbook. The sight of it reminded Angel of the shortfall on her rent. The day had worn on, and she needed to see Prancer and eat fudge.

Frank looked glum but said, "It won't be necessary." He ordered Angel, "Don't leave the globe. If you hear from either one of your parents, you need to contact me." He gauged her commitment to his conditions with a piercing look.

"You have my word." Angel would do anything to avoid jail, especially one not located in the globe. Besides, she had not promised Frank a timely response to any new information. The two women said their goodbyes. It was her turn to smirk as she walked out and saw Merry still filling out forms. The woman must be recounting every insult Angel had ever paid her. It could take a while.

She followed Vivian to a Rolls Royce golf cart. Her license plate read "#2;" Glacier, of course, had been "#1."

"I don't want to sound ungrateful, but why did you spring me?" Angel did not have bail money, and if what Frank said was true, her parents had left the globe. She had no opportunity to question him about the men stationed at the outer wall. If her parents had indeed gone, they would know when.

"Everyone needs to blow off a little steam now and again," Vivian said as she inserted the key. "Most people don't have the nerve to use a bulldozer."

"It's a front-end loader. Bulldozers only push."

Vivian laughed, and Angel felt a little foolish. The mayor's widow was not the type to operate heavy machinery. Stilettos and manicures did not go over well in construction, but she was sure they would be a hit with the men on the site.

"It took guts. I wish I'd have been there. Why'd you do it?" The woman gave her a gaze both admiring and curious, and Angel altered her previous assessment. Vivian had the nerve to do anything she wanted. If she wasn't already rich, Angel thought she would make an excellent jewel thief.

"Merry had no business horning in and taking over anything. She's not qualified to call Bingo numbers, much less represent the globe."

Vivian took a right at the corner. The cart's headlights shown halogen blue on the road. People still mingled under space heaters in outdoor cafés and watched a walrus balance a ball. He was one of Angel's favorite performers. She had a thing for exotic facial hair and may not have given Benny the boot if he had worn a handlebar mustache.

"Your cousin has a way of making things about her," Vivian said. "Are you still up for a drink?"

"I am, but can we make a stop first?" She needed to verify she meant so little to her parents they would move without notifying her. If they had, a good therapist stood to collect a lot of health insurance dollars. Assuming she did not lose her job first.

Though Frank had warned her, the fight whooshed out of Angel when she saw her childhood home. A few personal items remained on the walls and tabletops. She checked the kitchen cabinets and found all the dishware and utensils in their proper spots. Her mother's favorite tea kettle sat abandoned, and Angel felt a strong empathy for the once-loved object. A quick look in the bedroom closet revealed several Santa and Mrs. Claus outfits, but not much else. A pair of shoes Angel knew pinched her mother's feet sat in a corner, forgotten.

Vivian followed her and said, "They're really gone, aren't they? I don't see any notes telling you where they were going or why."

Angel shook her head in hurt and confusion. How had they walked away from their life's work and only child without a word? Neither of her advanced degrees helped her comprehend it. Her dad always claimed experience taught more lessons than she would ever learn in school, but why must they all be cruel? Give her music or ornithology any day.

"Sit down," Vivian said. "I'll find us something."

Angel did as she was told. Her parents had not taken much more than their clothes, but the house felt empty. The Christmas decorations, books, and hand-knitted throws did nothing to bring the space alive and meant nothing to her. She missed her parents and the life they used to share.

Vivian returned with the tea kettle and cups. They looked wrong in another woman's hands, but Angel held her tongue. Her opinion on how things should be had caused her enough trouble for one day.

"What will you do now?" Vivian asked after she poured their Earl Grey. She added two lumps of sugar. Angel had asked her the same question not so long ago. Both of their lives had taken unexpected turns.

"Find them." She could not tell the widow of her fear the pair were responsible for her husband's death. Nothing short of murder could have made them leave the empire they built. Somehow, they had known Frank planned to arrest them.

"Do you want my help?" Vivian sipped the steaming liquid and looked over the rim of her cup. "I know people."

Angel had not thought about how to approach her task, but she would use every resource offered to her. Pride was an extravagance she could not afford. "Please. Something is very wrong."

# Chapter 11

Angel could not sleep. She put on her coat and slipped from the house, hoping Prancer did not hear her exit. If he did, his protests at being left behind might wake the neighbor. Their relationship remained strained after Angel borrowed the frame to his poinsettia Christmas tree stand. She did not need a fight on another front.

The bars had closed, and the streets remained quiet. The golf cart started with a small whirring sound, and she held her breath. Angel did not switch on the headlights to avoid waking the bird. The street lamps gave off enough of a glow to navigate, and she left the switch in the "off" position. Moving down the street in the dark made her feel invisible. Holly Avenue, where the Harrisons lived, led toward the main exit. She needed to question the guard on duty and find out what he or she knew about her parents' departure.

They had left the house but maybe not the globe. If they took off, it would have been in the night like criminals. In the daylight, too many people would have questioned them. What would they have said in their defense? As she drove close to the mayor's mansion, gratitude filled her. Frank could have forced Angel out of the bubble and jailed her. She and Vivian had shared a moment and a regretful bottle of wine after Glacier's death, but no more. There was no reason for her to intervene in Angel's arrest, but she had.

Angel thought she glimpsed movement in the street and stopped. No wildlife per se lived in the globe. A few squirrels and birds called it home, but no larger mammals like foxes or coyotes. Suspicion and fear shot through her, and she considered returning home. The night brought out misshapen beings with teeth and tails, and she had no business out in it.

This was no animal. A figure bent to the ground, picked something up, and threw it. Angel pulled the golf cart into the shadows and proceeded at a crawl, curious but wary. Bravery was useless without physicality, and she had none.

A thwack followed each toss of the arm, and Angel understood. She had caught someone egging the mayor's house. The person carried on a conversation with themselves; they had not noticed Angel.

"Glacier didn't love you. He loved me." Splat. An egg hit the house near the red front door. The thrower wavered a bit, and Angel guessed they were drunk. Alcohol made bad ideas far more appealing. A case of eggs sat on the pavement; plenty of ammo to trash Vivian's home.

She scanned the street. The closest vehicle to the staging area sported a life-sized gingerbread man. Angel recognized the logo. With a flick of her finger, the headlights sprang to life, and she yelled, "Cookie!"

The café owner stopped, arm raised above her head, egg in hand. She used her elbow to shield her eyes, and called, "Who's there? Leave me alone. I'm busy." Cookie slurred the words, but the egg flew straight and splayed across the driveway.

She drove forward and shouted, "Stop!" hoping to force the rascal to flee. No one should add to Vivian's heartbreak. The woman had lost her husband, and Angel could think of nothing worse. Cookie took a step back, but not in retreat. She raised her right arm and let go. An egg shattered on the hood of the golf cart, and its contents sprayed Angel's dash with yellow goo. The woman wanted to see her dirtied—first the wine—now yolks. Both stained.

"You knock that off!" She looked for something to hurl, but the seat was empty except for twenty pounds of birdseed. Another egg sailed, and Angel ducked. She popped her head back up, and the next one smashed against the side of it. Her reflexes left something to be desired.

Mad at the unprovoked attack, Angel went on the offensive. She had just shampooed her unruly mess of hair and would now have to do it again. Two could play at this game. She gunned the cart and drove to the crazed baker's arsenal. Cookie ran back a few steps. Meanwhile, Angel seized the enemy's cache and placed it beside her. Without her supply, Cookie would have to retreat. Instead of getting in her cart and driving away, the drunk lunged at her.

Acting in self-defense, Angel threw it in reverse and pelted the psycho with eggs. The woman kept coming, and Angel swore. She was unhinged. Two more eggs connected with their target, and Cookie stumbled.

Things had gone too far. Angel had never meant to get into a war. Cookie and Glacier belonged to AA; she must have relapsed. Angel's heart went out to her. The woman had obviously been in love with a married man, a position no woman envied. It always ended in heartbreak.

"Truce! Truce!" Angel called as she drove closer to make sure the poor woman was not injured. She would never forgive herself for getting drawn into this. Cookie pulled herself up using the golf cart's frame for leverage. "Please, come in. I'm so sorry. Are you okay?"

She felt ashamed for having behaved this way. Cookie's assault had not forced her to return fire. Angel could have driven away; she had made another poor decision in a day full of them. Leaving the house had been a bad idea. The drunken woman's face contorted, and instead of getting in the cart, Cookie grabbed a handful of eggs and launched them at close range. "Stop it! I said truce!"

Two more of the fragile projectiles hit her chest. When Cookie reached in to re-load, Angel tore open Prancer's food bag and flung the contents. The sticky egg innards decorating her opponent's face and clothing made the seed stick. Had they been at the seashore, the woman would have been pecked to death by seagulls.

A loud voice caught both of their attentions. "What in the world is going on out here?"

Angel's assumptions proved valid. Vivian looked like a fashion model even when woken from a deep sleep. She felt sheepish and hurried to place the blame elsewhere. "I caught Cookie egging your house, and she came after me."

Vivian looked from one to the other of the goo-covered combatants. Her make-up-free face looked sad. "Haven't you done enough to me?" she said to Cookie.

The words hurt Angel. Vivian knew about the baker's infatuation with her now-deceased husband. How awful it must have been to find out about it when her husband announced he was leaving.

"I could ask you the same," Cookie said. She still held an egg in her right hand, and Angel prayed she did not launch it. Hurling the tiny explosives demeaned them all.

Vivian straightened her shoulders and pulled her robe closer. "He was my husband." Nothing more needed to be said. Women should never get involved with men who were spoken for; Angel had known it her entire life.

Cookie did not appear the least bit ashamed. She stood tall and said, "Glacier was leaving you, and you couldn't stand it."

Angel sat with her mouth open until a bit of raw egg dripped in, and she snapped it shut. No outsider should witness this intimate confrontation; the raw emotion made her sick to her stomach with second-hand heartbreak. No song could convey the loss.

"No, I couldn't." Vivian's voice reflected a deep well of pain. "He was the love of my life, and I didn't want him to go." She did not scream and call her nemesis names. The two women looked at each other, and Angel feared what would happen next. Vivian had not only known about Glacier and Cookie; she knew he meant to divorce her. How horrible. Angel's heart cried for the woman. Losing a spouse to death was unavoidable; watching one walk away with another woman was unbearable.

"You killed him!" Cookie had not kept her poise. She clutched an egg, and it broke in her hand the way her future had. Angel found it unbearably sad. Setting aside her compassion for the widow, she saw how much Cookie had lost. The woman could not mourn her love in public without being scorned. She was alone, and her dream had died inches from her grasp.

Glacier was a shrewd businessman, not the type to marry without a prenuptial agreement. Divorce would strip Vivian of her community standing and assets. How unfair it must have seemed to the wife who had done nothing wrong. Her husband could abandon her without cost.

Vivian shook her head, disputing Cookie's claim. Her tone suggested some empathy for the other woman. "We reconciled. He promised me it was over between the two of you."

Angel knew it usually happened just as Vivian said. Few men left their wives for their side piece. Most walked to the door and turned around, fearful of the losses. Glacier was an elected politician, and the scandal could have cost him his office.

The betrayed wife's expression changed. News of the affair and her husband's decision to leave had put her through the wringer. Then, the cheater died, and she felt robbed. "You got so mad, you killed him."

Angel ping-ponged between viewpoints. According to Vivian, Glacier had changed his mind. He stood to gain nothing by switching one wife for another and could lose his holdings and respect. He would have been torn. With Cookie as his mistress, he kept everything.

"You liar!" Cookie crumpled to the ground, a broken woman. "He didn't love you. We were supposed to be together." She held onto the fantasy with a death grip. To do otherwise meant the man she loved rejected her in favor of the status quo he claimed to hate.

The married and betrayed woman gave Cookie a look full of bitter understanding. "You were together; look at what it did to you. Go. You're better off without him. So am I." She turned and walked back to her big, empty house.

Angel watched her go and experienced an emotional weariness she had never known. Romantic love, parental love, even the platonic love she shared with Etta caused so much anguish.

Glacier's current wife retained his name, title, and resources. Everyone rallied around her as his widow and would have done the same as his abandoned spouse. She was the injured party—her husband, the scum who walked out on her. The same man promised Cookie all the recognition Vivian now experienced. She had waited, seeing Glacier at AA meetings and in other anonymous places. He had forced her to remain hidden, a dirty secret, and she internalized the shame. Cookie had been robbed of something she never had and was doubly damned.

"Let me take you home," Angel said. "It's very late." She still had business to conduct before it got light and before Prancer discovered her missing if he had not already.

"I'll drive myself." The woman did not look up but stared at her sticky fingers as if she did not remember how they got so dirty. Her clothes and skin were covered in small seeds, and Angel felt guilty. Prancer would not mind; he preferred fresh food. She tossed Cookie a package of Wet Ones from the glove box.

"You're drunk. It's not safe." She worried about loading a tiger into her cart, but the beast seemed tamed. Impaired driving was no joke, and Angel wanted to make sure the baker got home in one piece and did not endanger anyone else.

"Five years of sobriety out the window," Cookie said as she washed egg and seed from her face and hands. A pile of disposable cloths built up next to her in the street. "One slip and a person loses everything."

The news disheartened Angel, but she knew it to be true. No matter how carefully people planned, they had no control over the outcome. "How long was Glacier in the program?"

"Twenty years." The mayor was older than Cookie, and the age difference did not surprise Angel. Successful men never chased after females their own age. They sucked the youth and vitality from younger women. She stared at the results and wanted to cry for the destruction he had wrought.

"Was he sober when he died?" Ever curious, Angel wanted to

know if the two of them had resumed old habits together, but she had overstepped.

"Of course he was." Cookie's face radiated hatred once again. From her point of view, Angel had impugned the man's character. She alone appreciated him, and his marriage had died because Vivian failed the misunderstood man.

"I'm happy for him," Angel said to regain civility between them. "Glacier would want the same for you." Cookie wailed, and it twisted Angel's insides. "Come with me. I'll take you home." She helped the spent woman into her cart and drove.

Angel helped Cookie insert her key into the lock and offered to turn on the shower. The house was cozy, and the woman had handmade most of the furnishings. She would be a great wife and mother. Angel wished the creative soul had chosen a better man on which to lavish her love. Glacier was no prize.

Cookie entered the shower, and Angel searched for something clean for her to wear. The closet stood open, and she spotted a warm robe. While reaching for the slippers, she found a black boot, the kind her father wore the last time she saw him. It reminded Angel of her task. She was tired, but she needed to finish the job.

Once she settled Cookie in bed with a glass of water and crackers, Angel left. Visiting someone's home provided deep insights, but not as much as the two rivals had spilled in the street. Her heart ached for them both. She hoped to never pit herself against another woman for the love of a man. Everyone lost but him.

Glacier's selfishness and cruelty incensed her, and Angel berated him as if he rode in the cart. "You had it all, and it wasn't enough. Two women are devastated because you lied to them. You've ruined their lives, and neither one is going to forgive you—ever." She looked over to see his reaction.

The deceased mayor did not respond. What could the jerk say in his defense besides he did not mean to hurt anyone? She hated the flimsy excuse for cruelty. Another aging male had gotten bored and sought a young woman to make him feel better about himself.

Impressing oneself was demanding but more productive than external validation.

Angel felt an intense dislike for the mayor and told him so, but someone had despised the man enough to kill him. She wondered if either of the two disillusioned women had the stomach for murder. Glacier had humiliated and abandoned them; they both remained suspects in Angel's book.

Passion drove Cookie, but Vivian used a much more studied approach. Glacier's final resting place was so bizarre it defied classification. The location held personal meaning to someone, but the mayor wasn't talking.

Angel hoped not to be waylaid by any other strange occurrences; she wanted to go home. Always asleep at this time, she had no idea what took place late at night and was fascinated. She watched delivery men drop off supplies to local restaurants and stores. Two trash companies made their rounds. Other illicit businesses such as drug deals probably also took place, but she did not witness any.

Angel drove through the short tunnel leading out of the inner dome. The bubble's designer had created it as a colossal nesting doll that utilized a sophisticated airlock system. The inner core sat underneath a barrier dome used for climate stabilization and protection. Within the buffer zone, the architect had built a greenspace. Filtered sunshine from the outside world lifted the spirits of villagers tired of icicles and penguins. The park permitted school kids to play soccer and baseball as well as ice skate and sled, all while never leaving town.

In the summers, she came here to experience strong sunshine and greenspace, things she missed in the constant Christmas climate. This time of the year, it was a little warmer than inside, but not much. The trees had lost their leaves, and the park was not as inviting.

She crossed the buffer and made her way to the outside wall. A monument to the engineer responsible for the globe marked the entry. Dwight Franklin had been a visionary. He, her father, and Glacier had gone to high school together and had been the best of friends.

Franklin had been the hands-on guy of the group. He re-built his first car at age nine and sold a water reclamation design for untold millions while still a teen. The man held nine hundred patents when he died shortly after the globe's completion.

Her dad, Santos, was the group's leader. He envisioned a utopia where people lived and worked toward a common goal.

Franklin engineered the technology, Angel's father supplied the ideology, and Glacier brought his wallet to the table. His family owned the land on which they built the fledgling society. The three of them risked all they had to get the enterprise off the ground. Twenty years later, their dream thrived.

Only one man stood watch at the gate tonight. He looked around sixty and stood wide awake, surveying the no-man's land between the two bubbles. "Has there been a family emergency?" he asked, concern on his face.

"No," Angel said, confused. "Why?" The day had tired her, and it must have shown on her face.

He squirmed and stuffed large hands into his uniform pockets. "I'm sorry, ma'am. It's just with your folks leaving last night, and now you," he stammered but did not continue. Angel did not know the guard but was not surprised he knew her. Everyone did. Her face looked down on them all from billboards and out from the occasional television spot.

"Were you here when they left?" Angel asked. She needed information but did not want a stranger to know her folks had moved without telling her. Word would spread around the globe like wildfire, and the news could affect everyone's livelihood. All her life, her parents had drilled into Angel the importance of perception.

The globe worked because people believed in it. As soon as they didn't, the seams would tear as people jockeyed for position. Glacier's murder had unsettled the community. When they found out her parents had fled, people would lose faith in the system supporting them.

"Yes, ma'am. They came here late, like you." He studied her face, and Angel wondered if he guessed they had not said anything in advance.

She hesitated and chose her words with care. "Do you remember them saying or doing anything unusual?" Angel had tipped her hand but saw no alternative.

It was evident the man did not wish to say anything amiss, whether for the sake of his job or her feelings, Angel could not say. "Your mother acted as if wolves waited on the other side. I don't think she wanted to go."

Angel blanched. "But your father calmed her down, right enough," he hurried to add. "He sure looks different without the beard, doesn't he? Almost had me fooled."

Her father had shaved? The man had never done more than trim his trademark facial hair in her lifetime. Angel was not sure she would recognize him without it.

"It's incredible how much younger he looks," Angel said. "His skin is so white under there now. It hasn't seen the sun in years." She knew this had to be the truth and wondered if her mother thought to use bronzer to hide it.

"I didn't know about the scar," The guard confessed. "You sure couldn't see it underneath the full ZZ Top treatment."

Angel laughed, but her stomach lurched. She had no knowledge of a scar. Her father had never mentioned it or told stories about how it came to be. Maybe he found it disfiguring, but its existence disturbed her. Angel felt the true man hid beneath the beard, and she had never met him.

"They've never really traveled, and I'm a little worried about them." She twisted her hands together and hoped the guard will feel for her. "Did they take enough stuff?"

"Hardly anything, but they said they wouldn't be gone long. They just wanted to accomplish some business and hurry home."

Angel tried not to let her relief show too much, but she nearly doubled over with it. If her parents planned to return, they had not abandoned her. She was an adult, and so were they. They each ought to be able to leave town with no one making a fuss.

Her father's timing might have been a coincidence, and not a move to avoid arrest. What did Frank have on him anyway? He was seen driving a truck he owns at an unusual hour. Angel felt silly and had to stop herself from hugging the guard. She felt hopeful her parents had not been involved in Glacier's death.

"If you are on duty when they come back through, would you let me know, please?"

"I can post a note if you like. That way, whoever is working can give you a call."

She backed off in a hurry. "Please, no," she said and touched his sleeve. Her heart pounded, and Angel knew she had made a mistake. "I don't want to embarrass them with my overreaction." She hung her head and prayed the man would work with her and not start a rumor. "They're getting older. You understand."

"I'll do whatever you like," said the man. He seemed kind and did not look like a gossip. Most men weren't.

"Here's my number," Angel said and handed him her business card. "If you see them, please let me know. Even at night. If not, I'll catch up with them once they settle back in at home."

She thanked the security officer and got back into her cart. As she drove past Dwight Franklin's memorial, she wondered how much the globe would have changed if he lived. Men like him never stopped innovating. By now, Benny's shop might be unnecessary. Thermal power could heat every building for free.

Benny. She had not thought about him for several hours. When Frank threatened to send her to jail, Angel considered calling him for help but discarded the idea. Asking for bail the day after she dumped him was too much, even for her.

Angel set aside Sunday as a day of atonement. She played the organ for both church services and then went to see about making things right at the North Pole Complex. People worked here, and it served as the town's main attraction. Her unacceptable temper tantrum had cost innocent employees and shop owners' revenue.

When she and Prancer arrived, she found Basil supervising the last of the stage reconstruction. The front-end loader had been removed, presumably back to the garage where it belonged. She wondered if they moved the keys to prevent a reoccurrence.

"I want you to know, I'm very sorry." Her anger at Merry had gotten the best of her, and after listening to two sermons on living like Christ, Angel felt chastened. The Savior had once flipped a few tables, but not because of jealousy and hurt feelings.

Basil smiled, and her heart warmed. He did not hold grudges. "That was quite the thing. Got my blood going." Angel was glad he could laugh about it so soon after the event.

"You're pretty fast on your feet." She watched as a forklift replaced Santa's seat. Mrs. Claus's plush red throne sat off to the side, and the new cookie table seemed more functional than the one Angel had destroyed.

"I played a little ball." Basil pretended to tuck a football under his elbow and run down the field with one arm outstretched. When his former self reached the imaginary goal line, he spiked it and cheered.

Angel hung her head. "There's no excuse for my behavior." She sighed. "Things have been a little weird."

"Tell me about it. When Merry told me your folks were leaving, I couldn't believe it." Basil shook his head in wonderment. Angel felt sick. Merry had known they were going? Her betrayal could be measured on the Richter scale. Low-lying areas should be concerned about tsunamis.

Basil hugged her. "It's got to be hard. My parents never expected much, but it must take strength to disappoint yours. They're great." He said the words as casually as if he had not just ripped the heart from her chest.

She struggled for breath. "It was a shock, for sure. I went a little crazy." Angel's parents had planned her life. Her crime was not letting them.

From inside his carrying case, Prancer said, "Plum loco." His timing was perfect, and it gave Angel a moment to gather herself. She could not believe her parents confided in Merry and not her, no matter how disappointed they were with her life choices.

Basil laughed. "He's great; can I pet him?" He bent down to peer at the macaw. Talking birds fascinated people, including her. There was something irresistible in their intelligent faces and mimicry. He did not extend a finger and so got to keep it.

"I'm sorry, he's not great with strangers. He bites." Angel worried about tourist attractions using live birds for photoshoots. Someone could lose an eye. Parrots were not as domesticated as people liked to think.

Prancer agreed with the assessment, "Bad bird." He growled like a rottweiler and followed it with a mad scientist laugh.

"Amazing," Basil said. "How did you train him?"

"A few repetitions is all it takes. I wish I picked things up as fast as he does." Noticing her parents were about to go on the lam would have been useful. Angel prepared to leave but had one more thing to ask. "I just wanted to come by and make sure this got fixed, but it looks like you have it all under control."

"Of course I do." Basil beamed at what he took as a compliment. "Someone has to step up in a crisis."

She was happy Merry had not accompanied her husband. No matter how dire circumstances were, there was a limit to the number of times she would humiliate herself. "I have a favor to ask." The words grated.

"Shoot."

"I need a side gig. I'm a couple hundred short on the rent." Prancer's snacking on the textbooks hurt her, but she would not name him. Functioning adults kept emergency money, and she had neglected to prepare. Prancer was not the only one who had destroyed something this month.

Basil smiled and reached for his wallet. Angel stopped him before he extracted the bills. She would never be beholden to Merry. "Thank you, but I can't accept it. Work builds character."

"Go by my office then, and they'll set you up with something." He put away his billfold, and Angel felt a pang. She should reign in her pride. It was lucky she did not have to pay to rebuild her father's set as well.

"I appreciate it, thank you. And once again, I'm sorry about yesterday." She ate more humble pie than any other dessert.

"If I'm going to fill the big guy's boots, I've got to roll with the punches." He laughed at his own wit, but Angel did not mind. He was a good man. No one could replace her father, but Basil had what it took.

Once home, Prancer did his best to brighten her spirits. He challenged her to a gunfight, played dead, and they both spun on their backs, pretending to be breakdancers. Angel's phone remained on silent because she had no energy for conversation. A quick check every hour or so proved Benny still wanted to speak to her, as did Etta. Her parents did not.

Vivian had scheduled her for a shift at the Twelve Days of Christmas tonight. Angel wanted to cancel but did not allow herself the indulgence; work built character. The town needed the revenue, and she had promised. If committee members did not honor their word, they could not expect the townspeople to carry the load. On the way to provide her civic duty, Angel stopped by Basil's office. He had told them to expect her. His division of her father's company dealt with the buskers and free-roaming entertainment throughout the globe.

None of the performers passed a hat; their services were paid for on an hourly basis. Clowns twisted balloons into reindeer and sleighs, animal handlers encouraged their charges to bounce balls, speak, or just be cute. An introvert, Angel did not have the makings of a street artist. They would assign her to something much more mundane, like passing out free samples. She negotiated when to return and headed to the light display.

The park's transformation impressed her. Always lovely, with lighted paths and a gazebo, the drive-thru showcase had turned the peaceful place into a carnival of lights and activity. Christmas music played, bells jingled, and the merriment made her feel like a child.

Vivian's smile was weak, and Angel guessed she had wanted to call out as well. The acting mayor again relegated her to the first-aid tent, and she blessed her for it but wanted to make something clear. "You needn't worry; I won't be talking to anyone about your business." The middle-of-the-night-scene she witnessed remained confidential.

"I never thought you would," Vivian said. "It's for your protection. There's a nasty wind blowing tonight."

The climate-controlled globe did not allow Mother Nature to flex her muscles. Inside the safety zone, no hurricanes, tornadoes, or blizzards endangered anyone. The breeze Vivian spoke of blew through the villagers, not their homes.

Until the past few weeks, Angel had discounted the role of routine in all their lives. The same was probably true of people everywhere, but the inhabitants of the globe relied on predictability. Very few events had challenged their security up until Glacier's death. No one in the globe went hungry or homeless. Natural disasters did not take place, and people limited the man-made types to marital spats.

Everyone played their part, and in the rare instance they did not, Angel's father replaced them. Those disgruntled with snow globe life lost their homes and jobs. Living in Poinsettia Point was an honor, and those who sought it out did nothing to jeopardize their standing. A crime-free town full of goodwill and Christmas cheer was impossible to replace.

Vivian's words made Angel nervous. "Anything in particular I should know?" She felt paranoid and looked to see if anyone eyed her.

"No. It's just something I feel. People are restless." Glacier's widow seemed ill at ease with the topic, and Angel guessed she withheld a vital piece of information.

"If I'm in danger—"

The acting mayor looked as if Angel had slapped her. She hugged a clipboard to her chest and said, "Danger? I never said anything of the sort. Folks are worried. Your parents haven't been around all week, and without information, they're inventing stories better left untold."

Angel wore her heavier coat but felt a chill through the material. "They lost their long-time business partner. It shook them. Give them a little time, and they'll make everything right."

Vivian's snort pointed out the obvious. Whatever Angel's parents did would not bring back Glacier. The man had announced his intention to leave his wife, and though she had convinced him otherwise, Vivian would never know if they could have healed the rift in their marriage.

"They hadn't acted like partners in a long time. Glacier planned on calling in the provisions of their original agreement."

It was true—something had changed their relationship over the years. The former friends retreated to their corners and ignored each other. The only time they interacted was to disagree about the future of the globe.

"What provisions?" Angel's heart thumped around as if trying to break free. Had the move given her father a motive to kill Glacier?

Vivian shook her head. "I don't know. The fool was planning to leave me, so he didn't share a lot. After he changed his mind," she hesitated, "there wasn't enough time." Had the divorce caused Glacier to do something drastic? Did he want to limit his settlement to Vivian? Or give Cookie a consolation prize when he changed his mind? It was all too confusing. "There's one thing I thought you should know about," Vivian said. She opened her handbag and took out a folded sheet.

Angel did not extend her hand. She did not want proof of her parents' misdeeds. Her sanity rested on believing them incapable of heinous crimes.

"Take it," Vivian said and shook the paper. "It has to do with Benny."

She exhaled her relief. This had nothing to do with her. "We're no longer together." It wasn't any of Vivian's business, but Angel had witnessed the woman's embarrassment. Sharing some of her own leveled the ground between them.

"Take it. You might want to think twice before reconciling with him." How did Vivian know Angel's heart clenched every time she saw a message from the man? She had not yet listened to a single voicemail because it would hurt too much.

The printout was a letter from Glacier to Benny stating a secondary background check made him ineligible to remain in the globe. He had been given sixty days to close his shop and leave. Benny did not seem like a guy with a shady past, or she would not have gone out with him. He did not have a single tattoo and never raised his voice. The night they broke up, he had wanted to tell her something, but she had not let him.

Vivian watched her face for a reaction. "Glacier hired a detective." A rich man always got his way, and the mayor had wanted Benny gone. The two had fought from the start. The city council had allowed the heating business over Glacier's official objection, so the man had dug for dirt.

Angel retreated to the first-aid tent to be alone. She had been inside for ten minutes when a local came through the tent flap carrying a clipboard. "Want to sign a petition—" the woman stopped when she recognized Angel. "Sorry," she said and hurried back to the exit.

"What petition?" Townspeople presented them to the city council when they wanted change. Showing most citizens supported an issue carried a lot of weight with the group.

"It's nothing." The embarrassed petitioner hid the papers behind her back, and Angel had a sudden need to know. She crossed the few steps between them and grabbed it from the frightened woman.

The boldface print read: "Reclaim decency. Can the Clauses."

She could not believe her eyes. The town had turned on her parents as soon as they stopped fulfilling everyone's wish list. Did the adults really believe her dad was Santa Claus? They disregarded his decades of service without a thought. Angel clenched her fists and said, "Which coward started this?"

The woman did not answer. Angel flipped through the pages and found a hundred or so signatures. The first on the list was Cookie. Darn that baker to a place hotter than her kitchen.

"Get out of here," she told the unfortunate soul who had knocked on the wrong tent flap.

The timid woman held out her hand. "I need that." She had some nerve.

Angel unclipped the pages and held them to the blue flame of Benny's space heater. They caught and burned. "Here you go," she said and returned the empty clipboard. "You don't want to stay here."

The woman opened her mouth to object but fled instead. People had no problem whispering in corners but lacked the courage for uncomfortable confrontations. Angel understood. Everything terrified her, including what would happen when her parents returned to find their life's work counted for nothing.

# CHAPTER 12

Angel and Prancer worked in the office until time for class. Students learned better from in-depth discussions and hands-on experience. Still, today's session started with a lecture to introduce the topic of bird crops. She had spent hours preparing the slides and source materials and organizing them in an engaging manner. Angel even inserted a few cartoons to keep things light and was pleased with the content.

The classroom needed ten minutes of organization, and after she completed it, Angel tested the smartboard system. Everything was set, so she and Prancer went to lunch. Her boss would find no fault with her preparation today. With her parents missing and feeling out of sorts with Etta, Angel felt alone except for the macaw. Working helped, and she would dedicate herself to doing her job well.

The resolution empowered her. Maybe it was time to start an exercise regimen and get her endorphins going. When they got outside, Angel put Prancer's carrier in her golf cart. No one could expect her to lug him around while doing laps. Baby steps.

When they returned, she found several students, including Merry, already in their seats. Her cousin scowled, displeased Angel had not spent the weekend in jail. She might still hope to get her fired for the non-incident, but Angel knew of no anti-heavy-machinery clause in her employment contract. Her stubbornness in not allowing Merry a win lifted her spirits, and Angel decided to let Prancer show off his new trick. Her backpack held a set of toddler-sized bowling pins, and she lined them up in the traditional triangle.

"Watch, guys. He's a natural."

All the students except Merry formed a semi-circle around them. She handed the ball to Prancer, who pinched one of the finger indentations with his beak.

"One!" Angel counted, and the bird swung his head back in an arc. "Two!" Prancer did it again, and when she said, "Three!" he released. The ball traveled across the floor and knocked down four pins.

The group clapped and told him how wonderful he was. He loved the attention. Angel gave him a peanut, and he cracked it open, throwing the shells on the floor as if the classroom were a cowboy bar.

She reset the pins and said, "That was great, but let's try for a strike. Ready?"

"Ready," the bird said. Prancer shook his shoulders like an athlete getting loose. He only needed sweatbands to sell the look.

"One, two, three!" Instead of tossing the ball, the bird ran down the make-shift alley, tucked his head, and plowed into the pins. The students laughed in surprise and delight. Prancer took a bow.

"What if I was allergic to nuts?" Merry asked when Angel again rewarded the bird with his favorite treat.

"Then I would use fruit," Angel said. Merry was her cousin; they had grown up together. Angel knew she didn't have an allergy to anything besides work.

Ever persistent, Merry did not give up her needling. "And if bird dander bothered my asthma?" She narrowed her eyes in a challenge.

Angel would not fall into so easy of a trap. No way would she ever endanger a student's health. "Then, I would suggest you enroll in a different course."

Her boss appeared at the door to check up on her. Angel considered adjourning five minutes after he left to prove he could not watch her every move. With any other class, it would work, but stool pigeon Merry attended this one.

"Let's get started, shall we?" The students took their seats, and Angel placed Prancer on his stand with a quiet toy to amuse him. She brought up the first slide and began her lecture on a crop's function. Things were going well, and the students took notes. Without warning, her laptop lost its mind. The slide show minimized, and the web browser appeared. Before school, she had shopped for a new bra, and the picture of a push-up model filled the screen.

"What the heck?" Angel pounded the keyboard, but it refused to respond. Her eyes flicked between the laptop and the smart board, which reflected everything. Technology terrorized her on and induced panic attacks regularly. The next tab opened, and a picture of a muscular man filled the screen. Etta had told her to check out an actor, and she had been right; the guy was hot.

"Oh, la, la," said a student. Angel's face burned in embarrassment, and she hit the escape key with no result. Her startled mind tried to remember what other embarrassing links lurked on her device.

Taking more computer classes moved to the top of her to-do list, unseating "start an exercise regimen." Angel was a consummate user and understood none of the applied science. Her boss made a disgusted noise, and Angel cringed. She had forgotten all about him.

"Just give me a second, guys. This thing has gone crazy."

Her document files came up next, and the cursor sorted through the titles until it came to one marked diary. She let out a scream of dismay.

"Knock it off!" Prancer demanded when the room laughed at her obvious distress.

Angel unplugged the computer as fast as she could. The smart board's Bluetooth connection did not falter, and she cursed battery back-up systems. At last, she slammed the lid of her laptop and scanned the room in helpless mortification. The incident left her speechless and unnerved. She sat to collect herself and stared at the machine in horror. Until now, she had considered it her trusty friend. When her brain stopped jumping, Angel noticed something unusual. A tiny transmitter extended from her USB drive, the kind used to link external keyboards. With it, the system responded to a wireless mouse, or more likely, a phone app.

Angel yanked the offending hardware and held it aloft. "I guess someone finds my digital life fascinating. I assure you, it's not, except for my collection of parrot videos. If you want those, shoot me an email, and I'll send them to you."

"We're not interested in your private perversions. We came here to learn," Merry said.

Angel wanted nothing more than to teach her cousin a lesson. A frontal assault with heavy machinery had not worked, but she would find something that would.

"Do you intend on resuming, or is today's content bowling and underwear?" Her boss asked from the doorway and delayed Angel's plans for revenge.

"Of course. Now that our technical glitch has been resolved, let's finish the slides and prepare for our dissections." Several of the class members groaned, but Angel knew from experience they would press their noses into the specimens when the time came. Though distasteful, gross anatomy lessons intrigued even the most squeamish.

❄❄❄

After work, Angel took Prancer home. They turned on some music and went nuts. The bird bobbed his head, twirled, and even hung upside down from a branch while singing. The dance party provided the most fun she had all day, and Angel was grateful for it. It was impossible to worry too much while rocking out with a parrot. Prancer kept her in the moment, and for a woman with uncontrolled fears, he gave her a true blessing.

She got them both some cold water and grabbed the stack of mail piling up on the counter. Angel had avoided dealing with it because she lacked the funds to address the problems. Her shift tonight for Basil's entertainment division would change that, though. Logging a few more hours than necessary couldn't hurt.

Adding a paid part-time gig would lessen Angel's financial anxiety and improve her standard of living. She would walk to work and check off exercise from her to-do list as well. Empowerment flowed through her.

She opened the first envelope after checking to make sure no suspicious powder lurked on the seal. With a plan in place, Angel would deal with whatever bills remained. Even as a de-facto orphan, she would be fine. The usual suspects awaited payment: the power company, golf cart insurance, and cell phone bill. She tore open her checking account reconciliation and stopped cold. There had been a mistake, though this time, she had not been the one to make it.

Her bank listed two accounts instead of the solo one she had maintained for years. The person whose information they listed on her statement had much more money than she: $2,312.42 more. Angel laughed and wished she maintained such savings. She would not have to work all evening for minimum wage if she did.

A glance at the clock told her it was time to leave. She tossed the mail back onto the counter and locked up Prancer, promising to be home early.

"I love you," he said and made a kissing noise. Angel's heart broke a little every time she left him. The responsibility for his well-being weighed on her, even his boredom in her absence.

"I love you, too, bud."

She grabbed her coat and keys and drove to Basil's office for her assignment. He had not yet knocked off for the day and presented her with a few choices.

"I need someone in a goose costume to hand out coupons for the children's clothing store," he said and held up an outfit six feet long from breast to tail. It was cute, but the size of a ship, and she would be unable to sit while wearing it.

"Pass," she said. Angel knew the night would involve some level of self-esteem leveling. Still, she wanted to limit the damage to her fragile ego. An unmarried woman whose parents just ditched her did not need much help to question her lovability.

"Want to roast chestnuts in the plaza?" Basil said after consulting his list. He wore a suit to work, an anomaly in the globe. People here took business casual all the way down to flannel and work boots.

"Hard pass," she said. Once, when she was a child, she had stolen a large bag of the softened nuts and gobbled them in a single setting. The next twenty-four hours had not been pleasant, and Angel had sworn off them ever since. The smell alone nauseated her.

"Cookie needs a gingerbread man to hand out samples."

Angel considered it, but her presence might agitate the baker. She hoped to one day re-enter the café and not worry about being poisoned, but it was too soon. The woman had suffered a breakdown and would not forgive Angel for having witnessed it any time soon.

"She's not my biggest fan," Angel said by way of explanation.

Basil beamed at her. "She couldn't be! That's me." Angel wished she had met him before Merry had. He was everything she looked for in a man: handsome, good-natured, hard-working, and kind.

"What else do you have?" She gave her best smile but did not flirt. The guy was married to her cousin, and Angel would never go there.

Basil read from his list, "Penguin wrangler, someone to follow the carriage horses—say—you don't juggle do you?"

Angel told him she did not. Animal excrement was not what she had bargained for, either. She was getting discouraged—her new fiscal responsibility plan hinged on this side gig.

"How are you on ice skates?"

Angel lit up with joy. As a child, she loved the grace of the skaters and their dramatic outfits. Other girls wanted to be ballerinas; she wanted to be one balanced on a quarter-inch of steel.

"I'm great!" She exaggerated, but only because it had been a while, and she was unsure of her skill level. Angel had an image of herself gliding across the shimmering ice, her hair flowing behind her as she enthralled the crowd.

"Perfect. I'll be right back; stay here just a moment." Basil left the room, and Angel's heart sped up with excitement. What could be better than getting paid to have fun? She should have done this a long time ago.

Basil returned, his arms filled with a zipped up white bag, the type a bride kept her dress in before the big day. Angel unzipped it a few inches and swooned at sequined lace.

"I'm sure this will fit; you're smaller than Merry." The man could flatter her any time. Angel carried a few extra pounds but was not as plump as her cousin. To her shame, this meant something to her.

"How long is the shift?" She did have to work in the morning and had promised Prancer an early night.

"Seven until ten. Does that work?" Basil had gone out of his way for her, and she felt nothing but gratitude toward the man. She had pushed him off the stage, but he helped instead of punished her. It humbled her and made her reflect on Christian charity.

Angel smiled and gathered up the costume. "No, it's perfect." Skating counted as cardio, too, and would be fun. She drove to her assignment in smiling anticipation. A few people waved, and her spirits lifted. Angel wanted nothing more than a return to normal. Frank would solve Glacier's murder, her parents would come back, and life would be good.

The globe boasted three separate ice rinks, which were a destination for visitors and locals alike. The center held hockey tournaments, figure skating competitions, and one venue specialized in speed skating. Basil wanted her to interact with those on the family ice, and Angel could not wait. There was nothing cuter than small children attempting to keep their feet on the slippery surface.

Hot cocoa scented the air. Angel planned to grab one for herself later. Maybe, as an employee, she could skirt the line. The guy behind the counter issued her a rented pair of skates. Angel was careful to keep the blade covers in place; accidental wrist slitting featured in her death montages. She might buy a sparkly pink pair of her own skates if Basil made her a regular.

The women's changing room sat to the left, and the men's to the right. She headed to the ladies' in excitement about the beautiful lace costume in her arms. The corner locker, her favorite, was open. It was a good omen. Angel shimmied out of her boots and opened the bag. It was not an elegant figure skating outfit; it was a hippo. Basil had not forgiven or forgotten—he had retaliated. The lace she had so admired formed a neck ruffle and matching tutu around the purple behemoth. A large, molded head with jutting teeth completed the piece.

She placed the hippo's face over her own. It limited her view to the creature's open mouth, and the thing smelled like stale sweat. Her heart sank. The goose would have been better; at least she could have breathed fresh air. Tears pricked the back of her eyes, but she halted them with a thought. She would not cry. This was a job; Angel had come for the paycheck and would not leave without one. The best thing about the get-up was no one would recognize her. She changed in a hurry to avoid being spotted in her street clothes.

The hippo's body was made of foam, and though it did not breathe well, it was light. Angel found if she skated fast enough, she could generate a breeze. The DJ played upbeat songs, and the lights strung from poles across the ice mesmerized her. It had been too long since she had come and done a few turns on the ice.

Within ten minutes, Angel got over her embarrassment at being an oversized African animal transported to the tundra and embraced it. She borrowed six-year-olds from their parents and held their hands as they went around the rink. Younger children stared at her, but she did not approach or frighten them.

An hour into her shift, she started performing tricks for the crowd. Angel squatted her fake bulk on one knee, with the other leg out straight in front of her. She skated backward, her tutu flying. Small spins worked out every time. The hokey-pokey came on, and Angel led the group. Her exaggerated movements caused the kids to laugh and brought a smile to her face as well.

Then they brought out the limbo bar. Angel, riding a high of success, flew under the posts at their highest. A line of children followed her; most did not have to duck to clear the obstacle. She cheered for each in turn and made a second pass. It was close; the large hippo head tapped the wooden stick, but she had made it. Angel threw her arms up in victory.

The prop guys lowered the bar another rung. Angel started from further back and picked up speed; as she leaned backward to slide underneath the barrier, her skates came out from under her. Angel's heads, real and fake, thumped against the unforgiving ice. Dazed, she lay there for a moment, taking inventory of her parts. Strange hands pulled at her, urging her to sit. She complied. The crowd cheered, and she tottered off the ice. The game continued without her.

"Pride goeth before a fall," a voice said. She looked, and Cookie stood there, a tray of baked goods in hand. The woman was right, but Angel felt she could have asked about fatal injuries before scoring her performance.

"Come with me," the baker instructed. "I've got to drop these off, and I'll get you a hot chocolate.

"I'm so embarrassed," Angel said. She had gotten cocky and deserved to take a tumble. Her job was to entertain the children, not traumatize them.

Cookie snorted. "That fall? It was bush league. You want to know about making a fool out of yourself, you've come to the right person."

The pair walked around the perimeter until they reached the concession stand. Cookie said hello to the workers and dropped off the treats. She grabbed a carry tray, two hot chocolates, and a couple of the largest thumbprint cookies Angel had ever seen.

"Grab a squat," Cookie said, and they perched on a long bench. Angel arranged her costume to maintain her balance.

"Thanks," Angel said, though the headpiece altered her voice.

"You did fine, right up until the end." Cookie gave a rough chuckle. "So, did I. The danger comes when you think you've made it."

"What happened?" Angel asked, giving the woman an opening.

She kept her words to a minimum in hopes of getting Cookie to talk—and so the woman did not recognize her voice.

"I loved the wrong guy." Sadness filled the woman's eyes, and Angel felt sorry for her.

"Haven't we all," Angel said, and wished in her heart she had survived a tragic affair. She longed for a legendary love capable of burning a city to ashes. A series of near misses did nothing to validate her worth.

Cookie shook her head in agreement with the lie. "It wasn't the first time, but it was supposed to have been the last." Angel understood the dream of finding the right man and holding onto him for a lifetime. Women hoped to do it when in their twenties and avoid wasting a lifetime waiting. Doing so while young saved a lot of time. Angel's time had almost expired.

She patted the baker with one of the hippo's manicured hands. Loneliness and the overwhelming fear it would never end followed her everywhere she went.

"He was married." Cookie pushed the horrible syllables out, allowing Angel to judge her. She no longer did. If given a chance at married bliss, Angel could not guess what sins she would commit.

"It happens." Cookie did not know Angel wore the costume, or she would not have explained.

"No, you don't understand. We were different. Meant to be." The distraught woman was right. Angel had not yet met the man fate destined her to love for eternity, no matter the cost to her soul.

She patted Cookie once more, consoling her and granting permission to continue. "He told his wife he wanted a divorce. Most married men never do that, you know."

Glacier had announced his intent to leave Vivian, and it destroyed her. "I know." A lump formed in Angel's throat.

Cookie's face hardened with rage, and Angel shrunk back in fear. She had seen the woman lose it and feared physical harm. "On move-out day, he said he needed more time."

Angel's heart sank at the words; she could only imagine how

Cookie had received them. The woman laughed, but not from joy. "More time!" She repeated in disbelief. "I spent years waiting, and he chickened out at the last minute. She got to him."

"That's so sad," Angel said, and it was. She, too, had searched for a person to share a lifetime and failed.

"He was a good man, and he didn't want to hurt her." She looked as if she could chew through nails. "What about the heartache he caused me? Why was that any less important?" She burst into angry tears.

Angel thought the question would torture Cookie until the day she died. If Cookie had failed somehow, she could improve and do better next time. The blameless remained powerless.

"I'm so sorry," Angel said. "This was about him, not you." The words sounded lame. "He's weak and suffers for it." Angel caught herself before she spoke of Glacier in the past. As a stranger, she would have had no way of knowing about his death.

"No, it's about her. His wife didn't love him but didn't want me to have him. She yanked his cord, and he came running." It was clear Cookie was jealous. Bitterness filled her tone.

"He put you both in a terrible position," Angel said. "I'm sure he's in pain."

"No, he's not. He left, and he didn't take me with him." Cookie got up and walked away without saying another word. She had needed to vent and left when finished.

Break time had stretched longer than she intended, and Angel returned to the ice with a heavy heart. It took less effort than Angel would have imagined to pantomime having a good time and encourage the kids to do the same.

❄❄❄

The banging on her front door refused to stop, and Prancer screamed until Angel got up to answer it. Etta stood there with two coffees and a bag of bagels.

"We're doing this," the uninvited visitor said and opened the screen door. Angel took two steps back and allowed her to enter. It was time they put the fight behind them, but she had been unable to before now. Friends don't convince friends they imagined things. Angel excelled at self-deception; she needed no help.

"Rise, and shine, and give God the glory, glory…" Prancer did not want to be left out, so Angel brought him into the living room and excused herself.

When she returned, face washed and nerves steeled, Prancer and Etta shared an everything bagel. "Hmm," the bird said. "Good."

"Can I have some?" Angel asked. Etta handed a piece to the macaw who walked over and gave it to her. It might have been the sweetest thing he had ever done, and her heart swelled. Prancer believed food went from her to him, never the reverse.

"Forgiven?" Etta asked with hope in her voice. She put a thick layer of cream cheese on a beak-free bagel and placed it on a plate for her.

Angel accepted the peace offering and said, "I suppose. You didn't shoot anyone."

"No one did." The words brought her up short. She hadn't thought about the incident in those terms. A gun had discharged, but no one had gotten hurt. Those were the facts as they knew them. Neither of them saw Glacier pull the trigger. They only heard the aftermath. Angel needed to coax the entire story from her parents, but right now, they were MIA.

"Have you heard from my folks?" It was a long shot, but she needed to ask. They considered Etta a daughter and had trusted her with huge secrets in the past. Maybe they had done so again.

"No, and people are getting nervous. They want to call a town hall meeting." It wasn't a surprise that business owners worried about high season revenue and future leadership with both Glacier and her dad out of the picture.

Angel bit into the chewy bit of heaven slathered in creamy goodness and moaned. She should buy some of these and eat them every morning before work. It was not the best of ideas, so she pushed it aside but suffered the loss of a lovely dream.

"Do you think Vivian will be a good mayor?"

Etta used a knife and fork to eat her breakfast, and Angel felt uncouth tearing off large hunks until she noticed the cream cheese on Prancer's beak. Everything was relative. No matter how good or bad a person was, someone could always outdo them. Most people remained spectacularly moderate.

"I think so," her friend said. "The town could use some unity about now." Etta took a dainty bite, then said, "What about you? Will you step up?"

She almost choked. Etta knew her situation. As teenagers, she commiserated over Angel's parents wanting to keep control long past childhood and plotting out an ill-fitting future for her.

"You know I can't do that." Angel felt hurt. She did not owe anyone an explanation or apology for her decisions.

Traces of understanding, pity, and resolve showed in Etta's expression. "It's your parents' legacy. Without any of the original three, I don't know what will happen to us."

Neither did Angel, but the globe wasn't her problem. Years ago, she resolved not to involve herself in North Pole Enterprises beyond what it offered as pocket money. Her destiny lie in education, not the tourist industry.

"I don't have what it takes." She could not have been more honest. Accusing Angel of heartless disregard was unfair. Her father had not passed his charisma and wisdom onto her, and she did not want to be the empire's demise.

"Of course you do. Look what you accomplished for the Twelve Days of Christmas. People respected your vision, and they followed it."

"That's different," she argued. "It's behind the scenes. I can't take the stage." Life offered so many exciting options; she should not be sentenced to re-making the same one.

"You don't have to. Find the right couple for the stage work while you run operations."

It felt wrong on many levels. God had not gifted her to be

a leader, and she did not seek the role. Angel stopped eating her bagel, a sure sign of distress. "They're coming back, I'm sure of it."

Etta looked at her in pity; she did not believe they would. "We don't know what happened, but it was major. If your parents come back, they'll retire. It's over."

Angel got mad. Etta did not know the future; no one did. She needed to fix this. "Stop saying that!"

"What about a compromise? You take over North Pole Enterprises until they return. Win-win."

Why couldn't Etta side with her best interests? Angel dug in her heels and refused to be pushed. "I won't." Re-evaluating the largest stand she had taken in her life seemed like a bad idea. She needed to trust God and her instincts. He had placed her here and had not told her to move. She would stay planted.

Prancer broke into song. "Don't worry, be happy." The bird was the smartest creature in the room. Etta and Angel exchanged apologetic looks, sighed, and joined him. By silent tacit agreement, they switched subjects.

"Would you ask Eric to call me later when he has a minute?" Angel finished her bagel but knew more hid inside the bag. She talked herself out of second helpings, but only just.

"Sure, why?"

She tossed the erroneous statement over to Etta. Her husband worked at the bank and could fix the clerical error before it tempted Angel into taking unfair advantage. The money was not hers, and she would not steal to cover her shortfall.

"They think I'm rich." The idea struck her as amusing. Her balance hovered just over zero more often than she liked to admit. "The little account is mine, the other is someone else's."

Etta looked at the statement and then at her in confusion. "It would be a big mistake. They're super careful about these things. I'll have him call you."

Angel shrugged it off without much thought. "Someone pushed

the wrong button. I'm sure it happens all the time." The money would have been nice, but she would earn it.

The week continued with no word from her parents. Angel manned the first-aid tent, practiced the Christmas cantata, taught, and played skating rink host. She did not dwell on why they maintained radio silence.

When it seemed the gate guard had been wrong about their speedy return, she stopped Merry after class. "Have you heard from my parents?" Angel had waited as long as possible before broaching the subject but could put it off no longer.

The expression on Merry's smug face made her regret she ever asked. Angel cared about her folks, much more than they seemed to care about her, but putting up with this nitwit's gloating tested her limits.

"Of course I have."

Angel was at once angry and relieved. "Thank you, God," she said in silent thanksgiving. To Merry, she said, "That's wonderful. I just needed to know they're okay."

Merry's face hardened. "Really? You don't need to know where they are or why they left?" She wanted to flaunt inside knowledge and embarrass Angel for being out of the loop.

Pride was a sin, but Angel hung onto hers with a death grip. She would not give her cousin the satisfaction of measuring her pain. "They're adults and can make their own decisions. I hope they're happy." Angel did not buy into the hands-off version of love she espoused, but she sold it. Namaste. She would not place her abandonment neurosis on display for Merry's amusement.

Her cousin looked incredulous at Angel's assumptions. "Happy? They're miserable waiting for you to step up and do your duty."

They stood in the empty classroom and glared at each other. "I've just made sure they're fine and not lying somewhere in a ditch. My *duty* here is done." If they did not find her worthy of goodbye, how much effort should she put into looking for them?

"I thought when you took after us with a bulldozer—" Merry's face was pink, and she looked agitated as she shuffled from foot to foot, her hands waving in the air.

Angel interrupted, "Front-end loader." She picked up Prancer and placed him in the carrier. "Ready to go, big guy?" He gave her a kiss. The bird was always gung-ho for their next adventure.

"Peanut," he said. What used to be a bribe had turned into an expectation, but she could not deal with a fit and gave him one.

Merry shook her head as if she did not know what they were talking about anymore. She never was too bright. "What?"

"It was a front-end loader, not a bulldozer."

Exasperation showed on her cousin's pretty face, and Angel enjoyed it. The woman had enrolled to heckle her, and the joke had outlived its welcome. Angel had expected her to drop the class a week ago, but Merry had thrown herself into the prank. She even turned in homework assignments.

"It doesn't matter what it was, you maniac. You tried to kill me!"

Angel opened her mouth to protest otherwise. She needed to avoid jail time for attempted murder.

"But," Merry interrupted, testing to see if Angel would keep still, "I thought it meant you cared and wanted to take your rightful place."

Since when did Merry think of it as her "rightful place?" She had aspired to be next in the line of succession her entire life. The fact they argued over a piece of velvet-covered particleboard made Angel laugh. The furniture did not imbue power or respect. The person sitting in the chair had to shepherd the globe's inhabitants and put their needs first. Merry had never set her desires aside for anyone.

"Not that it's any of your business, but we settled this argument years ago. I'm never going to run North Pole Enterprises, and if my parents plan on staying gone until I change my mind, they should've packed more."

"Are you ready?" said a voice from the doorway. Great, now

Angel's boss wanted to check on her before and after class. Maybe he had read her mind about cutting out early just to spite him.

"I'm sorry. Have I forgotten a meeting?" She had tried hard to keep her schedule under control and prayed an appointment with her boss had not gotten pushed to one side.

Merry moved past her and said, "He's talking to me." She beamed at the man and took his arm with a final hair toss. "Let's go."

Basil would be so hurt. He worshipped the image of the woman he married. Angel did not believe he had met the actual person; she hid her true nature from him. He was a good man, and Angel would not destroy him by telling tales, but her heart wept for his deceived soul. Merry had also just suggested Angel's parents disappeared to force her into taking over North Pole Enterprises. The depth of manipulation required for such a stunt boggled her brain and steeled her will against compliance.

Merry's new interest in higher learning was no coincidence. She was a plant, sent to spy on her. Would her parents sanction getting Angel fired to further their own goals? She hated to think it of them, but it didn't stop her from entertaining the thought. Had Merry and Basil counted on Angel chasing them from the stage and assuming the role herself? Who did they think she would make into her Santa? Benny? The man no longer called; her refusal to respond must have registered.

Thoughts of her family's betrayal filled her head until she believed it would burst. If she had a stroke, it would be their fault. They had tried to force her hand but lost. Angel no longer cared if her parents spent decades building up the globe just to blow it to smithereens. She had not lit the fuse, they did.

# Chapter 13

Two nights later, while staffing the Twelve Days of Christmas, Angel asked Vivian for a meeting. They set one, and the next morning she arrived at the recent widow's home before work.

"No wine?" her impeccably dressed hostess asked as she ushered her into the foyer.

"It wasn't helping my career," Angel answered. Neither was her cousin cozying up to the boss. She followed Vivian to the same garden room they had occupied the last time she was here.

"I found a copy of the original charter for you. Do you have time for coffee?"

Angel had chugged half a pot before coming, and any more might result in aggression. Whatever was going on had only ended at the pear tree. She was certain its roots reached far into the past.

"I'm sorry, I don't." She hesitated and said, "You know everyone's getting nervous?"

Vivian sighed. "I've heard. I was hoping to get my feet under me and finish the drive-thru event, but it doesn't look like I'll get the time."

"You can do this," she said. Curiosity prompted Angel to ask, "Did you agree with Glacier about the gate charge?" Marital vows did not preclude separate opinions. Sometimes, they assured them.

"I think it's important to involve the shopkeepers in the decision. Glacier assumed a consensus I'm not sure exists." Vivian's smile was practiced. She would make a good politician.

"It would change us and our guests," Angel said. The globe drew city-weary visitors because of its kind and generous spirit. "An upfront fee would make them more demanding and us stingier."

Vivian tilted her head as if considering the point, "You may be right."

"There's one more thing," Angel said. "The town expects you and I to pick up for Glacier and my parents, but we don't have to." She lifted the charter document she had not yet read. "Three guys should have never held all the power."

Angel remembered Benny's clashes with the deceased mayor. The townspeople had not welcomed new blood, and without a transfusion of it, they would all wither and die.

Vivian walked her back to the front door. "Will you come to the meeting if I call one?"

The locals chased her out of the last one, but Angel would stand in for her parents one last time. She agreed, if only to hand their operation off to someone else. She picked up Prancer from the house and headed into work. Today's calendar centered around sacred hymns, and Angel was pleased Merry did not possess a musical mind. The organ absorbed her dark energy and transformed it into high worship. In the end, Angel felt clean and returned to her office energized. She had brought a salad and pulled out the city charter to read while eating it.

A knock surprised her; she had blocked the time slot. Angel considered keeping quiet until the student or whoever went away; she could not trust herself to be civil to her boss.

Unfortunately, she had not locked the door, and it opened without permission. Benny stood there, and Angel knew her instincts not to respond had been spot-on. The man looked angry, not boyish. His face was colored a dark red, and he clenched his fists. The only other time she had seen him this mad was the day he threatened Glacier. The mayor turned up dead the very next morning.

Angel shrank back, glad to have the desk between them. She looked to Prancer and then to Benny.

"If you never want to see me again, fine. But sending your goons around to squeeze me? I can't believe you'd stoop so low." He looked at her with disgust.

Angel worried he had lost his mind, and crazy people were dangerous. She did not know any goons and had not dispatched any to rough up the guy she still liked. "I haven't done anything," she said. "I have no idea what you are talking about."

Who did he think he was barging in here and accusing her of things? He was the one with a shady past he failed to disclose. It made him a liar and a criminal while her conscience stayed clear. He took three quick steps toward her desk, and Prancer screamed. Benny turned, as if only now aware of the large beak and talons. He tempered his voice to sound more reasonable and kept an eye on the flighted creature.

"It's no mistake; they were very clear you sent them. What's wrong with this town? You're all shake-down artists." He looked outraged but did not come closer or make another threatening move.

"Who used my name, and for what? I'm in the dark here." Angel searched her mind for anything the guy could have misconstrued but came up blank.

Benny stared as if she played a joke on him. "Are you saying you didn't send two thugs to Lump of Coal?"

Angel was single; she had no men to send anywhere. "Of course not. What'd they say, exactly?"

"They said the globe was pay for play, and if I ever wanted the street performers or animals near my shop, it cost extra."

She shook her head, "That's not true. North Pole Enterprises sends groups all around town. I do some work at the ice-skating rink."

"You do?" He looked surprised. The man had seen her trip over air; the idea of her on skates probably frightened him.

It wasn't important. "I needed a little extra cash." She looked at Prancer, who did not hang his head in shame. He should have; it was his fault.

Benny set his jaw again, "According to these guys, the best acts come with a surcharge. The crowds come to watch the penguins or whatever, then they wander into the store. It increases foot traffic."

"I work for the entertainment division; I'm not in charge of it. They make me wear a hippo outfit. Basil's the guy who runs it; he's married to my cousin."

"Why would they say you sent them?" He searched her face for answers.

Angel had no idea. Benny stopped pacing and took a seat. Prancer let his guard down a little and batted a bell while keeping half an eye on the intruder.

"To legitimize it, I guess. Nobody would've tried this nonsense if my dad was here. They're taking advantage of his being gone." They had no right to impersonate or use her to cover their crimes. Who hated Angel enough to do such a thing?

"When will he be back from vacation?"

The subject would not die; it haunted her and always would. Her parents provided no handy excuse for their bizarre behavior. They knew she would not speak ill of them, but it put her in an awkward position, and Angel did not appreciate their lack of empathy.

"I don't know." She tossed Prancer an almond, and he snatched it from the air.

Benny picked up one of the textbooks and started leafing through, looking at the color photos. They were some of the best Angel had ever seen. She loved wildlife photography. Maybe she would make a career change. It would be she and her camera, no boss around to belittle her effort.

"He's good," Benny said with admiration as the bird cracked open the soft shell. "Get him a glove and send him to the outfield."

"Better make him a catcher. He doesn't run very well."

The less-angry man looked at her for permission and picked up a nut. "Prancer, you want this?"

"Polly wants a cracker." The smart-aleck knew what strangers expected a parrot to say. He wasn't above hamming it up if it got him a treat. It worked, and Benny tossed him the gift. Prancer missed this one but scrambled down the tree stand to fetch it. He waited until he reached the perch again before savoring his snack.

"What happens in the meantime? Who's making the decisions?"

Angel knew her parents had counted on her stepping in to cover the slack, but she had refused. "Basil, I suppose. We have substitute Santas—there are never a lack of those—but my dad does so much more."

"They said he advocates for people, but the guy never told Glacier to stop charging me green fees."

Angel poked at her salad. It got Prancer's attention, and he dropped to her desk in hopes of sharing. "Did you ask him to?" She could not imagine her father turning down a direct request.

"No. I didn't know he was the union rep. There should be an orientation packet for newbies."

"Most families moved into the globe twenty years ago when it opened. They lined up to give it a try. Very few move out until after they retire, and even then, most stay."

Prancer squirted a cherry tomato onto her blotter. "Hmmm," he said, always appreciative of food. Soon, he would be too fat to fly.

"Honestly, I don't see why." Benny stretched his legs out and balanced his feet on his boot heels. The posture made her think of a cowboy. No one spoke ill of the globe, especially not someone who hadn't been here long enough to earn the right. He had no idea the work it took to keep the place running and its people happy. Benny continued, "Locals aren't as friendly as I was told, and twice people have tried to charge me for running my business. Someone should've mentioned the mafia before I sunk my life savings into this place."

Angel's temper flared. "You're the one with a secret! Glacier found out about your past and wanted you gone." A man with a rap sheet had no business knocking innocent people. Maybe the town had not rolled out a long enough welcome mat, but they didn't misrepresent themselves to gain his trust.

It was Benny's turn to get mad. He narrowed his eyes and

pushed back his chair. "Those records were sealed. The man hacked into them."

"But you don't deny they exist." To Angel, it proved wrongdoing. Courts protected juvenile offenders and some others, but it didn't mean they never broke the law.

"It's none of your business." It was all the confirmation she needed. Glacier's snoop had been right. Benny had been convicted of a crime.

"Did you kill him?" The sharpness in her tone made Prancer look up from eating her lunch.

"Is that what you think?" Benny stood now and headed to the door. He obviously wanted nothing to do with Angel or her low opinion of him.

"You lied to move here and fought with the mayor. Then he ended up dead." Angel had never considered Benny a suspect, but someone killed the man. She needed to find out who, so her parents could come home. Going forward, the globe would be more careful about vetting strangers, and life would get back to normal.

"Then you should watch out, because you were the last person to cross me. Tell your lackeys I'm not paying them a dime." He slammed his fist into the door and left.

Angel sat for a moment. Had he just threatened to kill her? Her first death threat had not been as fearsome as she thought it would be. Three minutes later, her boss showed up, a scowl on his face.

"Do I need to call security on you?"

She had done nothing but try to finish a salad in peace. Angel had not asked to be accosted by anyone and had caused no scene. "On me? How about him?" It would not have been the first time the guards encountered Benny.

"Personal visits aren't appropriate here. Especially loud ones." The man sniffed as if the subject were distasteful.

"I never asked him to come. We're not together," and never would be again, judging by their recent interactions. Angel felt a tinge of guilt over her meanness. Benny might have reasonable explanations, but she had not asked him.

The bow-tied buffoon said, "That's a private matter. This is a place of business."

Before she could stop herself, Angel let loose with the only ammunition in the clip, "It looked very *personal* between you and one of my students."

He left without responding, and Angel threw the last cherry tomato at the door. Prancer looked at her in disbelief. He had his eye on it.

She now knew the townspeople weren't lying when they accused her of extortion. It would have made more sense for the enforcers to say her father sent them, though. His name carried more clout than hers did—or had, until he ran from a murder charge.

The globe handed out brochures about how they constructed the dome. Behind the scenes tours showed how the men tapped the geothermal resources to provide endless heat and power. Angel read the charter agreement for a deeper understanding than the marketing materials provided. The partners had bequeathed their shares to each other to assure their dream's success. The men made decisions to protect the globe, not themselves, and Angel marveled at their fortitude in doing so.

Franklin never married or had children. His mind had been consumed with theoretical concepts, not human relationships. Once Glacier and Santos inherited his portion, they changed the provisions to provide for their families. It was fair. Had the married men died earlier, their wives and children would have been left penniless. They took a colossal gamble with everyone's financial security, but it was the only way big dreams were realized.

The engineer lived to see the globe through its opening year. Had he died sooner, it was likely everyone's investment would have been lost. Only he had the skills to see the project through to completion. Glacier recouped his money selling land and developing the globe's commercial real estate as the property belonged to his family.

Santos, the idea man, opened North Pole Enterprise and was granted exclusive rights to tourism development for the first twenty years. He had done such a spectacular job the globe remained unique in the world. People came from everywhere to experience his brand of love and year-round holiday cheer.

Angel continued to dig in, knowing the answers she sought lie in there somewhere. Prancer did not care for being ignored and reached over to the document. He tore off a corner of the tenth sheet.

"Hey, you. Knock that off." She waved a hand at him to shoo him out of her space.

He let go but started dancing. His bird shoulders dipped, and he bounced on his feet, singing about girls just wanting to have fun. "Fun! Fun! Fun!"

Angel laughed and said, "You're not a girl, but I get your point." She set the contract down and took a break. The legalese had given her a headache anyway.

Her sweater hung from the back of her chair, and she tossed it over Prancer's head. He said, "Ooh, I'm a ghost," and swayed side to side. It was a game they often played. His moans were less than scary. Three feet of colorful tail hung out behind him; it was not much of a costume.

She separated the fabric, looked at his face, and snatched them closed again. "Peek-a-boo!" he said from within the folds. They played "bang, bang you're dead," and a round of basketball.

"Break time is over," Angel said. "You can sit with me if you're going to be good." She placed the parrot on her shoulder and got back to her research.

After the initial twenty years, both men agreed to resign their positions. They had wanted each partner to benefit from their investment, but not hold the globe in a perpetual stranglehold. When two decades seemed an exceedingly long time, it made sense to them. Ten years in, the reality must have been difficult for both men, and they altered the contract. The updated version allowed for an heir to succeed them when the time came.

219

A forgotten memory hit Angel full-force. Glacier had a son about her age. He had lived with his mother outside of the globe and had drowned when he was twenty-one. She had never known the boy, but his death re-awakened Glacier's drinking problem. A few years later, he got straight and married Vivian. How horrible it must be to lose a child.

The document explained why her parents had tried to force Angel into the family business. With her in charge, their empire lived. Without her, the profits belonged to the city. Glacier had long since sold all the property, so the twenty-year mark would have meant little to him.

Her phone rang, and it was Eric, Etta's husband. "Hey, sorry it's been a few days, but I wanted to talk to you about your bank statements."

Angel had intentionally pushed the matter from her mind and limited her dreaming to the lottery. "It's not a problem. I assume you found out whose it is and returned it?" If she had the money, its rightful owner did not. It must have put them in quite a spot.

"I wanted to come over and talk to you about it. Are you still at work?"

Angel felt prickles in her spine. Why was their mistake her problem? But it was Eric, and he was one of the most thorough people she had ever met. He was an overachiever on anyone's scale.

"I am. We can meet here, or I could come to you."

Eric said, "I'm already out and about, so I'll swing by in a few." She heard a catch in his breath but figured he would tell her what was up when he came. Twenty minutes later, she heard the knock on her door and yelled for him to enter. Eric came through the door, but behind him, Frank did the same. Angel looked to the chief of police in concern.

"Are my parents alright?" Fear threatened to choke her words. "Please, God," she prayed. "Let them be okay." Angel looked to Eric for an explanation. If her folks were dead, wouldn't they have brought Etta to comfort her instead of her husband?

Eric stepped forward and said, "I'm sorry, but I'm required by law to do certain things."

"My parents?" She asked again, angry now neither had answered her question. The slowness at which people delivered bad news was understandable but aggravating.

"Your parents are fine, as far as I know," Frank said and sat in one of two chairs students used during office hours. "You haven't phoned, so I assume you haven't heard from them." He said it with a touch of sarcasm.

Eric took over and got to the point. "It's about your bank account."

"I told you, it's not mine. You guys made a mistake." Angel stood and placed Prancer back on his stand. She could not deal with him playing with her hair just now.

"No mistake," Eric said. "I researched it, and you opened the account online a couple months ago. Since then, you've been making weekly deposits of roughly two hundred dollars."

"With the money you coerced out of shopkeepers," Frank said. "I've been following up on their complaints."

Angel could not believe the audacity of either one of them. They had come here to accuse her of being a thief; it boggled her brain. "I told you, I never opened an account. When I found out about it, I reported it." She glared at the chief of police, "And I've never gouged people for money. Ever."

Eric looked uncomfortable. He knew how close she and Etta were, and as soon as Angel told her best friend about this, he would have heck to pay. "Who else could have done it?"

Angel stopped. She guarded her identifying information like a junkyard dog to prevent identity theft. If anyone were to spend her money or ruin her credit, she insisted it be her.

"No one."

Frank nodded his head. "I've had reports you sent collection men to local businesses, ordering them to pay up if they wanted to keep their shops."

Angel floundered. "I have not! Benny told me this morning; I had no idea. Someone's using my name, but it's not me."

The cop laughed. "You expect me to believe bag men are threatening people and depositing the money into your account without your knowledge."

It sounded ludicrous, but it was true. The problem was, no one would do such a thing. Nobody but the landlord cared if her rent would be late. "It doesn't matter what you think!" Angel said, her voice rising. "I had nothing to do with any of this, and you can't prove I did."

"You realize receiving dirty money is a crime, right?" Frank asked.

That couldn't be true. She had done nothing illegal, and he acted as if she went around breaking legs. "I've never taken a penny from anyone. I didn't know the money existed until a few days ago."

Eric nodded his head in agreement and broke his embarrassed silence. "There've been no withdrawals from the account." He looked eager to have the matter settled.

"Just because a bank robber hasn't spent the cash doesn't mean he's innocent," Frank said.

"Eric, tell him I had nothing to do with this." She looked imploringly at her friend. "You said it was all done online. Don't you find that weird? I walk into the branch all the time."

"She does," he said. "All the tellers know her."

Frank said, "So? People outside the globe recognize her. It doesn't mean she didn't set it up on the internet. Angel admits no one has access to her social security number."

Prancer said, "My social security number is 256-54-1514," in a perfect imitation of Angel's voice.

All three of them stared at the bird, mouths agape. "Alexa, turn on Prancer's playlist," he said because he had their full attention.

Frank said, "Date of birth?" and watched for the parrot's reaction.

The bird rattled it off, as well as her home address when the cop asked. Angel felt sick. Prancer had heard her provide the information countless times and knew it as well as she did. She had neglected to encrypt her parrot.

"It seems you did give out your information," Frank said. "Sharing it with anyone," he looked at Prancer, "lets the bank off the hook for any damages."

"What damages? No one ran up my credit card. They are *depositing* money into my account, not withdrawing it."

"Exactly," the cop said. "Who, besides you, would have a reason to do that?"

No one would, of course. Angel was single, and the accounts weren't joint. Once the money was in there, it belonged to her alone. "I have no idea." Angel floundered in the dark these days. She needed GPS to navigate her life.

Eric said, "The bird doesn't know how to read, does he? Or type? There's no way he filled out the forms."

Angel sighed in relief. Of course not. It had been silly. Prancer may know more than he ought to, but he had not opened another account or hired henchmen.

"Also," Angel said, "why would I put it a new one? If I was dumb enough to keep stolen cash under my name, why not use the account I already have?"

The men shook their heads. No one could make sense of the situation. Angel thought Eric might be on her side, if even for the sake of his marriage, but Frank did not believe a word she said.

"Am I under arrest?" If she were, Eric would have to deliver Prancer to Etta. With her parents gone, no one else was available to care for him. Frank had every reason not to trust her. He thought she might be implicated in Glacier's death, had filed a false kidnapping report, had stolen her neighbor's poinsettia stand, and had been accused of extortion.

The top cop considered the question. "Do you have any plans to leave the globe?"

"No." Her parents had left no forwarding address and might not welcome her to their hide-out. According to Merry, they only went to force her into compliance with their plans for her life. She did not wish to be anyone's puppet, even theirs.

"Not until I have more evidence; something seems off here, but I'm going to inform the gate to notify me if you attempt to leave," he said.

"Is that necessary?" Eric asked. He looked to Angel to see how she reacted to being under virtual globe arrest.

She jumped in before Frank could respond. "It's not a problem. I'm not going anywhere, but you need to find these guys and shut down their scheme before everyone hates me." Angel could forget the special treatment she had enjoyed; she would be wise not to eat in any local restaurant for the time being. With the conditions of her freedom set, the men left.

Eric returned two minutes after seeing Frank to the main door. "I never wanted to do this; I'm so sorry." He looked nervous. "I don't believe you're cheating the shops. You wouldn't do that."

He believed her and his words warmed her heart. They said a second goodbye, and he left for the final time. Angel kissed the macaw's beak. "Are you a spy? Do you work for the Russians?"

The macaw imitated a Russian accent and said, "Na Zdorovie, comrade."

She nearly dropped him. Prancer had a life before her, and unlike a new boyfriend, she was unable to question him about it. Words or phrases triggered responses she had not taught him, but he had not forgotten. The bird would outlive her, and when he did, his new owner would be surprised at how many songs he could sing. No matter how close two beings were, they never knew everything about each other.

# Chapter 14

Angel had several problems, and solving them required assistance from people who did not want to help her. She called Benny's number but was not surprised when he let it go to voicemail. She had accused him of murdering Glacier, and he probably planned on holding a grudge.

She dropped Prancer at home, and she settled him in before heading to the North Pole Complex. It was payday, and a legitimate influx of currency would perk up her mood. Basil was in the office working late; her father's absence had increased the man's responsibilities. Angel did not feel guilty about it. She had hired on as a bit player, not management.

"Thanks for the gig," she said. "I'm really enjoying it." She had learned not to hot-dog it too often, and things had gone well after the first night on the ice.

"Glad to hear it," he said and handed her the envelope covering the month's shortfall. "It's ongoing if you want. Things will slow down after the holidays, but I'm sure we can still feed you some hours."

"I'd like it very much, thanks." Angel planned an emergency savings fund and a few luxuries. If destined to remain single, she desired to be both pampered and prepared for emergencies.

"Are you coming for Thanksgiving?"

She had done her best to push the day from her mind. Most years, her family enjoyed a massive breakfast because her parents worked. Turkey day brought many weekend visitors to the globe.

Angel lied, "No, but thank you for thinking of me. I've got plans with a friend." Etta would invite her, but she would not go. Eric had a large family who loved to talk politics and hockey, neither of which interested her.

"We'll miss you. Come by if you change your mind."

"I will." She left and headed for Lump of Coal. Benny might not answer her call, but he would be in his shop, and she did not think there was a rear exit to the building.

Angel stopped at a specialty chocolate store on her way; she needed a peace offering to get through the door. It was manipulative but might work. The clerk suggested the English Toffee, and she bought two: one for him and one for her. Second paychecks came in handy.

Lump of Coal was situated on the famous Evergreen Avenue, one of the best streets in the globe. The many decorated Christmas trees lining the thoroughfare drew tourists and their cameras. She took a deep breath and pushed open Benny's door, setting off the chime. He had filled the showroom with various sizes of free-standing stoves. Angel liked the old-fashioned potbelly. She was sure they no longer used cast iron but could not tell from looking.

Benny came from the back when he heard her enter, and the smile dropped from his lips when he saw who it was. He looked behind him as if for back-up, but he was alone in the store. "What do you want?" His tone sounded curt; she had expected no more.

"I need to apologize. I brought these," she handed him the chocolate peace offering. He studied the box and her face. "I never thought you had anything to do with killing Glacier."

"Then why'd you say it?" He moved behind the counter to keep distance between them.

Angel looked down at the floor. She liked it; the hardwood gave off a homey feel. "Because I was hurt. You thought I sent gangsters here to threaten you."

Benny stiffened, "They said you did; it's pretty good proof."

The store bell rang again, and two women walked in and

exclaimed how warm the store felt. "Would you like some spiced cider?" Benny asked them. The scent had intrigued Angel since she arrived. It was a great idea, sure to make people feel at home.

The women took disposable cups of the fragrant liquid and oohed over how special it must be to live in such a wonderful place. One bought a stocking full of coal for her naughty husband, and they went back out into the night.

Angel said, "The village hasn't been very welcoming to you, and I'm sorry."

"You did the best of anyone." She blushed. The man would charm the entire town if they gave him a chance.

"Please forgive me, but I need a huge favor." Angel had no right to ask, but she could not do this alone. She dropped into a plush chair. Benny had done an excellent job making his customers want to spend time in the space. He should offer a few smaller items for sale, as most visitors would not purchase heating elements from him.

He gave a half-snort. "You brought the candy to butter me up so I would help you."

"I'll admit it. The candy was a bribe, but the apology was sincere. I didn't send people to scare you, and I want them stopped. Do you think they'll return?"

Benny squared his shoulders. "I told them I had bettered never see them again, but one said I wouldn't be so lucky."

A chill ran through Angel; these guys sounded serious. "How much money did they want?"

"Fifty bucks." Benny took a cleaning cloth from behind the counter and wiped down the glass until it shone. He moved to the first stove on the far left and polished it as well. The project kept him from meeting her eyes.

She had cashed her check at the candy store and took the requested amount from her wallet. "I want you to pay them."

The statement caused Benny to look up from his work. "No way am I giving in to intimidation." Angel sighed. This was not a test of his manliness; it was a trap.

227

"You aren't; you're buying information. When they show up, pay them, and text me. Try to keep them here a few minutes, and I'll follow when they leave. I need to know who they are and why they're pretending I sent them."

Benny did not take any time to consider. "I won't do it. I'll track them myself. It's too dangerous."

"It's fifty bucks." No mob boss sent out gorillas for such a small amount. She would be fine. This was still the globe.

A man walked in and wanted to compare efficiency ratings. Angel helped herself to some cider and waited while Benny spoke to him. He was good with people and knowledgeable about his business. The customer got answers to his questions and promised to return with his wife.

"Think he'll be back?" she asked.

"Half of them show up, the other half were never serious." Angel refilled her cider cup. The aroma soothed her as much as the drink itself. "It's not the money," Benny said. "They'll raise the ante if I pay. It takes guts to demand it, and that makes them dangerous. I couldn't live with myself if you got hurt."

She melted at his words. He still cared for her, even after she mistreated him. "I won't. I promise. Just let me know when they come back, and I'll do the rest. I would ask Frank to do it, but he doesn't have enough guys."

"Why don't we do it together?" Benny suggested. "It's the only way I'm involving you."

Angel bristled at his paternal attitude, but she needed him. These guys were the only lead she had.

"Okay," she said with reluctance. Benny held all the cards unless she intended to stake out the place herself. "You promise you'll text?"

He did. Angel thanked him and left. When she got in her cart, she noticed the other package of toffee. She had planned on eating it herself but decided to sacrifice it for the greater good. Evergreen Avenue met up with Tinsel Way, and from there, Angel took a right onto Holly and headed to Vivian's house.

The mayor's widow did not seem too surprised to see her show up uninvited. She opened the door, but instead of going to the glass-walled garden room, Vivian led Angel into the kitchen. A comfortable breakfast area sat to one side, and the women took seats. A beautiful bouquet of fresh flowers adorned the round table. Angel loved growing plants but could never cut them. They were alive, and all living things felt pain.

"How did Glacier feel about his upcoming forced retirement?" Angel asked when they settled with a cup of coffee. Socializing required consuming liquids, and it was best they remained non-alcoholic.

Vivian considered before answering. "You may find me silly, but I think it caused his affair."

Whatever Angel had expected her to say, this was not it. "How so?"

"He's was a man of a certain age who had worked his entire life. I think he wondered what he would do with his time. Tearing down one life and starting a new one gave him a project."

She made it sound like he wanted to replace a barn. "He'd still be mayor," Angel said. The job would have provided enough identity for most people.

"Not if we divorced. Villagers worry something like that will spill into their own bedrooms." It was true. Christian communities had the same problems as secular ones, but people felt an increased amount of guilt and shame. It was too bad, as they were the only ones who could be forgiven.

"How did you convince him to stay?" Angel had no business asking such personal questions but pressed ahead anyway. If she held all the pieces, she could form a clear picture.

Vivian took a sip of her coffee. "Why is this so interesting to you? You're not married."

Angel hated being considered as less-than based on her tax filing status. "No, but I hope to be. Someday." She looked at the cup in her hands. Requesting vulnerability required giving it as well.

"A woman's first instinct is to throw everything at the problem.

Seduce him, remind him he loves you, threaten to take half the money, and play the victim."

"It doesn't sound like you did that." Vivian's consistent composure interested Angel. She would love to present herself as pulled together as the recent widow, but such an image required commitment.

"If they're dumb enough to leave you, be smart enough to let them. It's a cliché, but an effective one."

"You didn't fight for him?" Part of her was disappointed. If she had a husband, she would not let go so quickly.

Vivian sighed, and in the sound, Angel understood she had done nothing but struggle to keep her man. She just used different tactics. Winning ones, it appeared.

"I wished his happiness over my mine. If he needed to leave me to find it, I would never stop him."

Angel felt unworthy of sharing the air. Hunting down love and holding it captive was not a solid game plan. Vivian had been through a lot in recent months, and she reacted with love, not hatred. "And Cookie?"

"Glacier was cruel; he tested us both. She failed. No man wants to be tied to a woman incapable of handling bad news. Life involves so much of it."

Angel gulped at the wisdom. She would remember it when choosing a partner. "Could Cookie have killed him?"

Vivian said, "I don't know her well, but she was mad enough." The woman had fallen off the wagon, egged Vivian's house, and attacked Angel twice since the man died. What else might she have done?

She remembered the small gift she had brought and pulled it from her bag. "These are for you. You deserve some sweetness." She hugged the woman and left a better person. Vivian Harrison had not killed her husband, but Angel wondered if his mistress had.

Benny's text came in at an unfortunate time, but if Angel wanted to catch the bad guys, this was her shot. With no time to change, she removed her ice skates and jumped into her cart, still wearing her purple hippo outfit. At least the men would not see her face. Anyone claiming they worked for her should recognize their boss.

She parked in the alley adjacent to the Lump of Coal and waited for the thugs to exit. Benny sent her frantic texts, but she ignored him. This was a one-woman operation, and she did not need his help to stalk them. Break-ups from ex-boyfriends had taught her the skill.

The well-dressed men left Benny's and walked down the street to a jewelry store. She crept along the curb and kept pace. A few minutes later, they re-emerged and continued along their route. They made stops at a T-shirt emporium, a specialty tea shop, and a stand selling funnel cakes. This was worse than she had thought. A few blocks later, the hired guns got into a rental cart. The streets were full of them. Angel did not think they noticed her, even though her get-up would have brought attention anywhere but the globe. Here, the streets pulsed with performers in costume, and she was just one of many.

They drove toward the North Pole Complex, and Angel followed at a distance. This was her turf. The men double-parked at the curb, and she hoped one of the nutcrackers had them towed. Angel need not worry about her vehicle; she used her parents' reserved spot. No one would mess with it.

The criminals paid no attention to the jugglers, stilt walkers, or mischievous elves cavorting on the plaza. They continued to the administrative buildings trailed by a purple pachyderm. Angel drew in a sharp breath when they approached Basil's office. She must have missed something. Merry's husband was family and her dad's right-hand man; a guy like him would not pull such a disloyal stunt.

She waited down the hall while the couriers went inside; Angel did not think they would be long. Their parking job indicated men in a hurry, but what business did they have with Basil?

It was time to go. No good could come from being found lurking here. She needed to find Frank and tell him what she learned. As she turned to leave, the office door behind her opened.

"Angel? Is that you? Is there a problem?" Basil had seen her.

Her back was to him, and she considered making a run for it, but physicality was never her strong suit. In desperation, Angel grasped the flexible foam she wore and ripped it.

Shifting to face him, she said, "I'm so sorry. I've damaged my costume. Do you have another?"

He looked at her for a long moment, then said, "Come on in, I'm sure we can find something that works for you."

Her heart beat so fast it made her weak. "You know, I bet I can sew this. I'll just take it home." She turned, but Basil grasped her arm.

"I insist," he said. The men stood on either side of the doorway like sentinels. Her cousin-in-law pushed her into his office and closed the door. She did not like the sound.

"I should really be going," Angel said. The atmosphere felt wrong, and she could not catch a breath. Basil leaned against the wall. She should not have come. This was a matter for the police—not an overweight, under-married woman fearful of everything.

"Why the sudden interest in business? You've prospered from the globe your whole life without caring how the money got made. Why now?" Basil did not seem his affable self. Darkness had crept into his eyes that she did not recognize or like.

"I don't know what you're talking about." Her head felt hazy, but she needed to think. She was in danger, and no one knew she was here. Blowing off Benny's help had been an incredibly bad idea, and she kicked herself.

Her phone was in her pants pocket, under the giant hippo. She took the costume off as if to replace it with another. If Angel pretended everything was normal, maybe Basil would too.

"I think you do. You read the charter agreement. Why?"

He had not moved from his position, but somehow, he increased his presence and loomed over the room. Angel had always liked his lumberjack physique, but he had never used it to intimidate her. Did he push Merry around at home? Is that why she made herself smaller and more childish in his presence?

"Frank thinks my dad killed Glacier. I was looking for the reason why."

Basil laughed. "Isn't it obvious? Our good mayor wanted to change things. Within a few years, he would have charged a hundred dollars a head to visit. People would demand carnival rides and fireworks every night."

"Dad would never kill him over it." Angel had flirted with the idea he had but knew it to be ridiculous. Her father would never lose control and harm anyone. "Besides, his twenty years is up at the end of December. Dad no longer gets a cut."

"Exactly." Basil acted as if she had just made his point, but she had no idea what it was.

"I don't follow." When the North Pole Corporation's profits went to the general fund instead of her family, it would reduce resident's taxes. Everyone's standard of living would improve, and she was sure her parents had saved enough for a long and enjoyable retirement. Her father had no reason to murder Glacier over a gate fee.

"He would no longer profit, but there has to be a successor." The look he gave Angel sent chills up her spine. She reached into her pocket, but Basil saw her. "I'll take the phone." Angel handed it over to him.

She stammered. "I'm not taking over; Merry can tell you. I've never wanted it." People defined Angel by her last name, but she refused to let it dictate her future. She got to choose her career, lifestyle, and partner.

"But the town wants you. Or they did until you started bleeding them dry." He gave a silent chuckle that lifted his giant shoulders.

"But I—" The pieces fell into place with a thud. Basil was her boss. He had access to her social security number and other identifying information. Her signed W-2 supplied him with a signature to copy. She did not use direct deposit, so all he had lacked was

233

her bank account number. It did not stop him; he opened a new account in her name.

"I know you didn't, but my guys were crystal clear about who sent them. Everyone knows it was you, and you have the money." He laughed again. This time it was real.

He had set her up to take the fall. She might go to jail for extortion, but even if she didn't, he had ruined her reputation. No one would put her in charge of anything. The townspeople might force her from the globe altogether.

"I'm not keeping it." She had daydreamed of using the money to dig out of her current hole, but now it seemed repugnant.

Basil stepped closer, and Angel shrunk back from him. "I deserve the job. You've done nothing to earn it; it was all handed to you." Angel resented the truth in his words. Her parents yearned for her to accept the gift of an empire, and she had rejected it.

She felt his body temperature rise in anger. He was too near for comfort. "You're right. It's yours." Angel wanted out of the room and away from North Pole Enterprises. The corporation had ruled her parents' lives and had come for hers as well. The entity created to make people happy suffocated them.

"It will be as soon you sign a confession stating you killed Glacier." The man had gone mad; Angel could see it in his face. Maybe he had always been loopy. He had chosen Merry.

"I didn't have anything to do with that!" Angel looked past him to see if there was a chance at the door. Basil would stop her before she left the chair. Claustrophobia clawed at her guts; she was trapped.

"Of course not. I had to do it; you're too weak. But once you kill yourself, it won't matter. They can't punish you then. It'll be fine."

Angel tried to remain still. Every minute she stayed alive gave God a chance to rescue her, and she prayed He would. "I'll sign it, and you can call the cops. Tell them I confessed to you. They'll arrest me, and you'll be a hero."

He considered the implication of her words but seemed doubtful. "What if you change your mind? I can't trust you."

"Sure, you can," Angel spoke in the soothing cadence she used to calm Prancer. The words did not matter; everything lie in the tone. If Vivian could change a man's mind, so could she. "The police will have my confession, and they'll promote you to replace Dad. You'll make it an even bigger success." Living in a cell beat no life at all. The apostle Paul had been imprisoned many times.

"And Merry could be mayor," he said as if imagining it. Angel felt sorry for the confused man. Others failed to appreciate him enough, and the frustration built until he did something drastic. It had happened to her, but the worst thing she had done in response was to consume a box of cookies.

"She'd be a great one," Angel said. "Give me a sheet of paper." Basil handed her a pad and pen. "Tell me what to say." She had faith God would extract her from the words later.

He dictated a letter explaining how she had found the mayor drunk and rambling about losing everything. Angel had seen her opportunity and taken it. With him out of the way, she planned to take over North Pole Enterprises and be set for life. No gate fee meant much more money in her pocket. She transcribed every syllable to buy herself time. When Basil claimed she forced her father to transport the dead body, Angel stopped writing. "You made Dad move him?" It made her sick. No wonder her father had started drinking.

Basil smiled. "It was perfect. I showed him proof of your shakedown racket and threatened to expose you if he didn't." The man beamed with pride at his cleverness. How had she seen him as anything other than opportunistic?

Angel winced in physical pain. Her father believed she was a thief who capitalized on his name. He had committed a felony to save her from disgrace.

"I won't write that. I'll say I moved Glacier myself." Angel did not want any blowback on her father.

"Frank won't believe you. You couldn't lift the man, and he has your dad on tape driving the truck."

235

Her tears came now, in a big gulping fashion. "How could you do this to us? We loved you, made you part of the family." Angel had wanted a husband just like him. She had since changed her mind.

Basil's face turned mean. "You made me into a stepchild, just like you did to Merry. She didn't count, and neither did I. Not really. We were fine for small things, but you refused us our full share."

The wanna-be St. Nick pulled a gun from behind his back; it must have been tucked into his waistband. No wonder the man wore a suit when no one else did. It hid the weapon. "You'll write exactly what I said."

Angel could not see anymore; the tears stung and blinded. Her poor father. He had done nothing to deserve any of this, and now she would be dead, and he would be implicated as an accessory to her crime. Her mother would lose them both.

"Write," he said and held the gun to the base of her neck. She did. "Now, tell them you can't live with yourself."

This was how it ended; there would be no dramatic hospital scenes complete with tearful goodbyes. She was glad Etta had agreed to take care of Prancer. The idea of him being alone was too much for her.

Angel signed the document. Basil folded and pocketed it.

"Why the pear tree?" Angel asked. It still made no sense to her, and if she could get Basil talking, maybe someone would find her in time.

He looked confused. "I don't know. It was your dad's idea, but I liked it. Glacier wanted to turn us into a spectacle, and we turned him into one. It's poetic, don't you think?"

Murder made a terrible art medium, and Angel thought she knew why her father chose the tree. He had not forgotten the day twenty years ago when the man took a shot at him and missed.

"Let's go," Basil said and nudged her.

"Where to?" She had once read a victim never wanted to leave the original crime scene. The second would be so much worse.

236

Should she make him kill her where she stood? Once again, Angel decided any time alive provided hope of escape.

"You'll see." They went downstairs. The gangsters had left. Would Basil stop collecting insurance money from the townspeople once he ran North Pole Enterprises? She didn't think so. He was greedy, and why abandon a revenue stream?

A nutcracker called out a greeting, and Basil poked her in the ribs. "Hey, great to see you," she said. She made frantic eye movements, but if the security guard noticed, he did not respond.

"Where's your cart?" Basil asked her after they crossed the plaza.

"Over there," she said and pointed toward the spot.

Basil jammed the gun into her side once more. "I should've known—only the best. You expect it all, don't you?" Angel had not used a fake disabled placard but felt as if she had.

They got in the cart, and he made her drive. She considered wrecking the vehicle to get away but worried about hurting someone. Basil picked up on her thoughts and said, "Merry tells me you have a talking rat with wings. How sad would it be if he died, too?"

What kind of a monster threatened an animal? Angel would not let anything happen to her feathered friend, ever. She dropped her plan of causing a disturbance. They lived in the globe. If she got away now, Basil would find her within hours, and he had her confession signed in ink and tears.

He instructed her to drive home. It made sense. If she were to commit suicide, it was the most likely place she would do it. Her brain scrambled ahead for anything to help her once she got there. The neighbor ignored her, and Angel did not think screams would bring him running. She should have reimbursed him for the poinsettia frame without delay. It moved to number one on the to-do list if she survived.

They arrived home without incident, and Angel unlocked the door. Basil looked around to see if anyone had witnessed his arrival. No one had not as far as she could see.

"Hello! Hello!" Prancer called in excitement when he heard her.

"Hi, beak boy," she said, but tears choked her voice. This might be the last time she saw him. Angel prayed God would deliver her. She promised to be a much better Christian if He did.

"Where are you going?" Basil demanded as she headed down the hall. He leveled the gun at her, but she kept walking.

"If I don't pet him right now, he will scream for hours. You don't want that."

"Be quick about it. I don't have all night; Merry is waiting."

Angel stroked Prancer's beak with one hand and spoke soothingly to him. She told him how good of a boy he was, and that she loved him. With her other hand pressed between her stomach and his enclosure, she thumbed the re-built lock to the open position.

"Hurry it up," Basil said. He took a few steps down the hallway, and Angel met him. She did not want him to hurt the bird.

"I'm coming." Her feet drug, and her eyes looked for anything she could use as a weapon. The duplex wasn't much, but it was hers. Framed photographs, mementos from college, and comfortable furniture filled the space. No fashion magazine ever came calling, but she had established her independence in this house.

"Sit down." Basil indicated a chair at the breakfast counter. Again, it was where she would have done the deed. The tile underneath the bar stool would be easier to clean than the carpeted living room. For the first time in her life, Angel was glad she did not have a husband or children. They could not find her body. Her parents and a few friends would grieve and move on in time.

Basil waved the gun, and she sat. She might as well be comfortable in her last moments. "I need to pray," she said as her captor set her false confession on the breakfast bar in front of her.

"You've got one minute." Having decided on his course of action, Basil looked resolved to hurry the result.

"Dear Lord, thank You for the life You gave me. Please forgive me for the sins I committed, especially those I did with a knowing heart. Thank You for sending your Son to save me, and please allow me into Your kingdom forever. I pray that Basil turns his heart to

You and is washed clean of this act. I look forward to seeing him in heaven."

"Shut up," he ordered and poked her with the barrel of the gun. "Time's up."

"Alexa, lights off." The voice was Angel's, but she had not spoken.

The lights went off; Angel felt a flapping and heard a scream. Basil fell away from her, and she scrambled to her feet. Prancer had launched an attack.

The big man thrashed on the floor, and the gun skittered away from him. Angel grabbed it and ordered the lights on again. Basil's face was bloodied, and he held a hand over a severely damaged eye. With his other, he beat at the bird who had not stopped his assault.

"Prancer! Stop!" The bird glanced at her, and she reached out her hand. He looked again at his victim and flew to her outstretched forearm.

Angel held the gun on Basil and told him not to move. He cradled his face. "I need a doctor. That thing blinded me."

"It's less than you planned to do to me," she said. "Alexa, call 911." When the operator answered, Angel requested Frank come immediately and for them to send an ambulance.

"I never would've done it," Basil said. "We're family. I could never kill you."

Angel did not believe him. "You killed for a job. What's worse is it would have been yours in January anyway." What a waste. Glacier died, and an entire village reeled over who sat in Santa's chair.

Basil attempted to stand, and Angel ordered him to stay where he was. She would take no chances. "Good boy, Prancer. Are you okay?" She looked him over but saw no damage. A visit to the vet was in order, just to be sure.

Frank arrived and ordered her to put down the weapon. "He's the bad guy, not me," she said but handed over the revolver.

"Baloney. Look right there, it's a signed confession. She murdered Glacier and tried to kill me!" Basil took the cake; the man would have said anything. Angel glared at him.

"He forced me to sign it at gunpoint. Basil shot him so he could take over Dad's job and collect all the revenue. The man died over gate fees." Angel was horrified, and her body shook.

"Lousy bugger," Prancer said. She could not agree more.

Frank's men arrived, and the next hour was spent giving statements in separate rooms. Angel kept Prancer with her, even though he made the deputy nervous. Having him near kept her sane. She would never let him leave her side again, and he could eat his weight in peanuts if he wanted.

When they finished, Frank took Basil to jail. Angel made a phone call. "Merry, I need you to call my parents. It's time they came home."

Before returning to the village, Angel's father cut a deal with Frank and the district attorney. He pled guilty to abuse of a corpse and resigned his position. The court sentenced him to community service.

The next-door neighbor could not handle living close to so much drama and moved. Her parents took over his lease.

Benny forgave her for not allowing him to play cops and robbers once he learned it involved firearms.

Vivian took over for her husband as mayor. She dissolved North Pole Enterprises and rolled its responsibilities and revenue to the city.

Cookie hand-delivered a plate of pah-rum-pum-pum-pums to Angel once she learned who really killed Glacier.

Merry was forced to take a job cleaning bathrooms while her husband awaited trial.

Angel resumed her efforts to find a husband.

CPSIA information can be obtained
at www.ICGtesting.com
Printed in the USA
BVHW040811190921
616890BV00021B/1026/J